IMRAN KHAN

IMRAN KHAN

Ivo Tennant

H. F. & G. WITHERBY

First published in Great Britain 1994
by H. F. & G. Witherby
A Cassell imprint
Villiers House, 41/47 Strand, London WC2N 5JE

A catalogue record for this book is
available from the British Library

ISBN 0 85493 228 3

Photoset in Great Britain by
Rowland Phototypesetting Ltd, Bury St Edmunds, Suffolk
and printed in Great Britain by
Mackays of Chatham plc, Chatham, Kent

Acknowledgements

I mran Khan is no ordinary cricketer and no ordinary person. You do not have to spend long in his presence in Pakistan or South Kensington to appreciate that. The route taken in researching this book illustrates the rich diversity of his life. From Tramp and Lord's to Jeffrey Archer's penthouse and Emma Sergeant's studio, then to the Shaukat Khanum Memorial Hospital in Lahore and overnight to a shooting lodge in the Salt Range Mountains; from the Department of Tourism in Islamabad, over which he presides as ambassador, to the offices of UNICEF, for which he is rather more than a figurehead, it is evident he is a man of numerous parts and as many reputations.

Imran has select friends and I am grateful to them and the cricketers, cricket officials and other individuals who spoke to me about him. I am particularly indebted to Jonathan Mermagen, Imran's closest English friend, for giving me much of his time and for reading the entire manuscript; to Emma Sergeant, who hitherto has never spoken to a journalist about her friendship with Imran; and to Dr Nausherwan Burki, Imran's first cousin, who during a brief visit to London took the trouble to explain at length the workings of the Shaukat Khanum hospital, the project which means more to Imran than his career in cricket. I am grateful to Worldwide Journeys & Expeditions of London for sponsoring my visit to Pakistan and for the hospitality of Pakistan's Tourist Board while there. Of those approached, two individuals, Majid Khan – another first cousin – and Salim Malik, the Pakistani batsman, declined to be interviewed for reasons that are apparent in this book.

My special thanks are to Imran himself for tolerating my shadow in Pakistan and in London. This is the first biography to have been written about him, which in itself is a surprise.

5

Richard Wigmore, my editor, made numerous helpful suggestions and John Pawsey was supportive throughout.

So for their help, I thank: Abdul Qadir, Lord Archer, Arif Ali Abbasi, Asif Iqbal, John Barclay, Chico Jahangir, Susannah Constantine, Sarah Crawley, Susie Dolby, Emma Gibbs, Oliver Gilmour, Charles Glass, Johny Gold, Dr Paul Hayes, Marie Helvin, Lulu Hutley, Ikramullah Niazi, Intikhab Alam, Javed Burki, Javed Miandad, Reynu Malla, Gehan Mendis, Jonathan Mermagen, Jacqui Muir, Mushtaq Ahmed, Dr Nausherwan Burki, Jonathan Orders, Qamar Ahmed, Sarfraz Nawaz, Emma Sergeant, Shahid Sadullah, Mark Shand, Gordon Smith, Abner Stein, Emily Todhunter, Guy Waller, Waqar Younis, Wasim Akram, Wasim Bari, Wasim Raja, Bob Willis, the Marchioness of Worcester, the Marquis of Worcester, Zakir Khan.

The following books were consulted: *Imran* (Pelham, 1983), *All Round View* (Chatto & Windus, 1988), *Warrior Race* (Chatto & Windus, 1993), all by Imran Khan; *My Dear Old Thing* (Stanley Paul, 1988) by Henry Blofeld; *Rhythm and Swing* (Souvenir Press, 1989) by Richard Hadlee; and numerous copies of *Wisden*.

Chapter 1

In Lahore, they are celebrating Basant, the coming of spring. It is a time for kite flying and as much conspicuous merriment as there ever is under the observance of Islam. At one of the oldest residences in the city, owned by a prominent politician of the Punjab, the buffet lunch is for six hundred. In Pakistan, open house means exactly that. There are successful businessmen, lustrous actresses, an honoured sir or two, journalists without any alcohol. And in their midst there is a strangely Koranic figure, robed in the national dress of Shalwar Kamiz, his dark curls framing a noble face as instantly recognizable on the antediluvian North-West Frontier as amid the hedonism of Tramp. East and West genuflects before Imran Khan.

On the roof terrace that overlooks a red-light area legalized only for dancing, everyone wishes to shake his hand, although the women are not so forward as they would be in London. He is unfailingly polite. Someone appears with a kite emblazoned with a photograph of Imran, depicting him as 'The Champ'. There is a further message: 'Fight the Cancer', in recognition of the hospital on the outskirts of the city that is now the focus of Imran's extraordinary life. In England, retired cricketers open pubs. On the subcontinent, they are given jobs by Pakistan International Airlines. Islam does not recognize any intermediary between man and God, but the throng who pump the flesh and the multitude waiting outside for a sighting or an autograph would have you believe differently. Imran is the father of his people.

Five hundred years of bloody tribal feuds merge in this deeply proud Pathan whose genes, more than the knowledge he assimilated in England, made him the cricketer he was. The red mists that clouded his eyes when he was hit for four made him only want to bowl the next ball faster. Pathans are an avenging race.

He is the greatest cricketer in his country's relatively brief history and one of the finest all-rounders in the history of the game, as 362 Test wickets at an average of 22.81, and 3807 Test runs at 37.69, would emphasize. It is a record that bears comparison with Sir Gary Sobers, whom Imran regards as peerless.

Yet as a sportsman, Imran is best remembered primarily for his leadership. Pakistan has long been the most troublesome of all sides to captain. The players can be self-serving, the administrators duplicitous, the press querulous, the spectators myopic, the umpiring incompetent, the groundsmen unskilled, the opposing captain censorious, the culture and the customs unappealing to touring parties. Understanding the lores of the land to which Ian Botham jibed he would not send even his mother-in-law is beyond most cricketers. As if coping with all this and needing to maintain his own considerable level of performance were not enough, Imran was for a decade the spokesman not just for his side but for his country. He was perceived by the West, where Islam is neither appreciated nor tolerated, as the one sane voice in a trackless deep of fundamentalism. The native is still seen as trying to do down his colonial master.

Imran is no apologist for his country. He is belligerent in his approach to its critics. English administrators, players and umpires who in one way or another are suspicious of Pakistanis are racists or bourgeois or both; the fish-and-chips tourist who brings baked beans and chocolate to Kashmir is beyond the pale. If it was not for the fact that most of his close friends are English, that he straddles East and West with remarkable ease and that he is above discrimination, Imran would be charged with practising racism.

Imran is scored for percussion. A supreme cricketer like Sobers can have the better of him in an argument, once baffling him by saying a batsman should be able to judge the length of a delivery the moment the ball leaves the bowler's hand. But with others, judgement is final. If a bowler who is at his peak cannot dismiss him, then he, Imran, will not regard that bowler as of any use, even if he is a Test cricketer. Imran's expectations are high, both for himself and others. He has time, but little use, for the journeyman cricketer. By forming an élite pool in his own country, and paying no heed to whether these individuals played any domestic cricket, he turned Pakistan into one of the best sides in the world.

Such dismissive opinions give him a haughty, almost aloof air, which can be a cover for a surprising shyness – surprising given the adulation he receives – and is the reason why he is so often loosely tagged as 'aristocratic'. His family are most accurately described as upper-middle class, and comfortably off rather than rich. From his father, Ikramullah, an engineer who was strongly anti-imperialist, Imran acquired his all-enveloping sense of pride and knowledge of his Pathan forebears. From his late mother, Shaukat, to whom he was extremely close, Imran gained his enthusiasm for cricket and, inadvertently through her death from cancer, his calling when his cricket career was coming towards an end.

His mother's family, the Burkis, are a large and gifted tribe. Eight of Imran's numerous cousins who grew up in his home suburb of Lahore, Zaman Park, became first-class cricketers. Among them are Javed Burki and Majid Khan, both of whom preceded Imran in going to Oxbridge and captaining Pakistan. Javed, to this day, retains a considerable influence over Imran. 'If he told Imran it was eleven o'clock at night, even now Imran would believe him,' said Wasim Raja, the Pakistani batsman who grew up as a contemporary of Imran's in Lahore. 'Javed is my hero,' said Imran. 'There are not many sportsmen with intellects in addition. There are exceptions.' Arrogance is a sin for a Muslim – it means a lack of belief in God – and Imran can couple himself with Javed without any realization that he might be construed as presumptuous.

He certainly was at the crowning moment of his career on the podium in Melbourne after Pakistan had won the World Cup in 1992. In such circumstances his opposing captain, Graham Gooch, would have said something along the lines of, 'The boys played well.' Imran's boys did not rate a mention. Apart from sounding as if he had won a single-wicket competition, the speech became a plug for his hospital project. He had no intention of promoting himself, merely what he saw as a national cause. Only later did he realize his mistake. The resentment of some of his players, coupled with their suspicion that money due to be showered on them was going instead to the hospital appeal, led to Imran pulling out of Pakistan's subsequent tour to England, and, indeed, to his retirement.

It would take one of Pakistan's most revered saints to survive the machinations and enmity of their cricketing politics. To play for them for twenty-one years, as Imran did, was as enervating off the field as on it. His career was scarred by in-fighting with administrators and prominent players. Majid Khan, his childhood hero, has not spoken to him since his Test career ended with a duck in 1982: Imran had dropped him in a manner Majid found unacceptable that summer in England. Sarfraz Nawaz, friend and new-ball partner of many years' standing, put the telephone down on him after a trivial row in 1989 and has not spoken to him since. Javed Miandad, whose relationship with Imran was never an easy one, was not on speaking terms for a while: he believed Imran was responsible for removing him from the captaincy after Imran had retired. Imran even had his disagreements with Abdul Qadir, whose career he had long nurtured.

That he was able to exert control over such a disparate group of excitable individuals owed much to an authoritative personality, even though the cricketers did not always find this appealing. It was a personality likewise shared by Abdul Hafeez Kardar, Pakistan's very first captain of all, and he was regarded as highly. Imran, whose game only benefited from the responsibility of captaincy, led Pakistan to victory in both England and India, and not even Kardar achieved that. If a plebiscite had been held, Imran would have been elected permanent president of his country. Jealousy, not least from the prime minister, Nawaz Sharif, was inevitable. 'But there was no point in envying him,' said Wasim Bari, Pakistan's long-standing wicketkeeper. 'What could anybody do? He will say he has been led by God. The man was God-gifted, he worked hard and he was fair.'

His success as captain owed much to his own match-winning performances. Becoming one of the finest fast bowlers in the world did not come as easily to Imran as it did to, say, Michael Holding. He was less naturally gifted than contemporaries such as Wasim Raja and Afzal Masood. The climate, the pitches, the history of his country, the opinions of Worcestershire, his first county club, were not in favour of him becoming a truly fast bowler. To be so, the first one Pakistan had unearthed, he had to practise and to train extremely hard. He eschewed alcohol. When young and running round Zaman Park to improve his fitness, a passerby, who had been taunting him for some while, shouted out, 'Look at that ponce!' Imran wheeled round and thumped him so hard that one of his own fingers was broken. Imran's closest English friend, Jonathan Mermagen, describes him as being 'so tough you would have to beat him until he is no more'.

As a fast bowler, Imran traded bouncer for bouncer with West Indians – and any side that he felt had a weakness against short-pitched bowling – without flinching or concern for the niceties of the game. He was but one of a number of his ilk responsible for cricket becoming, when they were bowling, about as aesthetic as a game of rollerball. In the mid-1970s a bouncer from Andy Roberts, a tailender to whom he had bowled too many short-pitched balls, almost killed him. When helmets followed shortly afterwards, the bouncers only increased. Not even leaving the laws to be enforced by international umpires, as Imran wished, was going to work in the age of player power.

If Law 42 on short-pitched bowling was flouted by Imran, so was the spirit of the game. Although in other respects a fair sportsman, he tampered with the ball on occasion, scratching the side and lifting the seam and once, playing for Sussex against Hampshire in 1981, asking the 12th man to bring on a bottle top. The upshot was that the ball began to move around as not before in the match. Sussex won and the umpires were none the wiser.

County cricket was Imran's finishing school. That, following an education at Oxford, made him in the eyes of the English media a product of their country. And yet in a long career, Imran preferred not to socialize with his county colleagues and never once spent an evening with an English Test cricketer. No one made sufficient impression on him. He found Ian Botham too much of a bully – although there was no animosity between them – David Gower too glib and Graham Gooch worthy but dull. He did, however, like Phil Edmonds, even if he took a while to work out Frances, his effervescent wife.

Although, as his friends stress, he is polite to fools and bores and gives everyone a chance – he is not so vain as not to talk to a girl whom he finds unattractive – the people he mixes with have to be intellectually stimulating. Some have a wild streak that he lacks; most, if not all, are well born and well educated. 'You're on your merit with him – he won't drag things out of people,' said Mermagen. 'Most of his friends are fallible and Imran is amused at the shambles they have sometimes got themselves into.'

Even a grudging respect from Imran is a commendation. For Sobers and Ian Chappell, the former Australian captain, he has rather more than that. Except when in such company, deference is not in his repertoire. Only once has he appeared overawed at a sporting event: when partnering Stefan Edberg in a celebrity tennis doubles match in London against John McEnroe and Richard Branson. Imran plays little tennis but he was flattered that Edberg, whom he felt was 'thoroughly gentlemanly', had watched him on television. He knew he was in the presence of a world star of comparable standing.

The flip side of a belief in mankind and holding forcibly expressed opinions is a naivety that manifests itself in his business dealings. 'Imran talks too much and doesn't find out what other people are like,' said Javed Burki, whose immediate family on one occasion discussed subjects Imran knew nothing about to see how long he would tolerate it. He exploded after thirty seconds. 'There is nothing bad about him, which is why he puts up with all these creeps who don't harm him but want to exploit him. He is hopeless at business. He is not a street-fighter, he doesn't have to worry about where his next meal is coming from – he is so good himself he thinks everybody else is good. Then he complains about them to me.'

Had he been more materialistically inclined, Imran's face would have been his fortune. By comparison with the likes of Edberg and McEnroe, he is a pauper, but his sensitivity towards his culture is such that there is a limit to the modelling assignments he undertakes. He is adept at deflecting an interviewer's line of questioning by recalling that his older sister, Robina, told him he was ugly when he was a boy; but he is aware of the hypnotic effect he has over women. He could hardly fail not to be when in England debs fall at his feet and on the subcontinent girls bombard him with telephone calls and proposals of an arranged marriage. 'Very few women seem to keep their decorum with him, partly because he has developed a relaxed, confident manner,' said Mermagen. If he does ever marry, and he himself feels it is now unlikely, the dowry will have to be a sizable one. Eligible bachelors are normally eligible for a few years. In Imran's case it is becoming a matter of decades.

He is more pinned up than down, which is a challenge in itself. He is the confutation of the English idea of a Pakistani as small, rotund and presiding over the corner shop with incomprehensible dialect. His appearance is at once masculine, athletic, handsome and intelligent. He has the face of a good man. His skin is sufficiently touched by the East to be exotic; his body, unpolluted by alcohol or cigarettes, is still in the condition it was when he was playing cricket. Other members of his family have the same Oxbridge drawl, only not so heightened. Some of his phraseology is distinctly English upper class, although he would not wish for that to be remarked upon since he and his family have long held in contempt those Pakistanis – the kala sahibs – who distanced themselves from their backgrounds and tried to ape their rulers. There is a feline ease of movement and an edge of arrogance. 'I have never heard anyone call him "Immy" and survive,' said Emma Sergeant. If the conversation takes an unexpected turn, the nostrils can flare: Imran can be stern enough when the occasion warrants it, but he has no side. Throw in his love of women, his politeness, intellect, outstanding cricketing ability, a reputation for an entourage that is the very stuff of gossip columns, and making his entry into cocktail parties 'with his back straight instead of scuttling in and fiffling and faffling around' as his friend Sarah Crawley puts it, and you have a rare mortal. 'No man looks as devastating as Imran,' said Marie Helvin, the model and a friend of many years' standing. 'Everyone falls for him. He has a scent that is very attractive to women.'

Emma Sergeant is the only girl Imran has ever truly loved. A Muslim can marry a Christian, or a Jew, but not always a Hindu, which meant that at a time when he was more attuned to the idea of an arranged marriage, he would not have proposed to Reynu Malla, the pretty, diminutive daughter of a Nepalese princess and the grand-daughter of a Maharajah of Nepal. They met in 1981 when she was only sixteen and studying in India, before Imran had made his way in London society. Any prospect of the relationship continuing was scuppered by her protective mother, who did not consider Imran sufficiently well bred. She was one of the very few people to have intimidated him. 'He is terribly uncomfortable with people he doesn't know and didn't make an effort with my parents. He was very shy and reserved, which led people to think he was arrogant – but that wasn't so,' said Reynu.

On the surface at least, Imran moves with ease between the cultures of East and West, following to the best of his ability, he says, the guidelines of the Koran. He sees his life as part of an extended youth which will be ended only if his sisters find him the perfect bride. At a dinner in Islamabad, his audience laughed when he spoke of not being ready to settle down. But if they found him to be having an affair with one of their daughters, they would shoot him. Pakistanis are aware that he is not

14

a virgin but so long as he does not flaunt women in front of them, it does not concern them. 'If I had married early, it would have held me back. I might have got further than I have, but I don't think so,' he says. He has long been careful in his handling of female sexual adulation. Scandalous stories, some lifted from English papers, have appeared about him in Pakistan but have died away as a result of his own discretion. He does not rule out marriage to an English girl but, as Emma Sergeant discovered, living in Pakistan is nigh impossible for a woman accustomed to the freedom of the West.

The likelihood is that he will never marry. As the years go by, an arranged marriage in his own country becomes increasingly improbable given that most girls are betrothed at a young age and that he is unwilling to give up spending much of the English summer at his flat in central London. Most of the girls he has been associated with are Europeans. There is a further, more compelling reason. 'He feels because he has not married he is being saved for something that should not be constrained by marriage,' said his friend Emily Todhunter. 'He feels he has had too much luck, that his career, culminating in winning the World Cup, has gone too damn tickety-boo. He has confidence in his destiny.'

Mystics in Pakistan, or, as Imran prefers to call them, guides, have long given that impression. His mother (but not his father) would journey out of Lahore to a village to see her own guide, who said – when Imran was but fourteen – that he would be famous in her lifetime. She never said anything so flattering to Majid Khan's mother, Shaukat's sister – even though he looked then as if he would become as good as any postwar batsman. Shaukat had great faith in her only son and this was affirmation of it. Imran has subsequently invested much belief in his own guide, not least when a stress fracture of his shin almost brought his career to a premature end. In 1988 he was told by a different clairvoyant that he would be assassinated if he went into politics. Six days later President Zia, who had been supportive of Imran to the point of bringing him out of retirement, was blown up in his own aeroplane. He had just offered Imran a post in Pakistan's government.

Imran declined a further offer of a cabinet position in 1993 from Pakistan's interim government, contenting himself with the loosely defined post of ambassador for tourism. 'He knows that if he went into politics he would have to change a whole class of rulers. He believes almost in revolution. There would be violence and it would be frightening,' said the Marchioness of Worcester, whose various causes Imran supports and publicizes. 'I told him that he had to be prepared to die for his country and he said he will go into politics when he is ready to die. I think he would be prepared to put up with this threat, to risk his life for the justice of his country.'

Even if he were not assassinated, Imran would lose the respect, to say nothing of the deification, of half the populace of Pakistan if he became a politician. His beneficence would be greater in social work, in the environment, in tourism. He is not enamoured of the grubby compromises of politics. His idea of a politician is, interestingly enough, not a front-ranking individual such as his Oxford contemporary Benazir Bhutto, but Ken Livingstone, the Labour MP, on account of what Imran sees as his compassion and care for the underdog, and Lord Gilmour, the elegant, profoundly un-Thatcherite Tory minister whose son, Oliver, is a good friend.

Since Imran retired in 1992, his study of the Koran has supplanted his assimilation of cricket. He does not hanker for the past. He is not a sentimentalist. He prays every day and punctuates his conversation with quotations from the Koran, which he feels encompasses the wisdom of the Bible and the Torah and is a practical guide to life. He is starting to sell religion. He follows the Koran's guidelines by identifying his needs and giving superfluous money away, in his case to the hospital that commemorates his mother. His determination after her death to see this project through from conception spoke volumes about his character: his ambition that includes an element of self-glorification, his dedication, his virtuousness, his naivety. The inevitable hangers-on appeared but their cheques did not. The business sense of his father and various trustees was required to ensure that Shaukat's death through cancer was not in vain. Even so, for the project to succeed, for the funds to be raised, Pakistan had to win the World Cup in 1992. To Imran, it was a question not of if they would win, but when.

In Pakistan, Imran's name 'will be revered for centuries to come', as Waqar Younis, one of his protégés, puts it. He has no especial fear of bouncers, of girls selling their stories to tabloid newspapers, or of losing his virility. Yet he does have one phobia. In Ahmedabad in 1987, a time when Pakistan were carrying all before them, his close friend Mark Shand was startled to see Imran terrified by an interloper leaping from the fan on to the sofa in his hotel room. Khan, the leader of the tribe in the estimation of the Koran, has a deep-seated fear of lizards.

Chapter 2

Pakistan is a complex ravelment of indigenous peoples, many different types and tribes having migrated there both from the north west and across the subcontinent of India. All left their mark on the culture of the land. Around 10 per cent of the population of the country formed after independence in 1947 was made up of Pathans, or Pashtuns, whose forebears once comprised all the ruling families of the states of India. Imran can trace his Pathan ancestry back to the Middle Ages when his father's tribe, the Niazi, arrived in India and his mother's, the Burkis, came from Afghanistan. The bloodfeuds and the pride are apparent across the river Indus to this day. Pride is a word Imran uses a great deal.

The Niazis and the Burkis talk in Urdu rather than Pushto, the language spoken in what are still known as the tribal areas at the North-West Frontier. Yet Imran is sufficiently taken with his ancestry to detail to anyone who cares to listen the running battles which the Niazis fought over the Punjab plains with Mogul emperors. Pathans have an insatiable thirst for vengeance, as in more recent times the Russians discovered in Afghanistan, and these genes have been relevant not only to the way in which Imran has conducted his life but to his development as a fast bowler. Pathans seek revenge when their bowling is carted to the boundary.

Imran talks loosely of his father's 'village', as if that was where he grew up. Mianwali, where the Niazis settled, is on the Indus, at the foot of the Salt Range Mountains. It is an area that Imran visits whenever he can. He is happiest not at Lord's, nor at Tramp, but here, encapsulating his distinctive union of East and West by driving his land cruiser in Shalwar Kamiz and sandals, Pink Floyd on the cassette machine, to shoot partridge for a day. From his ancestry and from journeying to these remote areas he can apply such Pathan imagery as 'fighting like cornered tigers' in the World Cup final.

Imran's family farm 200 acres of sugar cane and wheat 150 miles from Lahore, and a further 200 acres of crops 100 miles distant. Hence although not an aristocratic or upper-class family, or even one that dominates the modern economy of Pakistan, it does represent old money. Imran's father, Ikramullah Niazi, an engineer by profession, lives in a six-bedroomed house built in 1962 on the smartest street in Lahore. Since the death of Imran's mother in 1985 he has lived alone – other than when Imran is in occupation of the top floor – for his daughters all married. The area, Zaman Park, a small, residential suburb in which as many as fifty houses are owned by his relatives, is situated on the right bank of the canal that runs through the centre of the city. It is named after Imran's maternal great-uncle, Zaman Khan, who when he lived there was the only Muslim inhabitant. During Partition, the Hindu families migrated to India and the Burkis, travelling away from there, clustered in Zaman Park. The upshot was the congregation of an extraordinarily large number of relatives who produced an extraordinarily large number of cricketers.

Number 2 Zaman Park is of dark red brick and prominent blue tiles redolent of some of the finest architecture in the country. Red brick and blue tiles have been used in the design of the hospital, a further bondstone with the mother whom Imran adored. Shaukat Khanum would, said her widower, have been amazed at the achievements of her only son, whom she and her four daughters, Robina, Aleema, Noreen and Uzma, cosseted. A conventional family of similar background on the subcontinent would have had a subservient attitude to the departed English, but not Imran's. Both parents were fiercely anti-colonial. His father instilled in him pride about his background; from his mother he inherited strength of character and opinion. He has a chauvinistic attitude towards his sisters.

Imran's father, in his seventies, still works as a consulting engineer for the Republic Engineering Consortium in Lahore.

19

He was a government employee before setting up his own firm. Imran's childhood memories of him are hazy in that he was always working and knew little of cricket: the first the father was aware of the son's prowess was when Imran was selected for Pakistan's 1971 tour of England. Ikramullah had played only football as a student, concentrating, instead, on studies which culminated in reading engineering at Imperial College in London in 1946. As well as Imran, one of his daughters, Robina, was to follow him to England, to the London School of Economics. All five children were privately schooled, illustrating the importance he attached to education. This in spite of there being no great riches to be made from civil engineering in Pakistan.

In Lahore, Imran's family are considered rich only by the poor. When it was put to him by journalists that he was a playboy, Imran had a ready response: 'Playboys have plenty of time and money. I have never had either.' He was not given any trust fund, as were some of his English friends. His pleasures in growing up in Pakistan had more to do with nature and the wild than material possessions. He delighted in the monkeys, wild birds, jackals and foxes to be found at the foothills of the Himalayas during holidays. Imran was, according to his family, uncomplaining as a boy, not prone to tears even when he constantly fell down the steps of a house they rented in the country.

From his mother, who, unusually, had not married within her own wider family, Imran also inherited his love of animals, wild life and mountains. In Lahore, there was sufficient space in the garden and the fields behind the family's home and their servants' quarters to keep numerous animals, including a water buffalo. His mother gave Imran 'complete devotion, a blanket of security'. She had high hopes for him. Influenced by her spiritual guide, she really did feel he would become a true leader; and she lived to see this come about.

Her husband would have no dealings with any kind of guide or clairvoyant. Although a steadfast Muslim, he was too immersed in the practicalities of temporal existence. Strangely for a man who had such an absolute belief in the value of education, and who wanted Imran to follow in his own profession as an engineer, Ikramullah paid less heed to his son's schooling than to that of his four daughters. 'I never bothered about his studies but gave him a sense of responsibility for his own actions. I felt that if he was honest in his dealings and had a purpose, God would help him. My daughters were more academic, whereas Imran's reports were average,' he said.

Nevertheless, Ikramullah was intent upon Imran furthering, or rather finishing, his education in England. Of the two schools Imran went to in Lahore, Cathedral did not have the same standing as Aitchison College, which was as prestigious as any public school in undivided India and maintained its standards after the country was partitioned. The cricket grounds at Aitchison and the Gymkhana Club in Lahore were a match even for those at the Parks in Oxford and at Worcester, Imran's first county club. The standard was commensurate within the settings, and it was of a high order, too, in Zaman Park. Not that Imran could hold his own when a boy: his bowling, he said, was more of a danger to his own fielders and such innings as he had ended in swift dismissal and tantrums. He was out of his class and knew it.

Yet the game was rapidly becoming an obsession. Perhaps this was inevitable. Eight first cousins on his mother's side of the family had played first-class cricket, including two who had captained Pakistan. Javed Burki remains a hero to this day; Majid Khan was until he and Imran fell out in 1982. Majid's father, Jehangir Khan, was a Cambridge Blue who played for India and is best known for having inadvertently killed a sparrow while batting at Lord's. The bird is stuffed and displayed in the MCC museum. Two other relatives, Asad Khan and Ahmad Raza Khan, as well as the latter's two sons, also played first-class cricket. It was a hard but natural act for Imran to follow.

By comparison with his cousins and Wasim Raja, a contemporary who went to a different school in Lahore and who was a highly mature schoolboy cricketer, Imran did not appear to be gifted in his early teenage years. When a cousin, Javed Zaman,

21

took him partridge shooting as a teenager, he hit everything in sight. That, rather than batting and bowling, appeared to be his strength. Javed Burki had captained Pakistan at the age of twenty-four; Majid Khan, on his first-class debut at fifteen had made a century and taken six wickets. Cricketers of international standard matured at an early age on the subcontinent.

Wasim Raja, whose father played for Lahore Gymkhana, the Burkis' club, and who captained the Punjab under-19 side Imran played in, recalls a boy with a slinging action like that of Jeff Thomson, the Australian fast bowler. 'He couldn't come to terms with me having more talent than him – I did not have to work so hard,' said Wasim. 'Imran sprayed the ball about, almost killing the square-leg umpire, and could not understand why I took him off. He held a bit of a grudge over it.'

Imran could at least bowl fast, however waywardly. He was strong and tall and he had the inclination to do so. Playing under Javed Burki for a governor's eleven against a Punjab eleven, he took six wickets and surprised everyone with his speed. The wicketkeeper who greatly assisted him in this feat was Wasim Bari, who was four years his senior. 'I considered asking Imran to rebuild his action but thought better of it as he could get people out through sheer pace,' said Javed.

As a sixteen-year-old, Imran came into contact for the first time with boys from different backgrounds who had learned their cricket on the roadside. Class divisions were acute; as when he first played for Pakistan, there was an element of suspicion that he was not chosen on merit. On his first-class debut for Lahore against Sargodha, also when he was sixteen, Imran fell asleep during a delay caused by rain and did not wake in time to open the innings. The chairman of selectors was his uncle and the captain and senior player were his cousins, so inevitably there were those who felt the admonishment he received was not sufficient punishment.

After that match, Aitchison would not allow Imran to play any more first-class cricket for fear of disrupting his studies. Immediately after taking his O levels he switched to Cathedral

School and, resuming playing for Lahore at the age of ei[
achieved sufficient success to earn his first inclusion in *I*
Against Western Railways he scored 40 and took six for 54.
in that 1970–1 season Imran made an unbeaten half-centu[
a Pakistan XI against an International XI. He was rarely seen in
any cricket other than Test matches in Pakistan after that, but
it was an innings which helped gain him selection for the 1971
tour of England. He had not yet played in ten first-class matches.
The question of whether this was merited was to be asked for
the remainder of the year.

Imran was a bumptious eighteen-year-old when he was chosen
for Pakistan's 1971 tour of England. For that judgement we have
his own word. If that was not sufficient to make him unpopular,
his family ties were. The Khans and Burkis were seen as the
forces running domestic cricket and, because Imran had played
fewer than ten first-class matches, he was thought by some of
the senior players to have gained his place in the touring party
through family preference. He was, in their estimation, a
cricketer of less than average ability and they treated him as
such throughout the tour.

This was a view that Intikhab Alam, his first captain, did not
share. 'Imran was chosen on merit and I was keen to take him,'
he said. Imran was, to his mind, enthusiastic and willing to work
hard. He also had, as does many an eighteen-year-old, an inflated
estimation of his own worth. He did not contemplate a learning
process: he thought in terms of being the star of a series Pakistan
would win. No matter that England had just regained the Ashes
in Australia.

Imran's very first net practice at Lord's made him realize the
folly of this. His first ball, delivered in new kit and boots, sailed
past Aftab Gul's nose. This would have been almost forgivable
had Aftab not been batting in the adjoining net. Apologizing
profusely, Imran tried again. His next ball hit a spectator on the
side of the head. As well as not having a proper run-up, Imran
had made no allowances for the difference between the hard

surfaces at home and the soft turf of an English spring. For a long while he could not pitch the ball on a line with the stumps. One umpire, in addressing a batsman taking guard, summed up Imran's bowling when he peeled off his sweater as 'right arm over, anywhere'. That and a speech at Lord's by the manager, Masud Salahuddin, who told MCC members that they had been responsible for teaching his players how to hold a knife and fork, made for humour that was far from prevalent for most of the tour. It also embarrassed Imran, conscious as he was of a distinct subservience among Pakistanis of that generation. He became, for the first time, aware of racism. There were remarks, when he went out to bat, such as 'It's a bit dark here.' When the Pakistanis played Yorkshire at Bradford, one of the players was grabbed by a policeman from an alleyway as he walked down the street. They were perplexed, after having been brought up on stories about how wonderful the British Bobby and system of justice were.

In all senses, Imran was a callow tourist. He was the youngest member of the party, had never been out of Pakistan before and found the whole experience a complete contrast in culture. 'I had an idea of the Western way of life from seeing films at school and watching television at home but it was nothing like what hit me when I actually arrived,' he said. 'I was dazzled by the restaurants, the cinemas, the discos, even the shops. I am not at all the shopping type but I think every Pakistani is struck by this. When we arrived, we had a field day at Lillywhite's. In those days we did not have contracts with bat companies and we were just given an allowance and told, "This is where you buy your equipment." We were fascinated just looking at all the different bats.'

Normally, a tour party would not have had to consider such an inexperienced cricketer for a Test place. Pakistan, though, had problems. Two of their quicker bowlers, Saleem Altaf and Sarfraz Nawaz, were both injured, so the tour selectors had no option but to include Imran, who still had not sorted out his run-up, for the first Test. His first over at this level has stayed indelibly in his mind. It was bowled to Colin Cowdrey, who was playing first-class cricket before Imran was born and who two decades later was to be a fellow delegate in shaping the affairs of international cricket. The first four balls were full tosses, each one starting wide and going wider. Cowdrey was so bemused he failed to score off any of them, almost getting out through slicing one of them exceedingly close to his leg stump. The ball was swinging all over the place and Imran had scant idea how to control it.

Intikhab – whom Imran calls Skip to this day – told him to relax, not to become too tense when spraying the ball around and reminded him that an inswinger should start outside the off-stump. Soon after that Imran was taken off and was to bowl in only brief spells for the remainder of the match, although they were more tidy than those first five overs. What with having made just five runs in a total of 608 for seven – albeit running himself out when the declaration was imminent – it was clear that he would take little further part on what was only a three-Test tour.

In retrospect, Imran felt that if the tour had ended after that experience at Edgbaston, he would have settled for studying, gone into the Civil Service and not played Test cricket again. The remainder of his tour was not memorable. He was reported to the management by the senior players for a variety of reasons. He slipped out of his hotel to a disco after stuffing a pillow down his bed, was caught and fined £2. Saeed Ahmed, the most senior player in the party, reported him for breaking a curfew so that he would no longer have to share a room. Sadiq Mohammad went to see the manager after Imran refused to fetch him a cup of tea, saying he was not a servant. At one point on the tour two players sat discussing Imran's poor performances, well aware he could overhear them. Their remarks were to the effect that he was fit only for club cricket – not far off the mark considering that was more or less the standard he had been accustomed to in Pakistan. He felt so humiliated that he vowed there and then to make the grade at Test level.

25

England won the series through winning the final Test at Headingley, a match Imran took no part in. His 12 wickets on the tour, gained through ballooning inswingers, cost him 43.91 apiece. 'His success after that speaks volumes for his strength of character,' said Asif Iqbal, one of his more critical compatriots at the time. Other than his cousin Majid, who returned to Cambridge before the end of the tour, the player with whom Imran struck up a good friendship was Sarfraz Nawaz. 'Everywhere we went he was looking for milk. I took him to the Mecca dancing hall at Leicester Square and people fell about laughing when he asked for it. He would go after a girl who didn't fancy him, even if she was the ugliest in the room, because it was a challenge. But since he didn't drink, it was difficult to stay in a disco for long. On the field, I found he always wanted to learn.'

In later years, Sarfraz would teach Imran much about the art of fast bowling, particularly the controversial method of wetting one side of the ball that would lead to insinuations of ball-tampering. During the years of World Series Cricket, Imran would be taught still more by John Snow, just as Dennis Lillee was. For the time being, however, he knew that academic studies had to come first. His parents were particularly concerned that these should not be interrupted for long.

An approach from Worcestershire suited ideally, given that he could study and board at Worcester Royal Grammar School with a view to going to Oxford or Cambridge, as several members of his family had done. RGS was an independent institution (his father paid the fees) with an academic reputation. It was chosen in conjunction with the county, which was why Imran did not go to somewhere better known, besides which Ikramullah was not conversant with schools in England. He had to cram a two-year course in economics and geography into one year. Endless dark days, such as he had not experienced before, coupled with good teaching, enabled him to do so, although come the end of his first term (December 1971) the teachers did not feel he would pass his A levels the following summer. That he gained an A and a C was testimony to them and to his own intense studying.

He played some second eleven cricket before the end of the 1971 season, without much success, and worked on his bowling action in the school gym after taking some advice from John Parker, the New Zealander who had joined Worcestershire's staff at the same time. It was now that Imran developed a new action, culminating in a jump at the point of delivery that would ensure he would be side on and hence could develop an out-swinger. Sometimes it would take him too wide of the crease, but that leap would remain indelibly in the memory of cricket followers and commentators. 'For a moment his arms and legs, seemingly out of control, try desperately to detach themselves from his body. Then, miraculously, they rearrange themselves in an order that is as graceful as it is powerful and effective,' wrote Marcel Berlins in a profile for *The Times*. 'His left foot pounds the ground beneath it and his right hand releases the ball angrily at the waiting, apprehensive batsman. It is one of the breathtaking sights of modern cricket.'

If it was, Worcestershire's seasoned cricketers were as yet unaware of it. They reckoned Imran had the makings of a reasonable batsman – but would be nothing quicker than a swing bowler. 'Get it into your head – you're never going to be quick enough to be physically dangerous to batsmen,' said Glenn Turner. Since he was one of the best batsmen in the world, his opinion had to be given some credence. Imran's wages were reduced and, as he was told that he would be sacked if he did not get into Oxford, he felt no loyalty to the county thereafter. After he came down from Oxford for the remainder of the 1973 county season, he was moved down the batting order, made to bowl inswing to a packed legside field and proved effective only in the limited-overs matches. His stock stood almost as low as it had in 1971.

So it was not through any achievements in county cricket that Pakistan selected him for their three-Tests series in England in 1974. The way in which he had carried Oxford's batting and bowling had impressed the national selectors and, of course, he had the considerable advantage of being in form on English pitches. He was used as a third seamer, coming on after Sarfraz and Asif Masood had taken the new ball, and batted down the order, but contributed more than he had done in 1971. This was not borne out in terms of figures – 92 runs and five wickets at 51.60 in three Tests, although he averaged 31 with the bat in all tour matches – but *Wisden* evidently saw enough to claim: 'He should be a powerful figure in Pakistan cricket for years to come.'

Off the field, he found some players still distanced themselves from him. Asif Masood was one such. Wasim Raja, with whom he had played at under-19 level and who was making his first tour of England, felt that this stemmed from resentment towards Javed Burki when he had led Pakistan. 'Quite a few of Javed's players were ill-educated and thought he had a feeling of superiority because he had been to Oxford. Imran was spurred on by wanting to be like his heroes, Javed and Majid, and was also thought to have a superior attitude. People did not say this to his face but instead backed away and left him in his own castle.'

Imran still enjoyed the tour. All three Tests were drawn but he satisfied himself that he had greater pace and control than in 1971. Then, Wasim Bari had reckoned he would become a better batsman than a bowler. 'In his first Test he had asked me how to bowl a straight ball. He was directing it towards fine leg.' Now, the improvement was apparent.

The following year, his studies at Oxford complete, Imran returned to Pakistan for the first time in four years. After the disappointments of the World Cup and his sadness over finishing at Oxford, he had had a dismal remainder of the season with the bat back at Worcester, averaging ten in 11 matches. His bowling was more successful. Yet in Pakistan he determined to be a fast bowler – or nothing. The pitches were too hard and slow to dismiss batsmen regularly through standard medium-pace. He also resolved to master the hook shot, which he could not yet play with conviction, practising each day at the Lahore Gymkhana Club.

One reason for this was that he was receiving numerous bouncers in retaliation for the good many he was delivering. His first over of a spell with a new ball would often include four. In the mid-1970s the bouncer was overused by fast bowlers throughout the world, notably by Australians and West Indians. Administrators vacillated, umpires were seemingly impotent and player power prevailed. Imran admits he bowled too many bouncers when he was young but he remains unequivocal that it is up to the umpire to arbitrate when this occurs.

His genes had something to do with this approach to cricket. When he was hit for four, his reaction was an anger that rarely surfaced away from the game. The red mists came down, and so did the bouncers. There was no mistaking the temperament of a mean fast bowler.

His ancestry evidently had something to do with his becoming the first truly fast bowler to emanate from Pakistan or India. This was apparent when he excelled with bat and ball on a short Pakistan tour to Sri Lanka in January 1976. In the hot English summer that followed, Imran became, in the words of *Wisden*, 'identified as an all-rounder of world-class possibilities'. Uncapped at the start of the season, he finished it with 61 wickets, several of them gained with huge inswingers, and 1059 runs. Here, it seemed, was an overseas player who would shape Worcestershire's affairs for years to come.

Yet the attractions of Worcester, the quintessential county ground, were lost on Imran. No matter that it possessed a beauty similar to that of the tree-lined Aitchison College or the Parks, the town was, to the young Imran, a sleepy place. He declared it to be too boring. He particularly liked Basil d'Oliveira and had become quite friendly with John Inchmore, the stalwart county medium-pacer, but in terms of age and background he had little in common with anybody. After Oxford – three years of stimulating social discourse which had ended the previous summer – he was just existing. 'I was basically unhappy living there. I didn't know anyone. There were no friends. There was nothing to do in the town and I felt I was just wasting my life,' he lamented.

Worcestershire were convinced that Imran was wanted by another county. Or else that there could not be enough women in the town to satisfy him. 'If I had wanted to be dishonest, I could have said I was unhappy because I was not getting enough money or because I didn't like the team. I was honest and told them I couldn't live in Worcester. My reasons were purely social – they had nothing to do with cricket. I tried to explain all this to them but they never understood. I am sure they still don't understand,' Imran said. He had seen enough of London to know that he wanted to live there, or near to it. Having graduated from the motorcycle of his student days to a Mazda car, he would go to the cinemas and discos of the West End on his own: it was several more years before he would have his own circle of friends based there. He stayed at that time in the Shepherd's Bush flat of the journalist Qamar Ahmed, who would indulge his passion for food. Also lodging there from time to time was a young Pakistani who was playing in the Bolton League. Imran had begun his long, prickly association with Javed Miandad.

His disagreement with Worcestershire rumbled on. Their committee, claiming to have paid for Imran's education (in fact his parents had) blocked his prospects of playing for another county the following season. The Test and County Cricket Board's registration committee found Imran's reasoning not strong enough, only to have their verdict overturned by the Cricket Council. It transpired that Imran was allowed to play for another county – he had opted for Sussex – before the end of the 1977 season. A special registration could be completed on July 31, opposing Worcestershire's request that he should be made to wait twelve months before playing elsewhere. The saga was protracted and bitter – Imran was subjected to racial abuse in later years at Worcester – and culminated in Sussex hiring a lawyer to resolve the issue. There was talk of some county cricketers, upset by what they perceived as disloyalty, refusing to play against Imran, although that never came about.

Imran was delighted when he heard he could play some cricket other than for Worthing during the 1977 season. Clearly he was taken with the idea of bowling with John Snow, whom he had looked up to as a schoolboy. It was a case that was thought at the time to have cheapened players' loyalty to their clubs and to have sparked off a cricket transfer market but, largely owing to the Benefit system – a virtual guarantee of tax-free remuneration from supporters following ten years as a capped player – little movement of players ensued in the years that followed.

In the midst of all this, Imran became involved in wrangles over pay. He had his first experience of cricket politics in Pakistan when several players objected about their remuneration to the Board of Control. For the series against New Zealand they were each to be paid 1000 rupees per Test (around £50), which was less than any other country paid its Test cricketers. Six of their foremost players objected to this, including Imran, who said that he was more concerned with the lack of consultation than the money involved. No sooner had this been resolved and the pay increased to 5000 rupees a Test, than Imran was invited by Tony Greig, his prospective Sussex captain, to sign to play for Kerry Packer's World Series Cricket.

It was a flattering offer that he could not have dreamed of receiving two years, or even twelve months, earlier. The original fourteen Rest of the World cricketers who would take on the Australians included two other Pakistanis, Asif Iqbal and his cousin Majid. If the challenge was not enough, the money most certainly was. Greig mistakenly assured Imran that he would still be able to play Test cricket since a compromise would have to be reached with Packer. 'Tony probably brought Imran to Hove because he thought that here was a Packer man in the making,' said John Barclay, a team-mate who later captained Sussex. 'Tony was an addictive person, very persuasive, and had a glamorous touch to him. Imran was very attracted to that concept.'

The aspect of World Series Cricket which was not appealing to Imran was missing Test cricket that spanned eighteen months. No compromise could be reached between Packer and the International Cricket Conference and it was only through the intervention of General Zia, the autocratic president who was to play a significant and persuasive part in Imran's career, that Imran did not miss still more Test matches. Zia instructed the Board to pick the Packer players for the series against India in 1978, when rather more than just cricketing pride was at stake.

If this was an unsettling, peripatetic time for Imran (he had to apologize to Sussex for absentmindedly wearing a World Series shirt soon after joining the county), it was one that had an important bearing on his career. He revelled in the cut and thrust of World Series Cricket, gleaning aspects of fast bowling from John Snow that were denied him soon after he joined Sussex since Snow left the county earlier than anticipated. This, too, was the period in which cricketers attained, or had levied upon them, personality cults. They were marketed as never before. Relatively unknown for the first few years of his career, he now found upon returning to Pakistan in 1978 that many women were after him.

It was the period in which Imran would learn how to swing an old ball. Sarfraz Nawaz was, other than Imran himself, Pakistan's most potent fast bowler in the 1970s. He is both charming and contrary. To this day, his methods of swinging an old ball have been viewed in England with suspicions ranging from puzzlement, to downright allegations of ball tampering from his Northamptonshire team-mate, Allan Lamb.

Sarfraz blames the press for this as much as he does Lamb. 'Imran was very quick in the mid-1970s but I used to be able to move the ball. He asked me to teach him how to swing it when it became worn, so I instructed him how to shine it. In England, county cricketers don't look at what they are doing and shine both sides when they are returning the ball to the bowler, who then rubs both sides in the palms of his hands. In Pakistan, players only polish one side – the fielders are asked not to shine it at all.

'I used to rub an old ball on a clean and dry part of my flannels. Some bowlers used polyester but I always wore cotton, which gave a good shine, helped by sweat from my naturally oily skin and a lot of spit. This is straight swing, not reverse swing, but it does not work in wet conditions since both sides become polished,' said Sarfraz. 'Speed works a lot into it. Even school-boys swing the ball in Pakistan.'

Snow, Sarfraz and, upon joining Sussex, Garth le Roux all gave Imran the kind of help that only truly top-class fast bowlers can. In spite of Imran's natural disapproval of apartheid and lack of empathy with English county cricketers who spent their winters in South Africa, he forged his closest friendship during his eleven-year association with the county with this tall, decidedly quick Afrikaner. They roomed together and had a mutual respect that surprised some who knew them, for the process of dismant-ling apartheid had still to begin. Opening the bowling together, they were lethal. From his first season in 1977, when he was able to play in eight matches, Imran was described by *Wisden* as having 'mounted hostile spells down the Hove slope reminiscent of Snow'. He took 25 wickets and finished ahead of Snow and Greig in the bowling averages.

He and le Roux would visit clubs in the area while most of the players preferred to go to the pub. Imran could not under-stand why they considered him standoffish, given that they had seen him throughout the day. He got on best with the young players, but appreciated anyone with an enthusiasm for cricket and life. The kind of solid, conservative old pro, suspicious of anything or anybody out of the ordinary, was never to his taste. He lived, initially, in a flat in Brighton until the lure of central London proved too great to resist, surprised though he was to discover there was no Pakistani community there.

In those years, his was not the lifestyle of Prince Ranjitsinhji, his nephew Duleepsinhji, nor even the younger Nawab of Pataudi, all of whom had adorned Hove before him. He had yet to embark on what the *Independent* called 'a social life of extreme elegance'. He was not a maharajah, a rajah, a nawab, not even a zamindar. Yet he had joined a county with an affinity for promi-nent individuals from the Orient. It is not only the strokeplay of Fry and Dexter that comes to the mind's eye on late summer afternoons when Hove seems blessed with a golden hue.

At the time of Imran's joining, Sussex was not so much blessed as damned. He did have the occasional match with Snow – they bowled out a Hampshire side that contained Barry Richards – but it was no more than that. Snow left the county before the 1978 season, around the time Imran was developing into a world-class fast bowler, and Greig departed a few months later. Imran was fast discovering that to plan a cricket career, or indeed a life, was futile.

Chapter 3

O xford was the bedrock of Imran's intellectual as well as sporting development. His affection for the city, for his college, Keble, and the Parks, a ground whose beauty he equates with Aitchison College, is undimmed. Friendships begun with tutors and undergraduates remain to this day, although geographical distances are such as to preclude all but the occasional visit. In the 1990s, Imran is welcomed to Keble in the widest possible sense: as an honorary fellow of the college, he is entitled to eat there free at any time he chooses. Although the college is renowned for sporting excellence, Imran is their only fellow to have been elected for distinction in this field.

Oxford was not Imran's first choice. Majid Khan had been to Cambridge, where he had been renowned for a certain arrogance as well as cricketing brilliance and, if it had not been for their admissions policy changing, that would have been the obvious university for Imran. Yet he was turned down. His A-level grades would have gained him admission had he been of the previous generation; now, though, a games player of borderline academic prowess was as often as not rejected. Thus came the standard of Oxbridge cricket to be lowered, leading to interminable discussion over whether or not its first-class status should be retained. The admissions tutors shrunk by their own myopia.

A place at an English university would mean that Imran would be regarded as an English player for registration purposes and hence would be able to continue playing for Worcestershire. If not, he would be sacked. John Parker, a lesser talent, although not obviously so in 1972, had been registered ahead of Imran. It was a bleak outlook.

A cousin of Imran's, Asad Khan, had been up at Keble and commended him to Dr Paul Hayes, a fellow and tutor there since 1965. Hayes agreed to see Imran and, impressed with his intelligence as much as his sporting ability, offered him a place. 'He was on the margins but would not have been considered had he not had the academic interest and commitment. He played the game in that he knew he had been given exceptional consideration and was prepared to work hard. Sportsmen have respected that here, with only one exception.' It was agreed that Imran would read geography in his first year and then switch to politics and economics, his favoured subject. The reason for this was that a foreign language, in addition to his native Urdu, was a requirement of first-year study of philosophy, politics and economics. Studying geography could circumvent this.

Imran had also satisfied Gordon Smith, the geography tutor at Keble, of his intellect. 'Imran's A levels were perfectly respectable – it would not be fair to take a pupil just for cricket or rugby if he could not gain a degree. He was a run-of-the-mill student but he did his work on time, struck me as mature, and talked sensibly. He thought geography would be useful for agriculture at home. But status was important to him, which was why he preferred to read politics and economics. I was surprised in later years that he stuck with cricket.'

His tutors felt that, when he went up in the autumn of 1972, Imran was thinking of a career more in terms of the diplomatic service in Pakistan than as a cricketer. His intention was to follow the pattern set by his cousin, Javed Burki – a great deal of cricket and enjoyable socializing, some hard work at the end and then back to Pakistan to join the Civil Service. He managed all but the last. Although he did not lack self-belief as a cricketer, he was not the self-confident individual he was to become, and he knew that an Oxford education would give him wider career opportunities. It made him realize how the English class system worked: friends attracted to him through cricket had contacts he might not otherwise have met.

'This was obviously a formative age because a tight rein had been kept on him in Pakistan and there had been constraints at school in Worcester. He talked a lot about values and was uncompromising rather than arrogant in working out what he believed in,' said Dr Hayes. If there was a time when he would lose his sense of direction, go off the rails, it was now. Benazir Bhutto's brother had his problems adjusting to Oxford, as many a Pakistani would have done. Benazir herself was a contemporary of Imran's. The decade after Oxford it was a question of who was the greater luminary: the sylph of a prime minister or the imperious cricket captain. They were friends in their last year at Oxford but never discussed politics and had little contact thereafter.

The opportunities were there for Imran to try both drugs and alcohol. His own rationalization of the Koran led him to believe that it was absurd to ban alcohol in Pakistan. And yet he kept clear of it. It is said – erroneously – that the only time he had a strong drink, he spent the remainder of the evening talking about fielding practice. He did not dislike the taste but was conscious even at such a young age of the necessity to keep himself in prime physical shape if he was to bowl fast at the highest level. 'There was a lot of dope around in those days but he was not interested in it,' said Guy Waller, his closest friend from Oxford. 'He was very consistent about looking after his body.'

Waller, who was three years older and who played under Imran in the Varsity match of 1974, was impressed by the pride Imran took in his studies and in not letting himself down. This did not extend to his cooking: Waller and his wife taught him how to make curry after being unable to eat the fare Imran gave them for dinner. Imran lived at first in hall (the showers were in a separate block) and then catered for himself in a flat he shared with two other undergraduates above a fruiterer's in Summer-town, a suburb of Oxford. In his third year he moved to a flat in the city. He drove around on a battered Bantam motorcycle, as cold and miserable in the winter as he had been in Worcester. 'He was far less confident than he was to become and because he was shy and his English was poor when he arrived at Oxford, he came across as arrogant,' said Waller. 'He was very generous and warm-hearted but did not appear that way because of his lack of familiarity. Oxford totally liberated him.'

Imran's priorities were clear. In the winter he had to work harder than other undergraduates in order to leave as much time as possible for cricket in the summer term. In this way he brought a discipline to his game that was to benefit him throughout his career. He mixed among men whom he rarely came across in county cricket and, for that matter, women too. 'It was not unknown for him to lose concentration at the crease if he saw some beautiful girl on the boundary,' said Dr Hayes. 'Then he would hare off after her when he was out.' The female following that he had at Oxford was not exaggerated. Girls flocked around him, giving him a reputation for sexual success that made contemporaries thoroughly envious.

'Oxford was a complete education. It helped me to grow up, to find myself, and it matured me in a cricketing sense. I enjoyed it to the full,' he said. He might also, had he had the time, have gained a hockey Blue. He played for Keble, helping win the inter-college cup in 1973, but, in the knowledge that he had enough to contend with on the cricket field, did not attempt to compete at a higher level. In the summer terms he would have his tutorials either early in the morning or in the early evening. Those students who had to attend with him did not demur. In the vacations he studied, according to Dr Hayes, more than most did. Indeed, he took his work seriously enough to tell Pakistan's selectors that he would not be available for the 1975 World Cup until his finals were over. He had no trust fund, nor any pocket money from his parents: war had broken out with India and money could not be sent out of Pakistan. Their priority was his sister, Robina, who was then at the London School of Economics. In Imran's second year at Oxford he took a menial job before Christmas at Littlewoods in London, cleaning plates and cutting cheese – neither of which comes easily to him. After two weeks he was sacked 'by a battleaxe of a woman'.

Inevitably, the amount of sport he played affected his work, just as three years' acting would have done. Conversely, the responsibility of having to work helped make him a better player. Given the opportunity to bat at number four and open the bowling in each of his three years against first-class cricketers, Imran benefited to the extent that by the time he left he could bowl fast for lengthy periods and make large scores against both county and tourist opposition. His team-mates constantly cajoled him to bowl more quickly and, having been frustrated at Worcester by being asked to concentrate on line and length at military medium, this was a boon. He had the passion, strength and temperament to be a fast bowler, and he had become bored with negative second-eleven county cricket that served only to massage the averages of first-team batsmen.

Whether he had the action to do so was another matter. It would have been hard for any impressionable youngster to escape the strictures of Glenn Turner. Yet the advice of John Parker, coupled with a coaching session during one lunch interval at the Parks from Bill Alley, the Australian umpire, modified his action. It was not until Imran returned to Pakistan after leaving Oxford that he knew, for certain, that he wanted to become a genuinely quick bowler. There was scant profit in run-restricting seam-up in Lahore or Karachi.

The extent to which Oxford's sides were dependent upon Imran is evident from a cursory glance at the averages. 'The Oxford captain, Keith Jones, had an outstanding freshman in Imran Khan, who failed to gain admission at Cambridge, and his presence was immediately felt,' declared *Wisden* of his first season. Opening the bowling with Tim Lamb, later to join Middlesex, Northamptonshire and the Test and County Cricket Board, he was the leading wicket-taker (30) and made 469 middle-order runs. Having, in Imran, a Test cricketer in the same side was, of course, a novelty for undergraduates who were starry-eyed at the prospect of playing against their heroes in a way that he was not.

The following year, 1974, when he performed well enough to be recalled to Pakistan's party for the tour of England, Oxford did beat one county. The reasons for this were clear: Imran made 170 and took seven wickets. His splendid achievements – 767 runs including two centuries in one match against Nottingham-shire and 45 wickets – were marred only by some inept cricket in the Varsity match at Lord's. He had proved an inspirational captain but, perhaps because his was inevitably too much of a one-man side, could be dismissive of the suggestions of others. He made a lot of tactical mistakes.

He was ridiculed by his team-mates for attempting to develop a leg break in the middle of the Varsity match. Yet it almost came off when a Cambridge batsman dollied up what looked to be a straightforward catch. Waller, circling underneath, remembers Imran grinning broadly at him – until he dropped it. There was little else for anyone to be amused about, for this was a dismal match. Imran himself had done much to give Oxford every chance of winning, taking ten wickets and making 46 in his second innings. They needed 62 off the final 20 overs with wickets in hand and there was, according to *Wisden*, 'no excuse' for not gaining them. 'Imran's clear instructions to go for a win were disregarded by Edward Thackeray, who must shoulder the blame for a dreadful display.' Thackeray, who did well to get a job as a master at Eton after such damning comments, batted so slowly that Imran was reduced to poring over the rules of the game to see whether his innings could be declared closed. It could not. The match dissolved into a dull draw and the players were so upset about it that they never had a reunion.

On less intense occasions, Oxford's side would tease Imran mercilessly – as many of his friends would do in the future. Any pomposity was immediately punctured. 'There was a strange sort of stability about our lives,' said Waller, who left that year. The following summer, 1975, Imran devoted to his finals. He gave up the captaincy and played all too little cricket – four matches – and yet still topped Oxford's batting and bowling averages. For his third successive year, the Varsity match was drawn. He worked hard in the run up to his exams, as his tutor verified. The problem was that the World Cup was staged slap bang in the middle of them. It was the first of its kind, Pakistan had the talent to win it, and Imran naturally was keen to be included.

He was asked to play in their match against Australia, the day after taking two papers, and unwisely agreed. For there were more papers to come the following week.

Even at that age, though, skirting round challenges was not Imran's modus operandi. After sitting two papers on the Friday, he set off for Leeds, arriving at the hotel at 4 a.m. on the day of the match. Pakistan were beaten – disappointingly – and Imran's return journey to Oxford via British Rail proved as long-winded as the match had. He arrived in the early hours of the following morning, went down with flu soon afterwards and was in no fit state for his final two papers the next Wednesday. He gained a good second-class grade for politics but only a third for economics, a subject he had chosen because it had special reference to issues affecting the Third World. 'I was disappointed. I had done a lot of work in my third year. I thought I should have got a good second,' he said. His tutor, Dr Hayes, concurred. 'If you are asking me whether Imran was up to the intellectual standards of Oxbridge, my answer is yes. He was not a sportsman third class at all – it was a gross injustice to his intellect and the work he did. His proper level would have been middle second class. He was given one third class mark and another that was on the margin of a second and a third. He should have been given a viva.'

In one sense, it did not matter. Imran had by now decided to give himself a couple of years of full-time cricket before making up his mind about his longer-term future. He had determined not to be a civil servant in Pakistan. 'In the 1960s it was a very sought-after profession but in the 1970s it was beginning to lose its charm,' he said. But he continued to be enthralled by politics, especially those of the subcontinent. 'He was radical in his views and had especially strong opinions on the politics of Kashmir, but he was not a Marxist,' said Dr Hayes. 'And he was a jolly nice chap to have around.'

Although it was with sadness that he left Oxford, lamenting that Pakistan had been knocked out of the World Cup, he had been given a scholastic and sporting education that he profoundly cherished. The value of this was even more evident when he returned to Worcester and dispositions towards life and cricket that did not suit him. The structure of six- or seven-days-a-week county cricket, the one-day matches geared to containment, and numerous championship matches finishing in draws, left him frustrated. The company, with few exceptions, was inevitably one-dimensional. Evenings spent in the pub did not appeal, and not merely because he did not drink or smoke. Smells are abhorrent to Muslims. A county cricketer's idea of a night out – drinking beer, smoking and having a farting competition – left him cold.

'When I left Oxford and went back to Worcester, I joined the library and used to take out books virtually every day. A year later, the number of books I was reading had diminished. In the next few years I could count virtually on the fingers of two hands the books I read,' he said. 'It's a great pity. After a hard training session or a day's play I needed to relax, to watch television, perhaps. My eyes became tired and the last thing I could do was study.'

Chapter 4

Emma Sergeant's dreamy, pre-Raphaelite beauty is accentuated by lashings of golden brown hair that fall away to her shoulders in ringlets. Her figure is no less arresting. She is the daughter of an eminent City journalist, Sir Patrick Sergeant of the *Daily Mail* and *Euromoney*, a gifted artist and an eloquent conversationalist. She knows not a jot about cricket. Introduced to Imran at a dinner party in 1982, she became his 'very special friend', a euphemism necessary for consumption in Pakistan, where quotes from English newspapers are widely devoured.

There is mention of her in just about every one of the endless profiles of Imran, even though she never spoke about him in any publication. She is widely credited for introducing him into what is vaguely defined as 'society', although much of the credit for that belongs to Jonathan Orders, a Wykehamist and Oxford Blue whose brother had known Imran at university. Orders had already introduced Imran to one girl he invited to Pakistan, Susie Murray-Philipson, before he gave the dinner party in question while Pakistan were touring England. That same evening, Imran and Emma, seven years his junior, went on to a nightclub in London, making, for socialites as much as gossip columnists, an exquisite couple. The 1980s boom also helped. 'It was a great time for parties. Imran became part of that set,' said Jonathan Mermagen, who met him in 1982. 'I think what helped was that, unlike Hollywood, we do not have any star quality here. Imran has that star quality. He combines glamour with achievement.'

Orders had met Imran only earlier in that summer of 1982 but had seen enough to know what sort of guests should be invited to dinner with him. 'If there are no pretty girls, his mind wanders. Emma was good looking but also attractive through being very talented,' he said. That she was his first serious

43

English girlfriend surprised Mermagen. 'I've always thought Imran was a late developer. He was thrown into the party circuit seven years later than he would have been if English. We had all met debs at a much earlier age.'

In Pakistan, where a man should not be seen alone with a woman in a public place, Imran was simply not accustomed to there being so many women in train. 'It was as if he was in a candy shop at first,' said Mark Shand. Not only was Imran shy, but he could not comprehend the English belief in forming men's clubs. 'I have never understood women's lib and the idea of men and women competing. I think of them as complementing each other,' he said. 'Pakistanis are much warmer towards their women – they give them respect and protection. Men recognize that a woman is vulnerable.'

Thus, in his youth, Imran observed Pakistani customs. He asked one of the first English girls he took out, Susie Murray-Philipson (now Dolby), whether she wanted to bring a friend. A beautiful girl from a smart Leicestershire family, she met him, completely unaware of his cricketing fame, at a drinks party in London in 1982. 'He was charmingly bashful and flirtatious, not at all westernized. Everyone else seemed to know who he was and I realized he was a star when President Zia sent him tele-grams during that summer. But I didn't know what to talk to him about and wasn't impressed with the whole Pakistan set-up. I felt wholly out of place.' Imran had tried to make her feel at ease by asking her out only with his Pakistani friends; alas, by doing so, he had only isolated her. He invited her (along with other people) to stay with him in Pakistan. Her mother suggested that a letter to Imran's mother – who had implored him not to bring home a foreign wife – would be in order. 'But I thought that there might be another side of the bargain. I couldn't believe he was seriously interested in me, that I was an exclusive girl-friend. I felt privileged because everyone wanted to be in my place but I had a suspicion I might be stuck in a hotel room. Imran wrote to me saying how disappointed he was and that I had listened to gossip about him and girls. The next thing I heard was that Emma Sergeant had been there – it must have been the start of their relationship.'

Imran's days of wandering round clubs and pubs in the company of Garth le Roux were clearly over. However fashionable Brighton might have been, it was but a backwater compared with South Kensington – Imran's newly acquired flat in Draycott Avenue was about a mile from Emma's studio in Cornwall Gardens, the King's Road, where he attracted double takes in the way George Best once did, and Tramp in St James, the nightclub which Pakistanis referred to as 'his sitting room'. The 1980s, the Thatcher decade, were associated with champagne. So, too, even though he did not drink it, was Imran. 'He was always winning bottles which were bunged into Emma's bath with buckets of ice,' said Mermagen. 'There was a party there once a week, Emma always wandering around pouring it out. It was a fun period, definitely, the 1980s. If friends became paralytic, that was fine with him. But he felt people should have self-respect and he disliked bad manners.'

He had a method of dealing with bores which, like Best's, did not involve rudeness. 'Imran always tolerates the type of person who makes the wrong noises,' said Johny Gold, owner of Tramp. 'Someone will come up to him knowing perfectly well who he is, and say, "I recognize you, what's your name?" He'll just say, quietly, "Imran Khan."' Membership of Tramp helped launch him into café society, the world of Jeffrey Archer and Andrew Neil, of George Best and Marie Helvin, of Mick Jagger and Nigel Dempster. 'But where he differed from café society was that he would not be impressed by material standards,' said Mermagen.

Imran could not disguise when he was bored. At a barbecue given in Fulham by the *Daily Telegraph* cricket writer Geoffrey Dean, Imran could not hide his boredom when the food was a long time in appearing. 'Unlike people such as myself who give the lot for an hour at a party, sparks and all, Imran does not perform,' said Emma. 'His sense of dignity is such that he does not feel he has to make an effort with strangers.' He did not dress to impress girls. He saw them then, as he does now, on his terms.

Not that he had to make an effort, because there was always someone who wanted to talk to him. Archer, an avid cricket follower, embraced him into his circle of political and social friends by inviting him to his shepherd's-pie-and-Krug parties at his penthouse overlooking the Thames. 'I remember the prime minister and foreign secretary desperately trying to find someone to talk to while Imran was surrounded at the other end of the room,' said Archer.

Here was not only a world-class sportsman but a man of princely appearance from the Raj. The perception in Britain that handsome men from the subcontinent are alluring goes back many years. Queen Victoria is said to have taken a fancy to Duleep Singh, the exiled ruler of the Punjab, as well as to his koh-i-noor diamond. Prince Ranjitsinhji was the first cricketer to come from India, go to Oxbridge, play for England and socialize indefatigably. He was followed by his nephew, Duleepsinhji, and the Nawab of Pataudi. Majid Khan, Imran's cousin, was no socialite but he looked the part. He had been to Cambridge and captained Pakistan in recent times.

This is another reason why Imran is often described, erroneously, as aristocratic. He has not discouraged it. He was highly amused when John Woodcock described him in *The Times* as 'like a latter-day Maharajah'. Many public-school Englishmen had a greater affinity with him than they did with the products of what they perceived to be Micky Stewart's dreary work ethic. David Gower, the one England cricketer of like background and standing to Imran, had flattened his vowels, played for an unfashionable county and was too flippant to have the same presence. Imran knew the score. For so long as the company was amusing and attractive at the parties to which he was invited, he tolerated being displayed as a trophy. 'He's not under any illusions why he's flavour of the month,' said Mermagen.

'For someone who looks stony at parties, he loves chit chat,' said Emma. Imran likes a good gossip about his friends but has never much enjoyed cocktail functions. He has long favoured small dinner parties, eight people or fewer, when the cooking will be done by a caterer. In Draycott Avenue, guests sit on the floor and habitually spill wine on to the rugs he has brought to London from the East. He mixes Pakistani and English guests, usually successfully, although when Susannah Constantine, a friend of several years' standing, is invited she makes certain she eats beforehand. She cannot stomach Pakistani food.

Other than when he entertains friends, Imran rarely eats in his flat. He has never bothered to learn to cook. He relishes the choice of restaurants in London, not least those in Draycott Avenue itself ('although the best food in the world is served by the roadside in Lahore'). His favourite food is partridge cooked in hot spices and served with hot bread from a clay oven, as it is in Pakistan. He was so taken with an Indian restaurant in Bayswater, Khan's, that he sent for the owner to discover how he could run such an establishment himself. It is one project that he has yet to realize.

At his flat – more a maisonette since it is on two levels – he held court in the 1980s to all sorts. Cricketers, socialites, journalists flocked to see him, as they still do. His telephone rings so often that he keeps the answering machine permanently on, breaking into the message in English or Urdu, sometimes both, only when the call is personal or pressing. Enhanced by some re-decoration after a fire in his bedroom a decade after he bought it, the flat has been a sound investment (not that Imran is especially interested in decorations or investments). He dislikes shopping and is easily bored by financial matters. The entrance may be unprepossessing, sited next to a grocer, but that cannot be said of his own taste. There are rugs and small statues from Pakistan, numerous plants that evoke childhood views from his bedroom window, low-level chairs to ensure his visitors feel relaxed, trinkets on his sitting-room table that recall a bloody past on the North-West Frontier. A pleated gold canopy hangs over his bed and paintings of tigers are at the foot of it. There is all-pervading incense that has been burned in a tomb of one of

Pakistan's greatest saints, the most revered Sufi of Punjab, Dataa Ganj Bakish. It is only when you look out at the dome of the Albert Hall and alight upon silver trophies and autobiographies, few of them by cricketers, the telephone conversations alternating between English and Urdu all the while, that you begin to appreciate the effortlessness with which this man embraces West and East.

The dominant features are the paintings by Emma Sergeant. Three are in oils, one depicting Imran reading at the foot of the staircase. (Another portrait of him, hands in pockets, hangs in Barings bank.) A large watercolour of a woman with her head covered is from a series Emma did on Afghan refugees during one of her two lengthy visits to Pakistan. Imran bought it because the woman's face reminded him of his mother. There is also her pencil drawing of Lord Olivier. These tell not only of her talent. That they remain Imran's property several years after their relationship ended is also testimony to the affection she still inspires in him.

'Because we came from very different worlds I could make him think about other things,' said Emma. 'He is someone who has been an enormous influence on me. He taught me about pride, how to esteem myself – if I didn't hold my head high, no one else would – and about routine. He went about the day with his rhythm and his abstinence from drinking and smoking. I learned from him the importance of telling the truth.' She does not refer to their friendship, even now, as having been a relationship. She does not wish to cause Imran embarrassment in his own country. The guidelines of the Koran are that meetings between men and women are not allowed frequently unless for a specific purpose. Single women are not allowed to go out on their own; all social life is family orientated. There are no meeting places, clubs or bars in Pakistan. Not every Muslim follows these guidelines quite as closely as that, partly because any sexual relationship is hard to prove. Four witnesses are necessary for the act to be illegal.

But both Imran's parents were strict Muslims. 'If I was written about in the gossip columns in England and they heard about it, they sent me letters immediately,' said Imran. 'I hated being portrayed as a playboy. I wasn't one – cricket was always my obsession.'

There was no question of Imran being able to take Emma to his parents' home when she visited Pakistan in 1982. She never met his mother. 'It would have been very embarrassing for her and for Imran to meet me anywhere in their country,' she said. 'Society is black and white there and God forbid if you put a foot the wrong side of the line.' His mother's parting words when Imran left for England on the 1971 tour were: 'Don't bring back a foreign wife.' She was concerned because a cousin who had married an English girl had not been accepted by his father for many years. Shaukat Khanum naturally did not want Imran to settle in England, or to divorce his wife because she could not adapt to the way of life and the culture in Pakistan. Tradition dictated he should marry only a fellow Muslim, and that this would be arranged by his parents. He himself always assumed in his youth that this would happen, but also that his parents would accept a marriage which came about through true love.

Into this stern society arrived the 22-year-old Emma Sergeant. Or very nearly did not arrive, since she forgot to notify Imran when she was coming. At Karachi airport, PIA airline officials were not accustomed to single British girls landing without knowledge of their destination. She almost caught the next flight home. 'They were asking me whom I had come to see and so I told them it was a cricketer. Until I mentioned Imran's name it had not got home to me just how important he was.' She was whisked off to the VIP enclosure at Faisalabad, where Pakistan were playing Australia, and was enthralled by the difference between 'the mundane English grounds' and 'the rose petals and symbols and trumpets'. She was with Imran in Baluchistan when he received a kidnap threat – nothing came of it – and visited a section of his family's 400 acres of sugar cane, wheat and crops where she saw his father's amazement at the adulation Imran received from the populace. When she returned for a second trip in 1985, it was to paint Afghan refugees at the North-West Frontier while Imran was playing cricket.

It took Emma six months to find sponsors. She agreed that the proceeds from the sale of the paintings should go to help the Afghans through UNICEF (with which Imran also became involved). She lost her passport and documents upon arrival in Islamabad, dropped one or two clangers – 'One Pakistani was moaning about the influx of Afghans resulting in a Pakistani unemployment problem. I replied, "We have the same problem in Southall," which was silly and tactless' – and found the Afghans the most impressive race she had come across. After a three-and-a-half-month stay, with only seven rest days, she and another painter, Dominique Lacloche, returned to England with five hundred oil paintings, sketches and watercolours. 'My time in Pakistan opened my mind to how rich the people make their lives there,' she said.

Imran was preoccupied at that time with a series against Sri Lanka, following which he went to play in a tournament in Sharjah. Thus their relationship, as with any between the girl-friend or wife of a Test cricketer obliged to go on tours, suffered the strain of long separations. This was a contributory factor in it coming to an end the following year, 1986.

There had been other difficulties, not least that Emma had reckoned he would have an arranged marriage. Another cultural drawback arose during a Test match in Pakistan. It is customary for a visitor to a dressing room to ask the permission of the captain before seeking out a player. One irritating Pakistan Board of Control official, Rafi Naseem, was barred from entry by Imran and retaliated by making allegations that Emma had stayed in Imran's hotel room in Peshawar. Nothing came of this, save for Imran becoming thoroughly annoyed. He and Emma gradually realized that it would not be possible to reconcile their cultural differences. 'The things that mattered to him didn't matter to me, and vice versa,' said Emma.

Their lives diverged to the extent that, when the split came, it was a bad one. 'I realized that, where emotions are concerned, there is no room for logic,' Imran wrote. 'Sad to say, cultural differences and the touring life combined to end our relationship, but it taught me that I could no longer be sure how, when or whom I would marry.' Emma subsequently married an Italian banker, Riccardo dei Conti Pavoncheli, from whom she separated in 1993, moving to a flat-cum-studio in Notting Hill. 'I very much regretted losing Imran as a friend, which I had to do for a while,' she said. 'I feel privileged to have known him. But things happen because they are meant to happen. I'm very fatalistic. I don't think we could get back together again because he loves a very public life and that would kill me.'

Before Imran and Emma drifted apart, Imran's mother had become too ill to contemplate continuing to look for a potential bride for him, which she had done when he was younger. At one point he had said to her, 'When I am thirty, just marry me to whomever you want.' When he had reached that age he became, he said, scared at the prospect. Several of his closest friends were divorcing. He began to feel marriage had never appealed to him, although he saw the logic of one which was arranged: if it went through a bad patch, there would be greater family support to make it work than there would be in what he termed a 'love marriage'.

That he was still single in his early thirties fuelled speculation as to when he would marry, as well as to whom. Many celebrities would have tired of answering much the same kind of question from much the same kind of journalist (female, thirty something, women's pages of newspapers and magazines) but he dealt with them all with tolerance. His attractiveness to women was only increased by remaining single; so, too, some felt, was it by the fact that he was still thought likely to have an arranged marriage. The challenge was on.

Later, when he had retired, he needed publicity to promote his books and, especially, the hospital appeal; but during his career there were times when all that seemed to come from endless interviews were comments that would not go down well

51

at home. In 1982 in the *Daily Mirror*, Noreen Taylor began an article by writing:

> Imran Khan is worried in case I portray him as a sex symbol. This is possibly why Imran is stretched across his hotel bed wearing only a petulant expression and a pair of tiny, black satin shorts.

In the same article she asked Imran why a seventeen-year-old daughter of a British duke would not be acceptable to his parents. Imran was, apparently, holding his head in despair at this. 'Oh no, no, no, no,' he was reported as saying. 'It is not just a matter of virginity. It's that she wouldn't be one of us. And if she's not one of us she would not be able to accept the lifestyle.' It was as if he feared already for the upshot of his relationship with Emma.

After their split, he explained that there was no point in his becoming involved with a girl who was not from Pakistan. 'I've seen my friends marry foreigners and the strain of their trying to adapt their needs and natural inclinations to a society where women do not have the same freedom to express themselves as English or American women do is usually disastrous and very, very sad. A Pakistani girl can usually achieve the same freedom in the end but she knows how to go about it without offending everyone's standards of behaviour.'

As he was in England every summer, whether he was playing for Sussex or Pakistan, Imran widened his circle of friends. By the mid-1980s he was extremely well connected. 'He treats Tramp rather like his own room, which is the biggest compliment to me,' said Johny Gold. 'He does not really understand the English sense of humour – when I make a joke he doesn't get it. But he has always mixed well. Women always want to sit with him. Like George Best in his younger days, women appear out of the woodwork, whether they are debs or South Americans. Imran likes a touch of craziness in his female friends but you can't say, "Ah! there's an Imran Khan type".' He did not necessarily share their views, disliking the materialistic outlook of the Thatcher years, but he liked mixing in the upper echelons of society in London.'

Lulu Blacker, who knew Emma and who was a confidante of the Duchess of York, was one of several girls Imran invited to Pakistan during the 1980s before her marriage to Edward Hutley. She remains a close (and platonic) friend to this day. 'His ideals don't accord with the ideals of a lot of the people he mixes with but he loves his posh friends – he is a little bit of a snob. When Fergie became Fergie, people were in awe of her. Even close friends put her on a pedestal. Imran could have become cocky – and even did for a time, since girls were throwing themselves at his feet. But his real friends wouldn't take any rubbish from him. I certainly don't look up to him,' she said.

Imran had first come to Lulu's attention when her father pointed him out on television as a good-looking cricketer. 'I didn't think there were any, but by chance I met him at a party two weeks later. "You're the good-looking cricketer," I told him, to which he replied, "Oh." But he knows it really.' Lulu invited him and Emma to a barbecue at her parents' house in Hampshire where Lulu's father sat on the ground and fed Imran lamb chops. Her mother took offence because he arrived late, which only illustrated another cultural difference – in Pakistan it is customary for guests to arrive late for parties. In England, the aspect of Imran's character which most irritates his friends is his lack of punctuality.

Lulu emphasizes, as do all of Imran's friends, that his heart is in the right place. 'He will hunt out the best in people and give everyone a chance.' Marie Helvin, a leading model, fashion designer and television presenter, who went out with Mark Shand after the breakdown of her marriage to the photographer David Bailey, says that she has never heard him gripe about anyone. 'You sense he's a good person with a kind heart and the soul of a tiger. The sort of world I work in is fickle and shallow but he is sincere and I trust him.

'You don't get bored talking to him and he does treat women

very well, perhaps because he's a Muslim. Unless asked, you never hear him talk about cricket. All the girls I knew and know wanted to meet him – I forgot to introduce him to some girlfriends of mine at a ball once and they were all upset. A lot of them have asked me how it is that I stay platonic friends with him. I tell them it is because he and my brother Steve look very similar,' she said.

For all this, Imran remained a man's man. His prime interests were pursuits such as hunting and shooting. He was still essentially shy and became flustered when surrounded by more women than men. In the steadfastness of the locker room he could escape those female writers who made him, he felt, sound moronic by writing that he liked dumb blondes with long legs who had nothing to say for themselves.

That this was hardly the case became apparent when one particular girl had too much to say for herself. Doone Murray, a former girlfriend of the Marquis of Blandford, who worked in Jonathan Mermagen's office, manned his Benefit telephone line when Sussex made Imran their Beneficiary for 1987. Warned by Mermagen to maintain a strictly working relationship, she fell for him and disclosed her feelings to 'a close friend' who in turn disclosed them to the *People*. 'I was shocked by the number of cricket groupies around. When we were together in his room the phone would keep ringing with girls desperate to meet him. It was a bit offputting, really, but I could tell he was quite flattered – what man wouldn't be? In many ways he's a lovely man but I pity the girl that marries him.'

At much the same time, similar articles were written about Ian Botham, one of Imran's foremost rivals on the field. There was always the possibility of such lurid details appearing in the more salacious newspapers, true or false, and, in Imran's case, being picked up in Pakistan. The difference between the two great all-rounders was that Imran learned the art of discretion. In English eyes it mattered not a whit, anyway, because he was single: such articles served to make him appear more alluring, while somehow they seemed only to personify Botham as a yob.

In every interview Imran was careful to play down any suggestion of being a playboy or a womanizer. Even after his mother's death, he could not be seen in Pakistan to be flaunting an affair. This was particularly the case when he began to raise funds for his hospital appeal. 'Of course I have been photographed with lots of beautiful women,' he told the *Daily Telegraph*. 'If you go to a charity ball, you have to take a partner; it doesn't necessarily mean anything. Most of the women with whom I have been photographed have just been escorts for one evening, sometimes they were the girlfriends of friends.' No one has ever given him a tougher interview than Caroline Phillips in the *Evening Standard*, who announced in her first paragraph that Imran was 'not fantastically good looking'. He was sharp enough, however, to cope with her line of questioning without evading it or resorting to rudeness. His longstanding disagreements with cricket writers in Pakistan had culminated in an altercation on an aeroplane with Qamar Ahmed that required the intervention of Javed Miandad, but he has not been known to be discourteous to an English journalist.

'In Pakistan,' he told the *Evening Standard*, 'the mere fact that you admit you're having affairs upsets a lot of people's sensitivities. I respect my own culture and a lot of people look up to me. It's a big responsibility for me not to make these admissions in public. Everyone knows I'm a single man and a normal man. But there's no need to ram it down their throats.'

Evening Standard: Would you have an affair with a married woman? Imran: 'No, I think that is a sin. The biggest sin in my religion and my mind is when you hurt someone. There are guidelines in the Koran on adultery.'
Have you ever had a love child? 'No.'
What would you do if you got someone pregnant? 'Well, I won't.'
But everyone knows you have affairs. 'I didn't realize people think I have affairs.'

If nothing else, such interviews kept him in the public eye at a time when he was contemplating retirement. So did the gossip columns. He was linked to a stream of women including Sita White, the daughter of Lord White of Hanson plc; the actress Stephanie Beacham; Lady Liza Campbell, daughter of Earl Cawdor; television presenter Anastasia Cooke; Lord Rothschild's daughter, Hannah, and Natasha Grenfell, likewise a scion of the upper classes. He had a particularly soft spot for Sarah Crawley, a striking, intelligent brunette whose husband had been killed in an aeroplane crash. She appreciated Imran's 'wonderful cocktail of strength and self-confidence' – 'I felt as if I was with Gandhi when I went with him to Pakistan' – but, as with Susie Murray-Philipson, was determined to keep him at arm's length.

In Lahore, Sarah found that she and Emily Todhunter, an interior designer who went with her to Pakistan, could not go into a restaurant with Imran, such was the attention he received. It irritated her, but she shared the respect of the people for him. 'He has looked inside himself, whether in a moral or religious way, is incredibly unmaterialistic and has an amazingly noble bearing – so many people do lead such incredibly shallow lives. Each year a new generation of girls collapses at his feet – he can have any woman he wants and yet is obsessed by marriage and the feeling that it is not going to work. He brings the subject up all the time.

'His parents' marriage was only so-so happy and he wouldn't want to make a mistake. Nor would he want a wife and child subjected to risk if he went into politics. He has listened to his guru. Some people have the ability to see the future in a way that is not quackish.'

Imran felt that because he had not married, and had not been constrained by marriage, he was being prepared for a particular role by, as it were, a higher authority. Religion, and his analysis of the Koran, was becoming as significant and as important to him as the temporal game of cricket. 'I think he should aim to be a saint rather than prime minister,' said Emily Todhunter. 'He is blessed with such background, looks and style that it would be a shame if he did not put them to use. There is a magnetism. A lot of women have been in love with him and he is very attractive. But he is not a playboy – he just happens to be rather cool. I'm going to be fascinated to see which way he goes.'

Emily, formerly a girlfriend of Taki, the *Spectator* columnist, and an interior decorator of considerable success by the 1990s, was taken with how much Imran knew about the people and the different climates of Pakistan. 'We would leave a cricket ground when play ended and drive through the night so that we could wake up in a beautiful place. Usually we would stay with a host who would choose where we'd go shooting. The girls were supposed to talk to Imran – but in their place,' she said.

In Pakistan, girls walk a couple of paces behind Imran. 'In England I would skip up to him and put my hand on his shoulder,' said Lulu Blacker. 'In Lahore you stay two paces behind and respect their country. They can fit into our society and yet English people can't fit into theirs. They are the overdogs, not the underdogs – the purest people I know. I would rather see my Pakistani friends than three-quarters of the people I know in England.'

Lulu recollects the bizarre looks she received 'when I was given a crooked twelve-bore gun and the Pakistani men thought I was from outer space', and when she and five other English girls fell into the water on a river crossing. 'The men with us had never seen a girl's leg or bottom before. Imran rescued the stereo, not us, and we ribbed him sick about leaving us in the water. There were six strong women on that trip who weren't going to let him get away with anything.'

Imran was acutely aware that he was an unofficial ambassador for his country to educated people in England. He was thrilled to visit parts of Pakistan that he had not seen before; and was thrilled to show them to friends who came a long way to see them. It amused him that English people were constantly disappearing to squat behind bushes, even if his sense of humour was less apparent upon discovery that Mermagen was eating tinned food he had brought out with him – and then announcing that he was off to Marbella with his hair dryer.

Chapter 5

I mran did not so much embrace society during the 1980s as allow society to embrace him. However homogeneous the girls he courted or escorted, his male friends were a disparate group. Apart from Zakir Khan, a fellow Pathan who went to England on Pakistan's 1987 tour and who shoots with Imran in the Salt Range mountains, they are not cricketers. They are mostly English and well educated but, with one or two exceptions, not glitterati. 'For a man who does not drink, he has latched on to some wild people – possibly to make up for the lack of wildness in his own character,' said Oliver Gilmour, one of a small group of friends who will be contacted by Imran when he is in London. The rest he prefers to ring him.

Several of these friendships were forged in the early 1980s when he met Emma Sergeant and, through her and Jonathan Orders, numerous other people besides. Jonathan Mermagen acts as unofficial agent and adviser, primarily because Imran has never felt comfortable with an agent who would take 10 per cent of his earnings. After trying four agents and, in particular, not hitting it off with Bev Walker, who looks after several sportsmen, he opted merely to retain a solicitor. His attempts to be taken on by Mark McCormack's International Management Group came to nothing: Imran was told, at the height of his career, that they could make more money representing a fifteen-year-old tennis player.

So Mermagen, a businessman of similar age to Imran, who during the 1980s ran his own graphic-design consultancy specializing in corporate identity from an office in the King's Road, became Imran's part-time business manager in 1983. Mermagen's dilemma was how to utilize Imran's looks and charisma in a way that would not offend Muslims. Imran would not embarrass them by being photographed with models draped round him or embarrass himself by advertising hair gel. Parts in films held no interest for him. 'I then realized it would get to the point where he'd tell me I hadn't got anywhere,' said Mermagen. 'I said that I'd rather we remained mates.'

Cricketers, unlike footballers, tennis players and golfers have never made huge sums of money. Nonetheless, there is no doubt that Imran could have accumulated considerably more money for himself had he the inclination. Not being a particularly good judge of character and having had a comfortable upbringing, with no family to support and no interest in finance, he came to rely on his closest friend's judgement. 'Imran eventually sees through commercial people. He's got a lot better at it. But I'm not sure whether he could spot a crook,' said Mermagen.

In England, Imran's best opportunity of building up some capital was through the Benefit he was awarded by Sussex in 1987. He did not require an agent to run this. Friends such as Mermagen and Jonathan Orders would sit on his committee, and do so for no reward. Benefits were tax free and during this affluent period there were record sums made every year. In 1984 Geoffrey Boycott realized over £147,000. In 1985 Graham Gooch netted over £153,000. Imran was in this category of cricketer and, even though he could not hope to make that much since he was not playing for England, his glamour and consistent achievements for Sussex would weigh heavily in his favour. Yet he thought it was too demeaning to go round pubs asking for money, particularly from pensioners. Although grateful for the efforts of others, he could not concentrate wholeheartedly on the fundraising events. The captains for the friendly six-a-side matches that were staged soon came to prefer Javed Miandad ahead of him.

The highlight of the events was a gathering of 2000 at Hammersmith Palais, one of several parties and stag nights held in London on his behalf during the summer. Even that embarrassed Imran, who felt the Benefit system should be scrapped and players given a lump sum from their counties for services rendered. 'It is just legalized begging. I thought when I saw a sheet being carried around for supporters' money during Mike Procter's Benefit year that a great cricketer was being degraded. I vowed then that I would do things differently.' He made in the region of £100,000 but gained a similar sum through donations in the Middle East. In Dubai and Sharjah, generosity knows no limits.

Other business ventures did not come off. A monthly publication called *Cricket Life*, of which Imran was editor-in-chief, lasted for just thirteen issues before the majority shareholder, the Sheik of Abu Dhabi, closed it down. Imran received nothing in the way of salary or expenses: he ended up having to pay for his telephone calls to contributors all around the world. 'He was concerned about his credibility after something that he had put his name to had not done very well,' said Shahid Sadullah, the editor. 'He was concerned that it would affect him when he started to raise funds for his hospital.

'He had taken the project very seriously, discussing with me the subjects he wanted covered. He had no bones about what he wrote – no concerns about libel or political hang-ups. Once he came to a decision, that was final. I needed a pickaxe and dynamite to change him. He trusted to the hilt the people running the organization, and was not a good judge of business, but he did not lose his Pathan sense of honour, saying he would work with me again.'

Imran was at least well remunerated by the *Sun*, for which he wrote a ghosted column in the mid-1980s, and later by the *Daily Telegraph*. The intermittent articles for the *Telegraph*, always trenchant and often taking the very opposite view of their cricket correspondent, he wrote himself. Little sub-editing was required in the *Telegraph*'s office. Sunil Gavaskar, the Indian batsman, became so concerned at Imran's forthright views, which were often opposed to some aspect of English cricket, that he asked him to tone them down. Imran, Gavaskar reminded him, was the only Asian writing a column on the game in the British press, and he did not want there to be none at all.

Yet no one could muzzle Imran when he was giving a

dissertation, not even Mermagen. He existed in a sphere of cricket, social conscience and gossip about his friends, was amused by their human and sexual foibles and swiftly became bored if he had no interest in the conversation or values espoused. He understood why a friend such as Orders went into a career like merchant banking, appreciating that the bills had to be paid, but it was an alien existence to him. He preferred to advise his friends on their love life, although he was not so good at accepting their advice when he had similar problems.

Oliver Gilmour, who is chief conductor of the Bulgarian State Opera, and who had been with Imran at Oxford but came to know him later through Emma Sergeant, liked to wind him up by injecting controversy into a late-night argument. 'I've not seen him jump against colonial arrogance but the only time he loses a bit of objectivity is over accusations that the Pakistanis are cheats. When we discuss ball tampering he is on their side to too great an extent,' said Gilmour. A mistrust of English attitudes towards Pakistan, stemming from colonialism, was never far from his reasoning – even if he was acting slightly tongue in cheek. 'It's our problem because we can't come to terms with our relationship with Pakistan,' said Mark Shand. 'I've seen English people travelling abroad and still thinking they own it.'

In particular, Imran felt that English cricketers could not accept being beaten by Pakistan, as occurred in two series in the 1980s. Although he realized there was scant time for sightseeing on any tour, he was disdainful of the cricketer who did not want to extend his boundaries beyond the swimming pool, the bar and the unaccompanied women to be found there. It only exacerbated the feelings of English cricketers about touring Pakistan that all three were at a premium. These attitudes also contributed to Imran not spending any time socializing with England players. He regarded Ian Botham's jibe that he would not send even his mother-in-law to Pakistan as no joke at all, and felt it told more about Botham than about Pakistan. He was alarmed at the attitudes of the more strident English papers covering Pakistan's

62

1987 tour – 'Paki Cheats' was one headline in the *Sun* – and disturbed at what he saw as an increase in racism in Britain. 'I certainly never could live there all the time, mainly because of the racism,' he said. 'There was not much of an Asian community in Brighton and consequently not much racism. But my friends encounter it a lot more. I feel it as well when I go to certain places, Manchester for instance. I meet people and feel undercurrents.'

As Imran began to feel that Pakistanis living in England were increasingly downtrodden, so he started to see xenophobia in class terms. 'The ordinary county cricketer is fairly racist,' Imran said. He has a particular dislike of what he terms an uneducated English outlook. This, for Imran, was epitomized by Mike Gatting, captain on England's 1987 tour of Pakistan, who did not come to terms with the country or its umpires. Further examples were Micky Stewart, manager on Gatting's tour, Alan Smith, chief executive of the Test and County Cricket Board, and umpire David Constant; these last two, for Imran, were too overbearing towards the Pakistani touring party to England in 1987. When Gehan Mendis (born in Sri Lanka but educated in Sussex and at Durham University) requested an article for his Benefit brochure, Imran wrote that the selectors were racists for not having chosen him for England. The comment was removed before it reached the printers. By the time he was constantly defending fellow Pakistani cricketers from allegations of ball tampering in the 1990s, it had become a taboo subject even with his friends. It was a topic he saw not merely in the context of a cricket match but in terms of race.

Imran developed his increasing political awareness when he was designated to share a room with Charles Glass, the political journalist, on a holiday at Emily Todhunter's family's villa in Ithaca. This was instantaneously a successful pairing, even if Imran snored at night ('But then no doubt you'll find three or four thousand women who say he snores,' said Glass).

Glass, who while working for ABC News had been kidnapped and held hostage in Lebanon, talked late into the night with

Imran on the terrace, and became aware of how much Imran despised imperialism and what he saw as Pakistan's obeisance to America. 'Imran sees a class of people in Pakistan merely responding to Western interests rather than to their own kind. He is sensitive to the persecution of Muslims and to the way in which the Western media portrays Islam. He believes it is a much misunderstood religion.'

Glass realized that Imran could make an impression on Pakistan simply through the force of his personality. 'He can talk of exploitation and mean it. He feels the country should stand on its own two feet, that it should improve its productive capacity. But if he enters politics he will lose his credibility. It is very dirty in Pakistan and politicians are not respected.'

Imran was especially interested in Glass's views on Iran and the Islamic movement in Lebanon. Said Glass, 'He does not like the Mullahs, the Islamic clergy – he does not have time for their intolerance of other religions and their dislike of Imran's opinion that birth control is necessary and soil erosion should be prevented. Imran has atheist and Christian friends and a cosmopolitan outlook.'

At a dinner party given in London by the Marchioness of Worcester for him and the playwright Harold Pinter, a cricket enthusiast, Imran expounded his views on the manipulation of third world countries by America. Tracy Worcester, best known as an actress for her role in the television series *Cat's Eye*, sat between them to ensure that there was not too much talk about cricket. There was not, for Imran spoke instead of a greater game. 'He should go into politics. I think he should be prepared to put up with the risk of death in order to gain justice for his country,' she said. 'He would have to change a class of rulers, which would be frightening. I told him that he would have to die for it. He would be a martyr.'

Such profundities made the life of a touring sportsman appear trivial. Increasingly, Imran was finding the cricketer of average ability too one-dimensional and some of those who had made themselves into outstanding performers, such as Geoffrey

Growing up in Lahore. Imran with his father,
Ikramullah, his mother, Shaukat, and sisters
Noreen and (right) Robina

Batting for Worcestershire in 1976. The senior professionals felt he had more potential as a batsman than as a fast bowler (*George Herringshaw*)

Opposite: First tour. Imran, eighteen years old and a bowler of ballooning inswingers in 1971 (*PA*)

Ian Botham was a long-standing adversary. Imran fails to connect with a hook against him in the Gillette Cup final of 1978 between Sussex and Somerset (*Sunday Telegraph*)

Opposite: Imran bowling at Melbourne in 1981, when his three first innings wickets helped Pakistan beat Australia (*Patrick Eagar*)

Javed Miandad and Imran after beating Australia at Melbourne in 1981. Their relationship was not as sound as the picture would suggest (*AP*)

Another English wicket. Mobbed by his Pakistani players (*Patrick Eagar*)

David Gower takes evasive action as Imran drives through the off-side during his century against England at the Oval in 1987 (*The Times*)

Country house cricket has always appealed to Imran. Here he is joined on the boundary by the actor Michael Brandon (left) and his close friend Jonathan Mermagen (*Jonathan Mermagen*)

Bowled by Ravi Shastri after making 82 in MCC's bicentenary match of
1987. Bruce French is the wicketkeeper (*PA*)

Boycott, naive when they broached subjects outside their own sphere. Driving to dinner parties, such as that given by Tracy Worcester, straight after finishing a day's cricket with Sussex was not adding to his popularity with the players. When, before Pakistan's tour of England in 1987, a journalist asked why he was not playing county cricket, he replied, 'I'm just appearing for Harlequins and Pakistan.' The remark encapsulated the kind of company he liked to keep.

The jazzhat sides (as they were known to first-class cricketers) for which he occasionally appeared included one run by the Marquis of Worcester. Imran cut down his run up and spoke willingly about cricket but his greater involvement with the Worcesters, other than becoming godfather to their daughter, Isabella, was with Tracy's various causes. Disturbed at the number of trees being cut down in the rainforests around the world, he hosted a ball at the Hippodrome with her in 1988 to raise funds for their protection. Three years later he put his name to the World Development Movement, supported Friends of the Earth and was photographed cutting up his credit cards as a protest against banks' lending policy to the Third World (he has since acquired new ones). 'Imran cares what debt is doing to countries like his own,' she said. 'He was one of a few celebrities who protested. He brings the voice of his people and all the lower-income groups who are fighting against the exploitation of America. He would never be a part of a government that was not correct or just.'

Imran also undertook work for Save the Children and for UNICEF, visiting countries such as Bangladesh where his name meant more than did those of Peter Ustinov or Audrey Hepburn. In his role as a special ambassador, he appeared on posters to promote vaccination. 'I was shocked to find some people still don't know they should vaccinate children against diphtheria, tetanus, mumps, rubella, whooping cough and measles,' he said.

When there wasn't speculation about whether Imran would marry, there was conjecture about whether he would go into politics. Jeffrey Archer, who when he was not writing novels was helping to run the Tory party, found that in the late 1980s and early 1990s Imran had more interest in talking to him about politics than cricket. 'What struck me was his obvious love for it and keenness to talk about the political scene. He is desperately sincere and above the average brightness of politicians. He'd be a good barrow boy in the East End because his brain works on six levels. I would not be surprised if he becomes prime minister of his country.'

Archer would tell Imran, as courteously as he could, that cricket would have to become ancillary to politics if he was to change careers. 'He will find, as Seb Coe has done, that a reputation in another field will almost count against him.' Strangely, in meetings that have taken place over a number of years, Archer has never asked Imran what his personal politics would be. He surmises that 'democratic' would be a good label. 'If he said he was an outright communist, I would be distressed,' said Archer.

Imran was always circumspect about committing himself to any party (although in English terms it was clear he was left of centre) and also about his relationship with General Mohammad Zia ul-Haq, the president whom he described as 'not exactly a friend because he was the Head of State' but who had not only persuaded him to come out of retirement in 1988 but had also offered him a post in his administration. It was Imran's feeling that he could make scant impact, as well as the threat to his life, that made him deliberate over a future in politics. 'I would only go into it if I felt totally committed, that I could forgo everything and just concentrate on a political career,' he said in 1988. 'I suppose I'm spoilt in a way. To have been able to play something like cricket, which I enjoy, as my profession, and to have had so much free time – when I wasn't playing, it was all holiday – has meant such an easy life. Money and power don't motivate me but I am idealistic. There is a whole younger generation who look up to me – though it might not for very long because once a public figure stops doing what they are famous for, they very quickly fade from the public eye.'

Shand reckoned that whatever Imran did in the long term, he

represented hope for the people of Pakistan. 'I remember going partridge shooting with him and people would appear from nowhere. He represents the best public relations figure for the country. I see him as an old-fashioned roving ambassador since he wouldn't like to be bogged down in politics. I feel he could do so much good promoting his country abroad. Pathans don't give in,' he said. 'Never underestimate the fact that he is a Pathan.'

Imran's friends have never allowed him to take himself too seriously, however difficult that has been when the genuflection in Pakistan has gone far beyond anything accorded to the prime minister. Lulu Blacker (now Lulu Hutley), and Susannah Constantine, who met Imran through her, were adept at taking the mickey out of him, telling him he would be writing his own obituary. They picked him up if he began a conversation with, 'When I was a rising star . . .' which he took in good part, as he did when they asked him why a number of people were lying at his feet on a billboard poster in Pakistan. And they did not hold back in London. When Imran was asked to give awards for knitwear at a British fashion presentation – hardly his *métier* – Lulu yelled out: 'Oi! Imran!' A gathering of three hundred and fifty, politicians among them, turned as one. Imran bounded up the stairs straight afterwards, demanding, 'Which of you bloody girls did that?'

Susannah Constantine's Australian flat-mate, Emma Gibbs, pricked any pomposity in the antipodean way. 'The second time I saw him, I said, "God, how are you?" He just laughed. Anybody that much loved and worshipped must be envied but he is not a big stud, not superficial at all. He likes people for what they are.' Emma invited her best friend, Annie Henderson, to a barbecue given for Imran. 'She just sat there, staring at him and couldn't answer properly. He was so nice and made all the conversation.'

By the end of the 1980s Imran was not considered a foreigner at all in the social milieu of London. He was as much a part of Kensington as of Karachi. At parties he was quite above working his way around the room. He was not consciously aware of the impact he could make and he did not arrive on the doorstep in a wave of publicity. He stood in one spot, and everyone else gravitated towards him. The entreaties of hangers-on and the condescension of rude people went over his head.

The attention he was receiving from the press showed no sign of abating. When, in 1989, he started to be seen with Susannah Constantine, gossip columnists and feature writers alike were enthralled. Here was a girl who not only seemed to be at every party worth attending in London, but was the sometime girl-friend of Viscount Linley to boot. When the press associate Imran with blondes who have endless long legs, as to his chagrin they often do, they have her in mind. Even the cricket writers were enraptured. When she travelled to Australia to join him on his last tour there in 1989–90, John Woodcock wrote in *The Times* of 'Some stunning creature coming gliding into Imran's suite, bearing an armful of what looks like lovingly ironed shirts. The next evening they were to be seen together, as striking a pair as there was in the house, at the first night of the musical *Chess*.' Imran had attempted to hide her from Woodcock's view in his suite.

Aged twenty-seven when she first met him, Susannah would joke about 'his gorgeous legs'. They initially attempted to keep the relationship as much of a secret as possible, although that could hardly be achieved given that Tramp was a favoured rendezvous. As Emma Sergeant said, there was no need for the likes of Nigel Dempster to contact Imran by telephone; he was sitting at the next table.

Susannah also went to Pakistan with Lulu Blacker, where she gave up trying to explain who she was to the scores of females who would telephone Imran, and in the end pretended to be his secretary. Practicalities sometimes passed Imran by: it had not occurred to him to ask the hotel receptionist in Karachi to take calls for him. Susannah became taken with cricket to the extent of running on to the pitch with Pakistani supporters when England were beaten at the Oval in 1992, two years after she had left the ground at Adelaide while he was making his highest Test score. Emma Gibbs, who travelled round Australia with her, running up bills when she took Imran's favourite chocolate from his hotel suites, was given an earful of a different kind from Australians for telling them they should support Pakistan.

It did not overly concern Susannah that, wherever Imran travelled, girls aplenty would follow, or that they would resent her presence. 'With anyone else it would have been difficult, but I was not bothered,' she said. 'Imran taught me a lot about trust and not to be jealous of someone. He is seen as a huge ladies' man, yet he is not really that. For most women, his looks and Eastern mystique are the attraction but he is very honest and open.'

As Emma Sergeant had done, so Susannah – who coincidentally also had a flat in Cornwall Gardens – introduced Imran to yet more upper-class and upper-middle-class individuals far removed from cricket. She took him partridge shooting to Longford Castle in Wiltshire where, among the tweeded landed gentry, he appeared in jeans, gym shoes, astrakhan hat and Barbour mac, borrowed the Earl of Radnor's gun and spent so much time gossiping with Susannah that he forgot to shoot at the appropriate moment. 'He also wore a hideous sweater with pheasants on it, which was the equivalent of turning up at Burleigh with pictures of horses on his clothing,' said Susannah. 'It went into the bin. I did improve his dress sense and gave him shirts to take back to Pakistan, but he does have a liking for the Italian hairdresser look.' (What remained of his wardrobe in London, notably clothes given to him by his friend Shariar Bakhtiar, was later destroyed by a fire in his flat.)

Imran treated the shoot as he might a safari, unnerving the Earl's fellow guests by running around gun in hand. 'But in spite of that and his gear, he got on well with the people there,' said Susannah. 'He is one of the best shots I have ever seen.' Imran also shot in Scotland on a grouse moor rented by a friend called Andrew Fraser and went clay-pigeon shooting whenever he could. He preferred both of these to stalking because he did not like killing animals, a strange characteristic for someone who enjoyed shooting so much. Winding down his cricket career gave him considerably greater scope for such activities, not least in the temperate winters in Pakistan.

When they were not on cricket tours, at parties or on shooting expeditions of one kind or another, Imran and Susannah often frequented Tramp. Nightclubs were for several years Imran's prime item of expenditure, even though the subscription at Tramp was not exorbitant (renewing his subscription in 1994 cost him £300). Try as she might, Susannah could not entice him on to the dance floor ('I had a few laughs at his expense because he can't dance'). He was embarrassed at being watched by the numerous people grouped around. Try as he might, he could not persuade her to give up smoking or to eat Pakistani food, which, she said, he took as a personal insult. On her two trips to visit Imran, she existed on chocolate, bread, rice and baked beans. He was as cross with her as he was with Mermagen.

Since Susannah had a background in public relations, she helped Imran launch his ill-fated *Cricket Life* magazine in Australia during Pakistan's tour of 1989–90. It turned into more of a party than a press conference. 'It's amazing how so many of you know nothing about cricket,' said Imran in his introductory speech. On the same tour, she asked Imran to lead Australia on to the field during a Test match for the benefit of charity. 'Are you mad?' he asked. But he assisted Susannah in her fundraising work for Motor Neurone Disease and a lesser known charity, Serious Road Trip. He was always the first person whom charities would request to be present at the launch of any event since he invariably attracted a great deal of publicity.

After a year, Imran and Susannah drifted apart. Given his peripatetic life and the fact that she could not be with him throughout every tour, it became something of a long-distance relationship. Marriage was never countenanced. Indeed, Susannah feels Imran will never marry. 'He has nothing in common with a seventeen-year-old and can't marry a Westerner or a divorcee. I think he will always be involved with charity work, will get stuck into tourism and continue with the hospital. If he goes into politics he realizes he would be assassinated within two days.'

The passing of time healed their split. Susannah vowed that when she had children, Imran would be godfather to all of them. 'He is a very loyal friend who would do his best to help you even if he was on the other side of the world. He loves to give advice. When I have a major problem, he is one of the first people I contact.'

Imran was inevitably linked to other girls. One such was Homaa Khan, who came from a similar background in Pakistan and worked, during the 1980s, as an oral surgeon at St Bartholomew's hospital in London. She was appalled that her parents in Pakistan might be shown photographs of her socializing with Imran. 'My parents are very traditional and wouldn't like to think of me as a society girl,' she told *Today*. 'My father would not be at all pleased. Yes, Imran is charming, well brought up and nice to be with. But if you tell me that women envy me, I can only say, what is all the fuss about? There are many more attractive men about, I would have thought.'

If this was a means of deflecting attention, it seemed to work; she was not heard of again. Imran started to mix with young women from the Kitkat Club, a luncheon circle organized by Ghislaine Maxwell, and escorted Kristiane Backer, a German brunette who worked for a satellite music channel – contrary to one report he was still seeing her in 1994 – but he was no closer to marriage. By now he was openly saying that the best decision he had ever made, other than not drinking alcohol, was not to marry.

'I have no regrets about it, nor about not having had children. My sisters' children are my own. Cricket was my great love affair and marriage and cricket are incompatible. Of my ten close friends, six are divorced and it was awful to witness the misery they went through. Marriage has never appealed to me, though I am still open to the idea – I would have to be one hundred per

71

cent sure before I made such a commitment. I have only once fallen in love and then I only considered marriage, I didn't get near to it.'

Chapter 6

Without the spur of Test cricket, Imran would not have remained in the game for any length of time. To treat it simply as a profession, to work towards a Benefit and then retire on the proceeds, would not have stimulated or interested him. This was partly because he had never been short of money but it also owed much to his having mixed with gifted individuals all his formative years. It did not matter to him what an individual excelled at, so long as he excelled at something. 'To be respected by him you had to be good at something – he would respect a good musician more than the weaker members of Oxford's side,' said his tutor, Dr Hayes. 'This is not uncommon among talented people.' Hence the difficulties Imran had comprehending the county cricketer of modest talent, as epitomized by Sussex colleagues Arnold Long and Stewart Storey, who stays in the game until he is middle-aged. That one became his captain and the other his coach was not to his liking.

To Imran, the ultimate test of a cricketer was how well he performed under pressure against a strong side. Ian Chappell, the very model of an aggressive captain, was his kind of opponent (and, incidentally, the only cricketer other than Sir Gary Sobers to have been able to contradict him publicly in recent years). Australia was the cricketing country he enjoyed more than any other – for its competitiveness, its hard, fast pitches, its noisy crowds like those he had been accustomed to at home. Australia was, he felt, the best country in the world in which to play cricket.

In the six months in 1977 prior to joining World Series Cricket, Imran played in as many as 11 Tests. This was when his reputation as an all-rounder was forged. On the slow pitches of Pakistan he took 14 wickets against New Zealand in a series dominated by the batting of Javed Miandad, who made a century on his Test debut at the age of nineteen and averaged

73

126 overall. Then, on a short, three-Tests tour of Australia, Imran bowled well enough, and fast enough, to draw comparisons with Dennis Lillee – of pace bowlers the nonpareil in his eyes. Imran took 18 wickets in the series, five of these in one innings at Melbourne when Sarfraz was injured, and then 12 wickets in the match at Sydney, a Test which Pakistan won by eight wickets to draw the series. This was what persuaded Ian Chappell and Tony Greig that he was of a high enough standard for World Series Cricket.

Imran and Sarfraz made excellent use of the humidity and a mottled pitch, twice dismissing Australia cheaply. Imran's pace and aggression thoroughly disconcerted their batsmen – although this was partly a result of overdoing the bouncer. Both he and Lillee were warned by the umpires for too many short-pitched balls at non-recognized batsmen and on one occasion Rodney Marsh gestured at him angrily with his bat. In the second innings Imran bowled unchanged for nearly four hours, a shirt sleeve coming off in the process. His match figures of 12 for 165, coupled with a brave century by Asif Iqbal, enabled Pakistan to win a Test in Australia for the first time.

Asif, who had been critical of Imran on the 1971 tour of England (although he did not feel that the selection was a nepotistic one by Majid), now saw that Imran had the application to match his ability. 'Fast bowlers look for excuses if the pitch is not good enough but he wanted things to happen. He was a tremendous trier and would become very depressed and dejected when he was not playing. Sarfraz helped him a lot and during World Series Cricket he worked hard to attain the standards of the superstars. He was so involved in his bowling at that time that he didn't pay as much attention to his batting,' said Asif.

After returning from Australia early in 1977, Pakistan toured West Indies for only the second time. There, waiters feel they can bowl as quickly as recognized cricketers, even as quickly as Imran – who was seen as no more than a medium-pacer. In a sense he was not. He lost his rhythm and, on occasion, his temper, even if he did finish with 25 wickets in a five-Tests series that Pakistan lost 2–1. For the most part, his success was due to persistence, although in the final Test he did bowl quickly on a responsive pitch at Sabina Park. His figures of six for 90 were not sufficient to win the match, for this was a markedly strong West Indian side, but they were at least a retort to the jibe by Sir Gary Sobers that he was nothing like as quick as Lillee. Again he overdid the bouncer – it was a constant theme in his career – this time at Andy Roberts, and was almost decapitated in return. The regular misuse of the short-pitched ball was common to most fast bowlers during the mid-1970s – there were more than ever before – resulting, sadly and inevitably, in the introduction of the helmet.

In 11 Tests, Imran had taken 57 wickets. He had proved to himself that he had the requisite ability and he had proved to his team-mates that the charge of nepotism made at his debut was not just. County cricket afforded the opportunity to work on his action and World Series the chance to improve, aided as he was by the likes of John Snow and Mike Procter. He was now a personality, not least because Packer was targeting women through his television channel and needed some good-looking cricketers to do so.

Once Imran resumed playing Test cricket after the two years of World Series, it seemed that his enthusiasm could be dampened only by having too much of a good thing: a surfeit of matches. At county level, this was what occurred. Unlike domestic cricket in Pakistan, a summer spent with Sussex meant concentrated playing. Imran could not muster the enthusiasm to play seven days a week, and performed with only fitful success. If he had not found a reasonable level of social intercourse within the county, he would not have kept at it for so long. He said at the time that he enjoyed much of his stay at Sussex; in retrospect he takes a different view. He was always conscious of being thought antisocial for not drinking with the players in the evening.

John Barclay tried to cushion him from reactive senior

professionals but Imran found the cautious captaincy of Long alien to his nature and felt that Stewart Storey dismantled a decent side too early. In those first years with Sussex, they did win the Gillette Cup in 1978, Imran taking the vital wicket of Ian Botham in the final, and he had some enjoyable partnerships with Javed Miandad before Javed left to join Glamorgan.

'There was no moment when Imran did not try,' Barclay said. 'In fact he almost tried too hard, taking too much responsibility on himself in run chases. When I became captain I felt I had to make the cricket fun for him to keep him going. It was always a great challenge – what could we do on a grey day at Leicester to get the best out of him?' The two were friendly enough but not as close as might have been expected given Barclay's Old Etonian background. This was partly because Barclay was married but also because Imran felt that after leading the side well for two years – Sussex were runners-up in the championship of 1981 – Barclay then tried to style himself as a captain on Mike Brearley. This, to Imran, did not come off.

'The trouble with you,' Imran said to Barclay one day, 'is that you are all too set in your ways.' His viewpoint was that the side should challenge its own bowlers by making positive declarations. 'Imran had brilliant ideas on limited-overs tactics,' said Barclay. 'He had ideas on the shape of a game that differed from the seasoned old pros.' Imran always felt that no side should be afraid of losing. 'Most three-day matches are drawn and I find it dreary playing in games that are heading nowhere,' he said in an interview with *The Times*. 'It is unsuitable for the players and it is unsuitable for the spectators. Young people are watching other sports. Who wants to watch draws?'

Imran's pride and awareness of his own figures ensured he performed more than adequately. Until the infamous occasion when he arrived late from London for a Sunday League match in his last season, incurring the displeasure of his team-mates and leading to his premature departure from Sussex, he would be on the ground in good time to warm himself up properly before bowling. After he bought his flat in South Kensington in

1983, he would drive or take the train (an hour's journey) to Hove.

Other than with le Roux, Imran forged his closest friendship with Gehan Mendis, a good player of fast bowling who had qualified for England. Imran was aghast at the prejudice that he felt was shown towards Mendis by England's selectors (on account of his colour) and by his team-mates (on account of relationships in his private life). 'He was the first person with whom I would get into deep discussion about cricket after hours,' said Mendis. 'He would turn the car radio down and ask how I kept going if I was out early. I found him extremely approachable and he had a mental hardness that rubbed off on me. To have known such a person is brilliant.'

Mendis was not impressed, however, by Imran's reaction to racial abuse. Racism seemed particularly prevalent in Yorkshire, although when Sussex played a Sunday League match at Bradford, the Pakistani community that had come to root for Javed and Imran outnumbered everyone else. One day when he was abused at Worcester, his old ground, he responded by smashing the ball into the offensive section of the crowd. It came off, but could have lost him his wicket. 'It doesn't affect me too much because I know England is not my home,' said Imran. 'But if I had children, I would never want them to grow up here in an atmosphere where there was racism. I've grown up with a lot of pride and I would not want my children ever to have to develop an inferiority complex in a society like this.' And yet on another day, on a visit to the Asian community of East London, Imran felt that he was regarded as having integrated into English society to such an extent that he was considered to be white. There were times when straddling various cultures was not as easy as he made it appear.

None of this concerned women of all backgrounds in England. Those who manned the telephones in the office at Hove took an extraordinary number of telephone calls from females, most of whom Imran had never met. When those lines were engaged, they would ring through to the hut at the end of the pavilion,

77

thoroughly irritating the groundsman. There were other good-looking cricketers of Asian origin, such as Rehan Alikhan, who also played for Sussex, and Mohsin Khan, the Pakistan batsman who became an actor. But none had such a big mailbag.

In the aftermath of World Series and its heightening of players' profiles, adulation of Imran ceased to be confined to England. The game was marketed and covered by press and radio as never before in Pakistan. Posters of Imran and other players appeared in bookshops, airports and railway stations. News of their prowess penetrated even the rural areas, where there was little in the way of communications. Imran himself was particularly fêted, by men and women alike, after Pakistan had beaten India in 1978, in the first series in which they had played each other for eighteen years.

As yet, Imran had had nothing like the press coverage he was to receive in the 1980s. In Pakistan, his relationships with journalists were never as cordial as they were with the press in England. He talks of seeing the raised knife, especially when he became captain. Shakespearian education or fevered imagination? The insight of a sage is necessary to understand the nature of cricket politics in Pakistan and the supposed rivalry in the press between Karachi and Lahore, even though all the big newspapers are printed in Karachi. When Imran displaced Javed Miandad as captain, he was seen as a Lahorite taking over from the hero from the other side of the country, to say nothing of growing up on the other side of the tracks. Imran would complain of picking up a newspaper in Pakistan and finding it ran to only three pages. In England he was accustomed to a diversified media, a high standard of cricket writing and a broader outlook, among the quality newspapers at any rate.

The tension that Imran felt over this series with India in 1978, which on the president's orders was the resumption of Test cricket for the Packer players, spilled over into disagreements with his captain, Mushtaq Mohammad, and sections of the press. Both were critical of his short-pitched bowling at batsmen of the standing of Gavaskar and Viswanath, disregarding his reasoning

78

about the sluggish nature of the pitch. The first Test of a three-match series ended in a predictable draw, as had the majority of Tests between the two countries in previous years. Indeed, the previous thirteen had all ended in draws, which partly accounted for the ecstatic reaction when Pakistan won the last two Tests. At Lahore, Imran gained wickets but it was for his batting in Karachi that he was acclaimed. Pakistan needed 164 to win in 100 minutes against the celebrated spin attack of Bedi, Prasanna and Chandrasekhar, and they achieved this with seven balls to spare. Imran, still considered a batsman who could strike the ball hard and, on account of his experience of limited-overs cricket in England, score quickly, was sent in at number four. He responded by striking Bedi, India's greatest slow bowler, for two sixes and a four to bring about victory by eight wickets. 'Overnight,' he wrote, 'I became a star in Pakistan.'

In that series, there was another discovery. Kapil Dev was no star as yet, but he was to become the fulcrum of India's bowling as their spinners declined. It was the commencement of an extraordinary era in which four truly world-class all-rounders would come to the fore, evoking endless comparisons and debate. Although Imran regarded Kapil as a cricketer of different skills to himself, in that Kapil was fast-medium in pace and a wristy stroke-player, he admired his attacking instincts and his effect on Indian cricket.

Imran naturally has respect for the abilities of Ian Botham and of Sir Richard Hadlee – 'the closest of the three to myself in approach to the game' – but this is tempered by a belief that Botham should have achieved more against West Indies and that Hadlee was too mechanical a bowler to be judged as highly as Dennis Lillee. Imran, in fact, has as high a regard for Clive Rice and Mike Procter as for any all-rounder other than Sir Gary Sobers. South African though they are, he has sympathy for them for playing little or, in Rice's case, no Test cricket.

Comparisons were bound to occur beyond long-room bars, if only to fill column inches. Imran himself indulged in this during the period in the 1980s when he was contracted to write for the *Sun* (Ian Todd, who ghosted these articles, found him 'an imperious bugger') and assessed Hadlee a better player than Botham. But he found this difficult enough given that it was hard to compare different types of all-rounders just as it was hard to compare batsmen who had varying approaches to their art. 'I am often likened to Ian Botham but in fact he is a completely different sort of player: he is an aggressive batsman, whereas I try to build an innings; I am a fast inswing bowler and he is – or was originally – a medium-pace outswinger,' Imran wrote in *All Round View*. He felt averages and career figures were misleading in that they could not take into account how much cricket an individual played while at his peak. His overall view, though, is that a cricketer, batsman or bowler, can only be judged under pressure against the strongest opponents.

The great increase in the number of Test matches in the 1980s rendered averages less meaningful. For instance, Kapil Dev has played around twice as many Tests as Bishen Bedi, and thus played more often at his peak. By the time he retires he will have set a record that could well prove unassailable. But his wickets will have been gained at a greater cost than those of Imran and Hadlee, whose averages are almost identical. In 86 Tests, Hadlee took 431 wickets at 22.29, bowling more overs than Imran, who in two more matches gained 362 wickets at 22.81 apiece. In 102 Tests, Botham took 383, at an average markedly similar to Kapil Dev of 28.40.

As for their batting, there are similar inferences to be drawn. Botham has an average of 33.54, Kapil 30.25, Hadlee – who was less effective before the advent of helmets – 27.16, and Imran, having made 3807 runs from 126 innings, 37.69, only marginally inferior to Majid Khan, Asif Iqbal and Mushtaq Mohammad. It is a titanic achievement. In terms of bald figures as well as other assessments, Imran has the standing to trump any inconclusive argument about all-rounders.

Away from the game, Imran is not close to any of them. The vulgar streak in Botham's make-up was too much for both Imran and Hadlee. Imran laments the fact that few cricketers take the trouble on international tours to discover what lies beyond the game plan. Hadlee respected Imran more than Botham and Kapil Dev because of his consistency but felt that in his later years Imran had too much power for the good of Pakistan's cricket. In particular Hadlee questioned his opposition to playing Test matches and one-day internationals at one of the hottest times of the year in Pakistan. Imran in turn regarded Hadlee as small-minded for saying, upon congratulating Kapil over taking his 400th Test wicket, that he had reached this goal in fewer Tests.

Imran regarded Kapil as a far more dangerous proposition in India than anywhere else. By the time Pakistan toured India for a return series in 1979, Kapil was very highly thought of. For the Test at Kanpur, the groundsman left a considerable amount of grass on the pitch in the expectation that Kapil would be able to take advantage of it. Imran struggled throughout the series owing to a rib injury, which was another factor in making India's selectors and groundsmen optimistic, but Pakistan lost the series more on account of feeble batting than anything else. Not accustomed to the partisan crowds or quite such close scrutiny, they had to run the gauntlet when they returned home as outclassed losers. To be beaten by India was quite beyond the pale. Lurid accounts of womanizing appeared in the Pakistani papers, although the stories were not proven.

Nineteen seventy-nine had not been a notable year of Test cricket for Pakistan, or indeed for Imran. It had begun with a series in New Zealand that Imran joined for the last two Tests after the second season of World Series, taking ten wickets but finding the cricket anti-climactic after what he had grown accustomed to in Australia. He found the umpiring so poor that for the first time he felt that neutral umpires should stand in Test cricket the world over.

A hastily arranged short tour of Australia, designed by the Boards of Control to deprive Packer of television rights for the two scheduled Tests, pitted World Series players against non-World Series players and was nothing if not acrimonious. The disaffection felt towards modern-day Pakistani sides by numerous

Test players from other countries could be said to have stemmed from these ill-judged matches. The running out of Rodney Hogg by Javed Miandad when he wandered out of his crease to pat down the pitch was not cricket as the Australians knew it, but it typified the way the game was played in the back streets of Karachi. It was a clash of cultures as much as a clash of etiquette. Further distasteful incidents followed, including stumps being smashed down and an Australian batsman given out for handling the ball when his only intention was to hand it back to the bowler. Imran finished with seven wickets in the drawn series.

Mushtaq, who led Pakistan in Australia, was replaced as captain for the 1979 World Cup in England by Asif Iqbal, whose batting Imran regarded highly. Yet Asif, who like Mushtaq had experience of leading sides in county cricket, found that uniting his countrymen was altogether a hard task. They did reach the semi-finals, losing to West Indies, whose batting strength was no greater than theirs. Imran felt they were unable to perform properly under pressure. In four matches he took five wickets and in three innings made 42 runs.

It was as evident now as it was during the following two years that Pakistan were desperately in need of leadership. Asif, Majid, Mushtaq, Zaheer and Sadiq Mohammad were coming to the end of their careers. Asif was re-appointed captain for their tour of India in 1979–80, a tour in which they were overwhelmed by a side they had underestimated. He was not helped by an injury to Imran during the second Test that resulted in him being able to take little effective part in the third and missing the fourth completely. In five of the six matches he still managed to take 19 wickets but achieved little with the bat. When he was not injured he was suffering from a virus and when he was not struggling with painkillers he was concerned that he was not pulling his weight. He was advised by a specialist to miss the fifth Test at Madras but dared not tell his captain that he had picked up a new injury while recovering from an old one. Ionization treatment during each interval enabled him to bowl in five-over spells and to take his hundredth Test wicket. In all he finished with five for 114, but to no avail. Pakistan were defeated by ten wickets and lost the series 2–0. Rumours abounded when they returned home that the players had been involved in all kinds of debauched behaviour, when in actuality curfews had been stringently imposed. Asif foresaw what would occur and resigned before arriving home. The team's time of arrival was even kept secret.

Though Majid was the obvious successor to Asif, his form in India was such that a younger person was deemed more desirable. Javed Miandad was already relatively experienced and even in his early twenties had a sound grasp of tactics. He led the side in a short series against Australia, and played on such lifeless pitches that Dennis Lillee vowed never to return to Pakistan; in three Tests he took three wickets. Imran took part in two and was more successful in gaining six wickets, as well as finishing on the winning side. Victory in the first of these matches was sufficient.

Similar wickets were assiduously prepared the next season in Pakistan, when West Indies were the visitors. The difference was that this time the slow pitches did not inconvenience their fast bowlers, Clarke, Croft, Garner and Marshall. Imran put Pakistan's defeat – they lost the one Test that yielded a result – down to a lack of team spirit: he was not readily impressed with Javed's captaincy and neither, as it transpired, were his fellow players. This was not to say that Imran did not perform for him: in the first Test at Lahore, Imran enabled Pakistan to recover from 95 for five and ultimately draw the match by making 123, his first Test century, on his twenty-eighth birthday. It was the most recognizable sign yet of his growing maturity as a batsman, achieved under pressure against a strong attack. 'I was never motivated by statistics but their bowling was very strong and I have never concentrated harder.' He himself took ten wickets in four matches but West Indies were too good for a side that urgently needed to be revitalized.

This was emphasized later that year of 1981 when Pakistan took part in a three-Tests tour of Australia, again under Javed. It was not as close a series as a 2–1 defeat would suggest.

Imran, who became Pakistan's highest wicket-taker in the final Test at Melbourne when he gained his 144th victim, bowled consistently well throughout, taking 16 wickets. The series, though, was overshadowed and clouded by a confrontation between Javed and Lillee that epitomized why Javed did not have the full support of his players. In the first Test at Perth he was completing a single when he was obstructed by Lillee, who kicked him. Javed in response raised his bat over his head in a threatening manner. It made for a dramatic photograph of one of the most undignified incidents in the history of the game. Morale was poor throughout the tour, not least because Javed would complain that he did not have the side he wanted. When Pakistan returned home, the Board issued a statement that they had failed because the senior players had not co-operated with the captain. The players regarded this as summarizing Javed's views and were, inevitably, appalled. 'Sadly the captaincy didn't suit Javed because previously he was always so full of fun and he seemed to change his personality and his attitude to the team which wasn't always successful,' said Imran. 'His man management was poor and even though he tried his best on the field, he lacked the strength of character to drag the team along under his wing.' Ten players issued a statement that questioned Javed's leadership. They refused to play under him in the imminent series against Sri Lanka.

The Board, however, stood their ground. Thus eight senior players, including Imran and Majid, spokesman for the rebels, were left out of the first two Tests, returning only for the final match at Lahore, which was won more or less single-handedly by Imran himself. A compromise had been reached: Javed would lead Pakistan in this match but would be unavailable to captain them in the subsequent tour to England. However disagreeable recent events had been, he would continue to play under a new captain. In this match Imran illustrated that he was at his peak as a truly fast bowler. He maintained his speed over long spells in Sri Lanka's first innings, taking eight for 58, and in their second innings six wickets at the same cost. This was Sri Lanka's first tour as a Test nation and thus they could be excused succumbing in the face of world-class fast bowling. Imran's figures in their first innings proved to be the best of his Test career. Since Pakistan were desperately in need of someone to lead them in a forthcoming series that would be rather more testing, his performance was opportune indeed.

Chapter 7

It is not readily apparent to the West why Pakistan did not appoint Imran as their captain sooner than 1982. If his family background bestowed precedence, so, in the eyes of the populace, would his years in England. Javed Miandad was a cricketer of proven abilities when he was given the captaincy at the age of twenty-two, but he was not helped by a sketchy education. The immediate predecessors, Intikhab Alam, Mushtaq Mohammad and Asif Iqbal, were fine performers with long experience of the necessary disciplines of leading all manner of players, but even they had been unable to rally their compatriots into achieving more than the sum of several erratic parts.

The sticking point was whether a fast-bowling all-rounder could captain a side at Test level without his own game suffering. Of the most notable postwar all-rounders, Sobers led by inspiration rather than tactical acumen, and Botham's personal performances suffered to the extent that he gave up the England captaincy only just before it gave him up. There was no compelling reason from history to show that Imran would make a decent fist of organizing the Pakistanis, or, indeed, that his own game would benefit. He was told as much by one or two individuals whose advice he heeded.

Neither had Imran much experience of captaincy, having led Oxford for just one season and played too little domestic cricket in Pakistan ever to have had the opportunity there. His own ambitions had not stretched to captaincy, partly because fast bowlers were always considered unsuited to it. Then there was the manner in which various Pakistani captains had come to the end of their time. None seemed to retire gracefully. Imran was as aware as anyone just how hard it was to unite the Pakistani sides, given that there always seemed to be self-promoting factions within them.

One viewpoint, however, had seemingly been overlooked by Pakistan's selectors, although not necessarily by Imran. He was not yet at his peak, certainly not as a batsman, and it was quite conceivable that, since he thrived on responsibility, leadership might well enhance his game. This had occurred at university, albeit eight years earlier, and it was what finally decided him to take on the captaincy of his country. So his time at Oxford continued to have a salutary effect.

After his involvement in the ganging-up on Javed, Imran could hardly have expected an easy passage. 'The situation when I took over was very volatile. After what had happened, it would have been very difficult for anyone taking over,' he said. He dispelled the notion that players from Karachi and Lahore were not speaking to each other, but was under no illusions about the enormity of his task. For one thing, he was leading a party that contained no fewer than three former captains: Javed, Wasim Bari and Majid Khan. With Majid, his cousin and his hero, he was to fall out before the end of the tour.

This was counterpointed by one individual whose gratitude was considerable. Abdul Qadir had had scant success in England on the 1978 tour and was far from highly regarded at home. He was the one player whose credentials Imran needed to emphasize to his fellow selectors. That Qadir turned out to be so successful and so charismatic in 1982 helped Imran have his way with other contentious selections in the future. His judgement as to who constituted a good player, and who would become one a few years hence, was to prove unerring. It was a vitally important aspect of his success as a captain.

Qadir was the cricketer who made John Arlott's summer – and those of a good many others besides. Leg spin was out of fashion at the time and yet Imran utilized him both as an aggressive, unfathomable match winner and as a stock bowler. It was a brilliant ploy. Batsmen who had become conditioned to facing batteries of fast bowlers the world over did not have the technique to cope with this. To Qadir, Imran was 'my greatest friend after Allah'. The captain held the Dervish's hand throughout the tour, taking him to parties and treating him like a child, or, as Wasim Raja reckoned, like an unpaid servant.

Qadir took ten wickets in the three-Tests series, and at greater cost than Mudassar Nazar, which would serve only to emphasize Imran's feelings that averages can be misleading. His worth was far greater than that. One of the delights of the tour was watching Imran bowl in conjunction with Qadir: one of the fastest bowlers in the world coupled with one of the most guileful. It was a tour which on the face of it was no triumph, in that England beat Pakistan 2–1, yet this too was intrinsically misleading. Pakistan's cricket had always been highly individualistic; now the players came together as a team. By and large this lasted until the end of Imran's career, a decade later. Just as two decades earlier Frank Worrell had united a disparate group of West Indians, so a similarly gifted collection of sportsmen now began to play to their potential under Imran.

Imran achieved this above all by 'being the commanding figure of the tour', as *Wisden* put it. He was to be the commanding figure on most of his subsequent tours. Only when he was not, namely when he was injured, were the Pakistanis riven with factions. In 1982 he was fit enough, and good enough, to do much of the bowling and his batting came on apace, which he thought it might as the upshot of his added responsibility. It would have been hard for any disaffected player to find fault in a captain who so conspicuously led by personal example.

Not that his leadership was without criticism. The English press disliked his admonishing of umpires, in which he was unexpectedly abetted by Intikhab, Pakistan's even-tempered manager. In the one-day internationals, both of which Pakistan lost, Imran's tactics were heavily criticized. The inevitable comparisons were made with Botham, who was thought to have been overburdened only the previous year, 1981. By the end of Pakistan's tour there were numerous people, the England captain among them, who had tired of Pakistan's incessant appealing. 'Imran and I had respectful, friendly relations but their appealing was histrionic and Imran should have controlled it,' said Bob

Willis. 'Even someone as straight-thinking as him looks through one end of the telescope only. Pakistani cricketers adopt the attitude of press-ganging the rest of the world in what they want.'

What they wanted was better umpiring, or at least different umpiring. Imran was already calling for international officials. As with the controversy over ball tampering a decade later, there was a tendency to see certain incidents in a racist light. The antagonism the Pakistanis felt towards one umpire, David Constant, which had begun in 1974 when he insisted that play should go ahead on rain-affected pitches, was still apparent when they toured in 1987. Hence their incomprehension over Mike Gatting's row with Shakoor Rana later in 1987. 'They say, why have a go at him when there is this racial abuse thrown at them in Yorkshire. It is why Pakistanis have a bit of a chip,' said John Barclay, Imran's Sussex captain.

Yet such concerns did not spoil the cricket. The two countries were well matched, even in the absence of those England players who had opted to tour South Africa. Throughout the series Imran strove to attack, which was really the only way he could lead a side; he could appear uninterested as well as aloof when a match was going nowhere. 'He probably attacked too much but then he probably expected his batsmen to score more runs than they did,' said Willis. Other than Imran himself and Mohsin Khan, who made a double hundred in the Test that Pakistan won at Lord's, the batting was thoroughly disappointing. Hence the need for Imran to bat as effectively as he did. Although not yet accomplished at selecting his shots and stuck on the back foot too often for English conditions, he averaged 53 over the three Tests, making an unbeaten 67 and 46 in the low-scoring, deciding match at Headingley.

It had helped to have spent the first half of the summer in form for Sussex. Imran's approach stemmed from what he had described as 'a dreadful shot' in the first Test. He knew he could not chide others if he was losing his wicket in such a way. As for his bowling, although he might have kept himself on for too long this was for a purpose: Sarfraz was not the bowler he had been and was prone to injury. Other than Qadir and the medium-paced Mudassar, the remainder of the attack was relatively innocuous. Imran more or less bowled out England in their first innings on his own, taking seven for 52. He had not slept well on the eve of the match, feeling as tense as Bob Willis looked, and by the end of it was on painkillers as a result of a thigh injury. He took two further wickets in England's second innings but 313 for victory proved too much. Indeed, but for Imran making 65, an innings that in retrospect he felt to be a watershed in his career, defeat would have been greater than 113 runs.

There was a further reason for Imran's charged state of mind. In finalizing his side, Imran had left out Majid, his mentor and, more significantly in the context, his first cousin. Majid had continued to feel he should exert some influence over Imran. 'He made no bones about trying to turn Imran away from discos, which were a far cry from Majid's pastimes of reading and watching westerns,' said Asif Iqbal. 'But no cricketer changed Imran's lifestyle.'

As a cricketing decision, the dropping of Majid was understandable. He was evidently past his best as a batsman and yet, being a proud man, he thought he had one remaining series in him in which he could go out of the game with a flourish. It never happened. He did play in the final Test, without success, but had been cut to the quick. He has not spoken to Imran since the tour, not even when Pakistan won the World Cup. 'Majid is very stubborn but he thought he had been stabbed in the back,' said Dr Nausherwan Burki, a cousin of them both. 'Imran accepts that the way he dropped Majid was not right.' Even in an educated family, tribal traditions in Pakistan still run deep. Pathan first cousins traditionally hate each other. It was fortunate for Imran that Majid became a selector only after Imran had retired.

Majid was not chosen for the second Test because of his lack of runs in four innings the preceding week: there was no compelling reason to retain the same batting order. Yet Pakistan's first innings of 428 for eight was a match-winning total.

Willis was not playing, having ricked his neck in the first Test swaying away from one of Imran's bouncers ('I was scared stiff'), and this was not a propitious match for David Gower to captain England for the first time.

Pakistan's innings was dominated by a superlative double century by Mohsin Khan, who became only the second postwar batsman to play such an innings in a Test at Lord's. Half-centuries by Mansoor Akhtar and Zaheer Abbas helped enable Imran, who was caught at the wicket off Botham for 12, to make an overnight declaration. The sense of this was shown when Sarfraz soon removed both openers and thereafter England struggled to make any headway against Abdul Qadir, unaccustomed as they were to coping with leg spin. The abiding memory of this match, other than of Mohsin's double century, is of Qadir's loop and guile complementing Imran's extreme pace down the slope. Here were two world-class bowlers on top of their game – and on top of England, for that matter.

No one England batsman managed to progress beyond the 30s, although Gatting, shepherding the tail, enabled them to come within three runs of saving the follow on. When partnered by the last man, Robin Jackman, he accepted an offer to come off for bad light. In the morning, having taken a single from the third ball of Imran's first over to try to keep the strike, he could only watch helplessly as Jackman was lbw to the last. It was no surprise that Imran had taken it upon himself to gain that last wicket, nor that he maintained his hostility when England followed on in spite of having to bowl 42 overs in the innings. Sarfraz and Tahir Naqqash were not fit, and yet he was not without support. Mudassar was capable of wobbling the ball around at a gentle medium but was regarded as no more than a useful change bowler. Now, however, he achieved enough swing – and enough luck – to take the wickets of Randall, Lamb and Gower in six balls without conceding a run. Chris Tavaré, batting as obdurately as anybody since Trevor Bailey, enabled England to avoid an innings defeat, taking nearly seven hours over 82, and there was a half-century by Botham besides, but a further spell by Mudassar was too much for the lower middle order. He finished with six for 32, leaving Pakistan to make 76 from 18 overs. Imran wisely sent in Javed Miandad with Mohsin and Javed's ability to improvise and snatch quick singles meant that they reached their target with four overs to spare. It was only the second time they had ever beaten England, the first having been under Kardar's captaincy in 1954.

The publicity emanating from this victory brought Imran a wider public. 'The press created a role but his physique, Oxford education and performance were all a part of it,' said Sarfraz. The profiles of him were cricket-related, unlike some that appeared a few years later, but they focused to a considerable extent on extraneous detail. Even in *The Times*. 'The handsomeness of his features is complemented by an outward manner that some call aloof and haughty and others describe as arrogant. He is not unfriendly or unapproachable, but there is always a reserve. It has been taken by some to be an insufferable expression of an attitude of superiority,' it thundered.

Bob Willis was one such person, finding Imran to have 'a bit of a strut' and to be 'slightly pretentious', although he had great respect for him as a cricketer. To the *Sunday Times*, once they had informed their readers that Imran had 'the kind of rugged good looks that are only enhanced by a day's growth of beard', there was respect for 'the way he swung the ball through the air at ferocious speed. Imran and Michael Holding are probably the only bowlers today who can consistently propel the ball at over 90 mph.' At Lord's, David Gower, England's foremost batsman, didn't know which way the ball was going.

The tabloid press had not yet latched on to Imran, partly because he had still to be linked to an English girl. He was not yet a member of Tramp, the St James nightclub, and was not appearing in gossip columns. The Pakistani side of 1982 was one which leafed through model agency telephone numbers as opposed to being pursued by the glitterati. The attention Imran was beginning to attract not only increased the likelihood of some of his colleagues gaining acceptance in smart circles on his shirt tails, it heightened the standing of Pakistanis living in England.

The close proximity of the Asian population at Bradford to Leeds, venue of the final Test, meant that there was no shortage of support for Pakistan. What let them down – as in the first Test – was their batting. Other than their appealing, it was the one aspect of their game over which Imran had yet to exert discipline. Again he would have to perform to the very limits of his ability since Sarfraz and Tahir were still not fit, and again he demonstrated just how his game benefited from additional responsibility. He won the toss and chose to bat on a pitch that would give some help to the seamers throughout, as pitches at Headingley invariably did, and found himself having to reorganize an innings that had slumped to 168 for six. Given some support by Wasim Bari, Imran finished with an unbeaten 67 and enabled Pakistan to reach a reasonably respectable total of 275. The onus was now on him to bowl England out in such conditions, especially since Ehtesham-ud-Din, a replacement brought in from the Leagues, was not sufficiently fit.

Imran responded indefatigably. Three of the first four wickets were his, including that of Tavaré. After Gower and Botham had batted competently enough to give England a chance of gaining a first innings lead, he returned and dealt with the tail. His figures of five for 49 were testimony to his hostility. Alas for him, Pakistan's lead of 19 soon proved worthless. Willis had Mohsin and Mudassar out in his opening over and although Javed made his second half-century of the match, their innings was immensely disappointing. Imran's disciplined batting contrasted markedly with this. He was last out for 46.

England required 219 to win, a target that was seemingly well within their compass when they had reached 168 for the loss of only Tavaré. They then lost their way and five wickets to Imran and Mudassar before bad light brought an end to play for the day. Botham was out early the following morning but with only 29 needed, Vic Marks and Bob Taylor ushered England to victory. Imran finished with eight wickets to add to his 113 runs and the man of the match award for the second time in the series. Yet that was no consolation for a 2–1 defeat overall. He gave vent to his feelings with an unprecedented attack on the umpiring, not least on account of what he perceived as the reprieve Gower had at an early stage of his first innings of 74. His antipathy towards David Constant was to spill over into the next series and lead ultimately to fractious behaviour in Pakistan five years later. But with much justification, he blamed Pakistan's defeat in the series upon the ill-discipline of his batsmen.

How sound a captain was he at this early stage? He had shown astute judgement in championing Qadir, even though he admitted he did not know how to set a field for him and was criticized for over-bowling him in the final Test. He had shown strength of character, as was to be expected, in dealing with players and in tactical decisions. He would not, for instance, take the new ball for the sake of doing so, just because it was due. He was an attacking captain and deployed the strengths of his side accordingly. Above all, he showed conclusively that his game was enhanced by what other all-rounders would consider an encumbrance.

Tactically, Imran relied more on Mudassar Nazar than on Javed Miandad, whose approach he found too defensive for his liking. He looked to uphold standards of sportsmanship. 'I always told the players to be fair. Three times in my career as captain I recalled batsmen who were wrongly given out.' His natural aloofness enabled him 'to rise above the common herd' as *The Times* put it. This gave him the detachment from his players necessary for a captain. He could be harshly realistic in the dressing room if he lacked confidence in individuals not noted for their consistency. If so and so doesn't do well and such and such doesn't come off, we'll lose, was his standpoint on occasion. Those who resented this did not admit as much to Imran's face, believing that any antagonism towards him would spell the end of their career. Brought up in a dictatorship, they had a deep-seated fear of the Khans and Burkis. Imran was seen by one

94

or two players to be valuing the advice of friends more than professional cricketers. He disputes that. ' I always talked cricket, always encouraged the younger players to give advice.'

He did not take criticism lightly but his personality was such that he could transcend jealousies, rivalries and intrigues. Poor cricket irritated him but he did not show it, nor would he make a fool of a colleague in public. He was critical of umpires on that tour, as on subsequent tours, yet accepted their decisions without acting in a way that would annoy spectators. Overall, he could be compared with Pakistan's most authoritative captain of all, Abdul Hafeez Kardar.

Imran was thirty in 1982 and hinted that he might not still be playing when Pakistan returned to England in 1987, although the reality was that he had no inkling of what he would do next. The Civil Service no longer held an appeal for him and he did not want to 'drown in an organization'. *Wisden* made him one of their five cricketers of the year, comparing him favourably with Botham and speculating that his future wife would have to wait until he had finished playing, which would not be for 'two or three years at least'.

He had unquestionably been man of the series on either side, and yet he was all too aware that the career of a fast-bowling all-rounder was a short one. It was another point to be taken into consideration in any comparison with Botham (of which there were plenty in 1982) and Kapil Dev, both of whom were essentially medium-pacers. Nor was Hadlee, once he had cut down his run, as quick as Imran. In the three Tests on the tour of England, Imran had carried a succession of injuries which resulted in the need to take painkillers at Headingley. 'The risk of injury is always there and we have got to get used to bowling through the pain barrier,' he said. Until, that was, he aggravated a stress fracture of the shin later that year. It was to lead to the most problematical period of his long career.

Having bowled more overs than anyone else on either side in England – 178 – Imran was now faced with nine Tests in Pakistan, against Australia and India, in which he would undoubtedly do as much bowling as anyone, with the possible exception of Qadir. The initial series, against Australia, was played at one of the hottest times of the year in Pakistan – September and October – which Imran disliked and in time avoided (although he chose to take part in lucrative one-day matches in Sharjah at that time of year). He objected in principle to countries touring Pakistan during these months, so that their own seasons would not be interrupted. Australia were thrashed, beaten in each of the three Tests. Imran gained eight wickets at Lahore but had scant opportunity with the bat given that the specialist batsmen atoned for their poor performances in England. Qadir took 22 wickets in the series, proving, if proof were needed, that he was not simply a Lahorite in the side at the behest of his captain.

The best fast bowler and the best spinner in Pakistan's history were now at their peak. India, who were hardly short of seasoned batsmen, were trounced. Imran reckoned he bowled as fast, and as well, as at any time in his life. In the six Tests he took 40 wickets, taking his tally to a record 88 for the year. When he wanted to produce a particular type of delivery, he could do so, which had not necessarily been the case against England.

At Karachi, Imran took eight for 60, the best analysis by a Pakistani against India. On the dead pitch of Faisalabad, which had defeated the likes of Lillee and Hadlee in the past, he had a match analysis of 11 for 180. He equalled Botham's record, also against India, of ten wickets and a century in the same Test. At Hyderabad, he took six wickets in India's first innings, including a spell of five for three when he reckoned he bowled as fast as he ever has.

Fit though he was, something had to give through bowling so fast for so long in such a concentrated year. It was his left shin bone, which broke through the constant pounding of his leg at the point of delivery. Partly as a result of a lack of suitable diagnostic equipment in India, the injury was not identified until the end of the series, by which time Imran was a limping medium-pacer. Not that this affected his capacity for taking wickets. His 40 for the series cost only 13.95 apiece.

The cure for this large fracture was to be a year's rest from bowling. Highly worrying though this was, considering that he was at his peak, Imran was at least able to give his batting the attention his talent merited. He was specifically asked by Pakistan's Board to play in the World Cup in England in 1983 as a batsman, if at all possible.

This he did, although with some reservations since he would not be playing for Sussex before the competition began in June. While he had some success batting at number five, making a century against Sri Lanka and gaining the man of the match award for an unbeaten 79 off New Zealand, Imran was frustrated that he could not bowl. Although Pakistan qualified for the semi-finals with England from the weaker of the two groups, they were no match for West Indies in the semi-finals, losing by eight wickets. To make matters worse for him and Pakistan, India unexpectedly beat West Indies in the final. Scorn was heaped on Imran for this as much as for his side not reaching the final. Since international one-day cricket was not then accorded the significance it gained in later years, winning the World Cup did not have the kudos it carried when Pakistan won nine years later – unless of course you happened to come from that tract of the subcontinent.

For the remainder of the summer of 1983 Imran reverted – unwisely – to county cricket at Hove. Injured or not, he was simply playing too much cricket. Nevertheless, he topped both the Sussex bowling and batting averages, striving, in the understated words of *Wisden*, 'almost impatiently to regain fitness'. Off a short run he took 12 wickets at 7.16 apiece, including six for six and a hat trick to boot against Warwickshire. Immediately after that, the pain returned and X-rays showed that the fracture had opened up again. He realized not only that the injury would take much longer to heal than he had anticipated but that it might even affect his batting. He missed another series with India, this one drawn, in which Pakistan were led by the more conservative Zaheer Abbas.

Zaheer continued to captain Pakistan in Australia that winter of 1983 when, initially, Imran could not participate. The Board was split as to which of the two should lead the side and, indeed, whether Imran should play under Zaheer. The President, Air Marshal Nur Khan, eventually sacked the selectors and reinstated Imran. In retrospect, Imran felt that by going to Australia at all, and by being able to play only at half cock, he gave those detractors who resented his authority the wherewithal they needed to try to remove him. Able to appear only in the last two Tests, as a batsman (and as captain), he produced at Melbourne as fine a piece of batting (83 out of 470) as he reckons he has ever done. *Wisden* was in accord as to its excellence. He followed it with an unbeaten 72 in the second innings that helped ensure the match would be drawn.

Nonetheless, Imran made two low scores in the final Test and the series was comfortably lost. In the subsequent one-day competition, Pakistan were thoroughly outplayed. This sparked off endless further manoeuvres at home, where the Board was ousted and Zaheer reinstated as captain. Worse, Imran was told after further X-rays early in 1984 that his career was over. He had now to face the prospect of leaving the game as a humiliated cricketer, like numerous other Pakistanis before him. Such was the press he was receiving in Pakistan that a story was published in one newspaper claiming that the trouble began when he kicked a local boy who ran on to the pitch when Imran was batting. In revenge, the boy put a curse on Imran's leg and it was not removed until Imran tracked the boy down and made atonement. 'Complete nonsense,' said Imran. 'Actually I kicked him with my right foot and it was my left shin which had the stress fracture.'

Other than his mother's death from cancer, this was the lowest period of Imran's life. Indeed, it was the first time that anything had gone seriously awry. Conflicting advice from various doctors did not help. One option remained, albeit a drastic one: a form of treatment still at the experimental stage which involved electrical currents charged through the leg. General Zia saw to it that this would be subsidized by the government.

For six months Imran's leg was in a cast. 'For ten hours a day

I could hardly move. The instrument inserted in the cast had to be plugged in to produce the therapeutic electrical cycles. It is not easy for a sportsman accustomed to perpetual exercise to adapt to being completely deprived of it,' he wrote in *All Round View*.

Fairweather friends, male and female alike, started to melt away. One woman said to him: 'I suppose you are going to get fat now.' In *All Round View*, Imran expresses brief but profound appreciation of Emma Sergeant, without whose support and counsel he would have been in still greater despair. 'It was extremely opportune that Imran knew her during this period,' said Imran's friend, explorer Mark Shand. As well as introducing him to new friends, she widened his range of interests to the extent that he pursues some of them to this day.

'People all over the world were throwing stones at him. It would have been a humbling experience for anyone, but it was a long way down for Imran,' she said. 'Jealousy is such a prevalent feeling among people dissatisfied with their own lives. His interests had to shift. He started to read and write much more and to think about his own country. I thought it was time he listened to opera, so we went to see *Carmen*. He saw the shattering end when Carmen was murdered, put his finger up in the way an umpire does and said, "That's out! That's back to the pavilion."'

In London, Imran's new friends tended to be people entirely unconnected with the game. He found that, unlike in Lahore, where he would always see more or less the same individuals, in London he encountered eclectic groups. Among cricketers, he had, as we have seen, become friendly with Gehan Mendis, and he developed a deeper, more analytical friendship with him during this period of recuperation. Wasim Bari, a colleague of long standing, felt Imran matured during this time. But most of his Test and county colleagues and, for that matter, opponents, were not of like intellect or outlook. Besides, he hardly wanted to spend his recuperation discoursing with fit and able sportsmen.

'I was very down for a time but then I had to rationalize it,' he said. 'It changed me. Maybe it made me into a nicer person,

I don't know. It made me realize how uncertain things are. I was at my peak and suddenly written off. Everyone was saying I would never play again. That and my mother's death are the two things in my life that have had the biggest impact on me. It was the moment when my awareness of God began.'

As well as the support he received from Emma Sergeant, Imran was given succour in particular by Mark Shand, an author and film-maker of similar age who had travelled widely in India. His sister is the friend of the Prince of Wales, Camilla Parker Bowles (whom Imran has never met). Shand, too, was going through a depressed period. 'We spent Easter together in a morose state. You get to know people best when at your lowest ebb and he helped me greatly through his determination,' said Shand. 'When you talk to him he makes you feel you're the only person there. He has a very human side to him which you don't gather until you get to know him and he is one of the few people I've met who is totally honourable.' Shand stressed the point that for much of 1984 Imran was concerned that he would never play cricket again. In Pakistan, the belief was that a miracle was needed. This fatalistic viewpoint was accentuated by the fact that the country had few fast bowlers in its history. Those who were seriously injured were not heard of again.

Imagine, then, the joy felt by Imran – and his friends – when X-rays in October 1984 showed that his leg had healed completely. There was no guarantee that there would not be a relapse, nor that he would be able to bowl as fast or as well again. Indeed, many felt he was never again quite the same bowler. Yet he was able to resume training and that, as he put it, felt like being freed from a cage. He trained in Hyde Park with Shand, who recalls 'hideous sprint sessions'.

Imran had determined not to resume playing in Pakistan until he was properly fit. He signed, instead, for New South Wales for the Australian summer of 1984–5 and gradually built up his pace and his fitness. They won both the McDonald's Cup and the Sheffield Shield, Imran finishing on top of the national bowling averages with 28 wickets. The cricket was competitive; the comeback as judicious and successful as could have been expected.

He could be thankful for once that there was another sequence of one-day internationals in Australia that winter. The 50-overs-a-side day/night matches, in which he needed to bowl no more than ten overs an innings, also proved to be recuperative. In his absence the captaincy had yo-yoed between Zaheer and Javed Miandad. Now, bowling with a whippy left-armer called Wasim Akram for the first time, Imran bowled and batted with sufficient success to help Pakistan to reach the final. They were beaten by India, as they were when the caravan moved on to Sharjah and yet another sponsored limited-overs competition. Among those who recall the details is Imran, which is not as surprising as it might sound. In the most telling spell he ever produced in the one-day game, he took six for 14 against India – and still finished on the losing side.

In England in the summer of 1985, Imran was no less effective. He played in only thirteen championship matches for Sussex, yet again headed both their bowling and their batting averages. Any concerns he had with self-motivation were not apparent in his performances. His rhythm, not his old injury, was the key to whether he bowled in long or short spells. 'His effectiveness was to come on at, say, 85 for two for his second spell,' said Barclay, recalling one match at Eastbourne when Derbyshire lost their last five wickets without addition.

That October of 1985 Imran took part in a short series against Sri Lanka at home. Although this was a one-sided affair, it was nonetheless ideal since it was the first Test cricket he had played for two years. In his absence, new batsmen had come into Pakistan's side and Imran found himself going in no higher than number seven; but he played one innings of 63 and was the most successful bowler on either side, taking 17 wickets and effectively winning the first Test match to have been staged at Sialkot.

What was more, during this series Zaheer Abbas announced his retirement and Javed Miandad said that he would be resigning as captain. He had been criticized strongly during the year, not least for losing three consecutive matches to India. No matter that they were one-day internationals: to Pakistanis they might as well have been wars. Thus, with Wasim Raja not having been chosen against Sri Lanka – it transpired that he played his last Test in 1984 – there was no one other than Imran with a notable claim to the captaincy, even if there were doubtless plenty with designs on it. Clearly the leadership should revert to Imran. Yet only the previous year he knew he would be fortunate even to put on a pair of flannels ever again.

Chapter 8

No sooner had Imran started to recover from his stress fracture than his mother became ill to the extent that, once properly diagnosed, she was almost inoperable. Cancer was known as a rich man's disease in Pakistan in that only well-off people could afford to fly to Europe to receive treatment. There was no national health service in Pakistan and, when Shaukat Kanum's family wanted her to be given chemotherapy, her doctor was opposed to it. Government-run hospitals in Pakistan theoretically provide free treatment but in reality are too poorly equipped to do so. In spite of flying to London and having an operation at Cromwell Hospital in 1984, Shaukat died the following year in acute pain. Imran's next career was thus determined. When he retired from cricket he would build the first cancer hospital in Pakistan in honour of his mother. This became an obsession.

'It was the most traumatic and painful period of my life,' said Imran. 'My mother was sick for six or seven months and suffered terribly during the last three months. Most of the time I was with her. I felt her pain. I knew she was going to die but there was nothing I could do. I could afford to give her the best medical treatment yet I couldn't help her.' She could have been given morphine, although the main painkillers were heroin-based and banned in Pakistan through the narcotics laws. There was no hospice, no care for terminally ill patients. All Imran could do, as he shuttled back and forth to play in Australia, was to try to make her more comfortable. For two years after her death he blocked out the memory of her last months alive; he could not bear to think of them. 'It is the most helpless feeling anyone can go through to watch someone you are close to in pain and not be able to do anything about it.'

In Pakistan, doctors were unable to follow the progress of a patient because of the numbers of people they had to see. They would spend, on average, just three minutes with each patient. Individuals who could afford to do so would pay the doctors to treat them privately. 'Medicine in Pakistan is a disaster,' said Dr Nausherwan Burki, Javed Burki's brother, who returned home from America to do what he could for his favourite aunt. 'Doctors in Pakistan go into medicine not for a vocation but to make money. Government hospitals are a disaster with one or two exceptions. Doctors put all their resources into private treatment since they know that is where all their money is coming from. The army has its own hospital which is much better than anything on the civilian side.'

At her local hospital, Shaukat had her stomach pains misdiagnosed as a minor illness. 'My mother died because the hospital facilities in Pakistan were so dirty, overcrowded and very primitive,' said Imran. 'By the time she realized it was something very serious and got a second opinion, it was too late.' In Britain, specialists come to a decision as to whether to inform their patients that they have cancer, whereas in America they are more blunt. The last two lines in the letter sent from the Cromwell Hospital to Shaukat's doctors in Pakistan explained her condition in a roundabout British way. They did not understand it, but Dr Burki did. Upon seeing it, he told his mother, Shaukat's sister, to call other members of the family back to Lahore. Shaukat did not have long to live.

His mother's death and his own serious injury made Imran appreciate just how precarious was the existence he had taken for granted. He was at his peak as a cricketer only to be told he would not play again; his mother, a constantly reassuring presence in his life, suddenly was dying. He reassessed his values and sense of direction. His visits to hospitals in Pakistan, when he would see three or four children suffering from cancer having to share a bed and uneducated people unable to afford basic medicine, made him appreciate just how desperately the poor needed specialist cancer treatment. He vowed to raise five million pounds to build and equip a hospital in Lahore, his home city.

'I'm almost ashamed that I managed to ignore the appalling conditions for so long,' he said. 'Now there is nothing else I want to do with my life but to see this hospital through to the end.'

Business was not Imran's forte, and it was an emotional rather than a rational decision. 'He goes into these things without planning,' admitted Javed Burki. In addition to having to extend his career to ensure that he and the hospital gained sufficient fundraising publicity, he was risking not only his own reputation but that of his family, too. He could not afford to fail.

Even though the government of Punjab donated 20 acres at Jauher Town on the barren outskirts of Lahore, it was to become apparent that five million pounds would cover only the initial phase. The costing had to make allowances for bribes in a society which Imran realized was suffused with corruption. When eventually the construction was complete and the equipment installed, the running costs would be such that Imran would be shackled to the project for the rest of his life. Initially, it did not dawn on him that this would be the case. 'What he is doing places him above any other sportsman in Pakistan,' said Wasim Bari, who arranged to have hospital brochures printed, mostly free of charge, through Pakistan International Airlines. 'It is out of this world for a country like Pakistan, whose people think of nothing other than themselves. Such a man has to be different.'

Imran offered to do any favour in return for the brochures, to be told by his old wicketkeeper that he arranged this 'for the cause'. Thousands, if not millions, would respond in like manner. What was questioned – by some – was the structure. 'People would benefit more from clinics all over the country rather than from one hospital since cancer is a rare disease,' said Qamar Ahmed. (In a country of around 110 million people, 200,000 new cases are diagnosed each year.) There was a concern that by personalizing the hospital Imran would gain less support than might otherwise be the case: the official appeal was called the Shaukat Khanum Memorial Trust but it was associated with Imran's name in England. Dr Burki suggested that Imran should

105

endow an existing institution with his mother's name. 'Crooks were coming out of the woodwork and saying, "I had a relation die from cancer and I'll help you." Someone sent Imran details of a district hospital and told him, wrongly, that this was what he wanted,' said Dr Burki.

Although fundraising offices were soon established in New York, under the direction of Imran's sister, Robina, and in London under Jacqui Muir, who had a background in advertising and marketing, the venture was attracting individuals who were more concerned with self-aggrandizement. 'Imran has boundless optimism and self-confidence which is not misplaced,' said Dr Burki. 'He does deliver. But there were people offering to help who were after their own gain and a minority of people within the media and cricket wanted to pull him down. There was negativity through envy. Doctors in Pakistan were saying that it couldn't be done.'

Some doctors who had been told they would be given roles when the hospital opened in 1992 were concerned that they would lose their practices. By May 1990, Imran was at the end of his tether. Fundraising had begun but there was no data to help him work out the costings. His father was starting to panic over the financial implications and whether donations were being properly channelled. He admitted he had not realized what a sizable project his son was taking on and felt that shame would be brought on his family if it did not come to fruition. Imran told the appointed trust governors, who included his father and the chairman of the directors of the Cromwell Hospital, that they had to have Dr Burki on board. Imran accordingly telephoned Dr Burki at the University of Kentucky, where he was on an education and research exchange, imploring him to come back to Lahore.

Nausherwan Burki, the only member of his family not inter-ested in cricket – he had never seen Imran in action – now became the foremost player in the design and implementation of the hospital. In Lahore he outlined to Imran a masterplan, basing his data on an equivalent institution in America. Imran's intention had been that treatment should be totally free for every-one but Dr Burki decided patients would be charged if they had the means to pay. For the majority, treatment would be palliative, not curative. Those who were dying would want to be near their families rather than in hospital.

It was decided that a quarter of the necessary finance would come from patients and the remaining three-quarters would be raised through donations and endowment funds. The governors would be responsible for fundraising and Dr Burki, having pre-sented his masterplan to them and returned to the US, would take a year's sabbatical from Kentucky to become chief medical adviser when the hospital opened. He would be responsible for staffing. 'I thought the governors did not have the first idea how to set up a hospital,' he said. From Lahore, Imran inundated Dr Burki's office at the university's medical centre with faxes about plans put forward by the doctors already engaged on work at the hospital. Dr Burki, meantime, was seeking advice from the head of the lymphoma biology section at the National Cancer Institute in Maryland. He took his masterplan to the trust governors in December 1990, unabashed that the hospital's office in Lahore saw him as something of an ogre. This was no surprise since the administration he was envisaging had not existed hitherto in Pakistan. His three-phase plan included detail on square footage and personnel and would, after ten years, result in a tertiary cancer centre that would be a centre of excellence and provide every diagnostic treatment. There would be sixteen town houses on the campus for visitors undertaking research at what would be an ideal training site for the Third World. 'I want the US to come and turn green with envy,' declared Dr Burki.

The first phase established a facility that could cope with the assessment of 5000 to 15,000 out-patients, including a large number of children, and 60 in-patients. The second phase would extend to a total of 150 beds as well as further operating theatres, and the third, after ten years, to 250 beds, a number of which would comprise a hospice. The basement walls were designed to be seven foot high by seven foot deep to prevent radiation.

Doctors and nurses would be accommodated in housing around the hospital. A lawn would be laid in front. 'We don't want this to be a depressing place for patients,' said Imran. In a long article in the Karachi newspaper, the *Herald*, it was said that Dr Burki had not emphasized any attempt by the hospital to prevent cancer. Dr Burki replied that it was not the hospital's job to stress prevention.

The non-profit-making Shaukat Khanum Memorial Trust was formed in February 1990 and the foundation stone laid by the then prime minister, Nawaz Sharif, in April the following year. Nothing that he had achieved in cricket, declared Imran, gave him the same satisfaction as seeing the model of the proposed four-storey building turn into a skeleton of reality. Now there was the small matter of furthering his fundraising.

Under the Charity Commissions Act, independent auditors would oversee that funds were properly channelled into a deposit account in Pakistan. Trustees were appointed in Britain, the United States and Australia. One such was Jonathan Mermagen, who later resigned to try to raise funds through marketing. Imran's appeal went worldwide: 'Let us not be too late with too little. We have it within our power to control the destiny of those who suffer. I, therefore, urge you to send a generous contribution or participate in any way possible, for this humanitarian cause.'

However good the cause, would the populace of Pakistan accept Imran's new vocation? 'For many years the people of Pakistan felt cricket was my great offering to my country, but now even the public have changed their minds. Somehow, this time round, I know they will accept my retirement because keeping the people healthy and alive is more important than any sport,' he said in 1990. 'This time round', however, did not come about for a further two years. To raise money in countries where cricket was played, it was imperative that he maintain a high profile, which meant continuing his career at the highest level. He remained fit enough and, in spite of losing some pace in his mid-thirties, good enough. He was making sufficient runs to justify his place solely as a batsman. As captain of his country, he was the nonpareil. His one concern had been whether he could motivate himself to keep playing when there was little left to achieve. Now he had a spur.

Imran even cut back on his socializing in London. 'The hospital project is taking over my life and I'm glad,' he was fond of saying. Did he feel guilty about his own well-off background? 'No, not guilty,' he replied. 'Just lucky.' He had to contend now with beggars outside his father's house in Lahore, which he disliked as much as he did going cap in hand to firms and individuals for contributions to the hospital. His desire to be left alone when he returned home after being in the public eye all day meant that occasionally he would snap at anyone begging for money. Sometimes he would accede, at other times he would tell them to get lost. He was always remorseful if he felt he had caused hurt.

The involvement of Imran's father and of prominent businessmen had helped allay any concern that the gathering of funds was not being properly supervised, but Imran was still worried that less money would be given to the appeal than would otherwise be the case because corruption in Pakistan was so widespread. Charities in India fared better. He knew that the Pakistani community in Britain would support him but he was aware that other British people might not be so inclined to contribute towards a project that was out of their sphere: there were numerous other charities closer to home and recession was imminent. He also felt that Americans, who knew little of cricket, would not necessarily have heard of him. It was important that he should involve other celebrities who were friends or acquaintances. They, after all, had often been keen to use him for their own projects.

Fundraising events in Britain took the form of dinners, concerts, floodlit matches and receptions. One reception was held at the Victoria and Albert Museum in London. Imran asked Lulu Blacker to bring the Duchess of York, who at the time was not separated from her husband and was causing waves of publicity through the press. The upshot was plenty more, both for herself and for the appeal. Marie Helvin, Mick Jagger and Jerry Hall brought further coverage when they attended fundraising dinners in London. Paul Getty, the philanthropist for whom cricket had become an infatuation, staged a match at his new private ground and was not best pleased when Imran arrived late and left early. Their relationship, however, was not impaired for long: Imran became a regular guest at Getty's box at Lord's. A series of fundraising dinners were held in South Africa, a country where Imran had never played cricket, and which attracted the Prime Minister F. W. de Klerk, Nelson Mandela and Dr Christiaan Barnard, the famous heart surgeon. Pakistani taxi drivers refused to accept fares for transporting Imran to an exhibition match in New York, part of a hectic trip that also took in a match in Toronto. Two of his sisters, Robina, in the United States, and Aleema, in Lahore, oversaw fundraising.

A great deal of money was forthcoming at receptions given by banks. Shaukat Aziz, a senior executive of Citibank, undertook a considerable amount of work in Singapore. In Bahrain, during a fundraising visit to the Middle East that also took in Abu Dhabi, Dubai, Kuwait and Sharjah, Imran was greeted by women who hugged him and presented him with their gold bangles. 'One considerably poorer woman presented him with a cheque for US $8000 – her life savings,' said Chico Jahangir, chairman of the appeal in London and chief co-ordinator internationally. In two days in Bahrain Imran raised US $170,000. Wherever he went, the Pakistan ambassador would welcome him and see him off when he left, a courtesy normally extended only to government ministers. When he visited Southall in west London, traffic came to a standstill – and this on a Sunday. At three restaurants in this predominantly Indian community, he was presented with cheques totalling £10,000 as well, of course, as plenty of food. Kerry Packer, his old employer, offered to introduce Imran to contacts in Australia.

Among cricketers, Sunil Gavaskar was particularly helpful. When floodlit exhibition matches were staged in England,

Pakistani and Indian elevens were represented by their best players and not, as can occur, by also-rans. The matches themselves were hugely successful in terms of takings but were chaotically organized. One floodlit encounter at Crystal Palace in July 1992 attracted 15,000 people and realized £73,000 after expenses, but started late and had to be abandoned at midnight after numerous pitch invasions and fights between stewards and spectators. Warnings over the loudspeaker, one by Imran, were completely ignored. The Pakistani and Indian spectators gave even a 35-overs-a-side exhibition match a patriotic significance lost on everyone else.

Indian doctors offered to give up their holidays by going to work at the hospital when it opened, testimony to the affection in which Imran was held in their country. So, too, did English doctors and nurses. Large companies such as Glaxo offered free equipment, and the Royal Marsden, the famous cancer hospital in London which had recently concluded its own appeal, donated some of its older equipment. A few of Imran's flights around the world were sponsored, notably when he went to South Africa. Other flights he paid for himself: he did not put one bill to his charity.

In Pakistan, Imran was particularly touched that schoolchildren would send him cheques. Emily Todhunter recalls how moved he was when a poor man got down from his bicycle and thrust five rupees, the equivalent of ten pence, into his hand. Another man gave Imran 80 per cent of his salary. This was not much – but to a poor person it was everything. Imran's shyness and lack of self-promotion were highly visible on the occasions when babies were thrust into his arms: evidence, if it were needed, that he was no political animal. He found the saddest aspect of his fundraising to be that those with the most money would often give the least. One rich individual, whom Imran estimated had assets of US $14 million, insisted on being given a complimentary ticket to one of the concerts. Richness, felt Imran, was a state of mind and not conditioned by bank balance.

His belief in fate, that his life was being shaped for him,

strengthened his faith, which had wavered after his mother's death. He had long believed in adhering to the guidelines of the Koran as he was best able to do. It was not practical for him to attempt to pray five times a day when he was playing cricket but he would say prayers every morning on a mat facing Mecca, when his belief in God had returned. His study of the Koran satisfied a desire for knowledge that could no longer be sated by text books on cricket. Opinions became a matter of certitude. 'The more you read, the more your awareness opens up. In Islam, the hoarding of wealth is the biggest sin. The moment you identify your needs you can give the rest of your money away. When you hold money you become a prisoner of your own greed,' he said. Wealth was a test and fame was a test. 'Maybe I can believe in God because the world is so cruel. This is a transitory place and we redeem ourselves in the way we deal with other human beings. God gives people unequal powers as a test.'

Before the death of his mother, Imran had never questioned his own faith. He did not now see himself as 'born again' because he had always been a Muslim, but if he had any doubts over his belief in the Koran he would visit his guide, Mian Bashir, who always refused payment and hence upheld Imran's belief that as soon as money changed hands, power of insight was gone. 'This holy man told me things about my mother no one else could have known. My own inability to control my future has made me realize there is another power,' Imran said. In incipient middle age, as the single-mindedness that had sustained him throughout his cricket career began to wane, Imran became submissive to what he saw as the will of God. His fundraising and his faith were interfluent, although he would not impose either on anyone else.

Some in the Pakistan side had a different viewpoint. They had their suspicions that gifts from wealthy and not so wealthy individuals which might have been theirs were going instead into the hospital appeal fund. This came to a head after Pakistan had won the World Cup in 1992 but such thinking had been prevalent since the appeal was launched three years earlier. It was customary on the subcontinent for businessmen and rich individuals to lavish money on successful cricketers. Javed Miandad, who was never afraid to ask for money, once collected US $100,000 for winning for his country a spurious one-day competition in Sharjah by hitting a six off the very last ball. It was a team game but he chose not to share this booty with his fellow players, whose resentment was doused by Imran. He told them their time would come. Evidently they felt it had by the end of the 1980s when, under Imran, they were as strong a side as any in the world.

During the World Cup Imran would find bundles of Australian dollars left at reception desks of the Pakistanis' hotels. They were evidently intended for the appeal. Yet it was unclear whether some monetary gifts were intended for the players or for the hospital, although, as Imran pointed out, this should have been made clear by the donors. Javed Burki, one of the leading figures in Pakistan's cricket, felt it to be a grey area. Imran, who had had scant material ambitions for himself since his earnings multiplied during World Series Cricket, may have been naive in not realizing just how motivated his colleagues were by money since the great majority of them – Javed Miandad especially – came from considerably poorer backgrounds than he had done. The players saw largesse over and above their match fees as part of their livelihood and wanted to decide for themselves how much money should go to the fund.

Once Pakistan had won the World Cup in 1992, having looked in the early part of the competition as if they would do well to win a match, the players felt there was every prospect of being showered with presents. On the journey home from Australia, all of the party bar Imran, who had stayed in Sydney, stopped at Singapore for a reception given by the Pakistani ambassador. A cheque was handed over for money raised by the Asian community in the area. Imran had felt it was intended for the hospital; some of the players, notably Salim Malik and Ramiz Raja, the articulate younger brother of Wasim, thought it was for them.

'It took me two weeks to realize what was going on,' said Imran. 'One or two players were blinded by greed and this infected most of the side. The players' perception was wrong. There was only the one incident in Singapore when there was uncertainty over where the money was going. The ambassador had been raising funds before the World Cup started. It never arose that I decided whether funds should go to the players or the hospital. But even the players who liked me were affected. Salim was no good when the chips were down but I had not expected it of Ramiz.' Already angered by Imran's speech on the podium at Melbourne, in which he had mentioned not them but the hospital, they told other players they had complained to the Board of Control, telling the administrators that it would be best if Javed Miandad led the side for the forthcoming tour of England.

Javed would have been quite content to have had Imran under him, even though he had made his own form of protest. Upon return to Pakistan, he had announced that the players would be making various appearances around the country unconnected with the appeal. His motives were evident. Later that year, when he played for Imran in fundraising matches in England, he returned his appearance fee, as did some other players. Imran took this to be an expression of guilt. 'All their complaints about me were behind my back,' he said. 'But if there were so many, how come they gave this money back?' Realizing he was not wanted and that, more significantly, fundraising in England could be impaired by such accusations reaching the press during the series, Imran decided not to tour. He went to England for much of the summer and continued to raise funds, unobtrusively.

Imran had given his own prize money from the World Cup, £85,000, to the appeal. By the following year he had donated £200,000, the extra contribution coming from his shares on Wall Street. His was the single largest private donation. He had invested also in a supermarket in Lahore and pledged that a proportion of the profits would go to the hospital. It had taken more than two years to raise the first one and a half million

114

pounds: in the six weeks immediately after the World Cup the same amount was raised again.

After the World Cup, Imran felt for the first time that there was a conflict between performing successfully for Pakistan and collecting the great sums of money required for the hospital. The good relationships Imran generally had with the media throughout the cricket-playing nations had not applied to a section of the Pakistani press. At the start of the World Cup they attributed the side's poor performances to Imran promoting the hospital rather than paying sufficient attention to their cricket. There was a clear correlation between lack of success on the field and lack of funds raised off it: at the start of the competition, when Pakistan were trounced by West Indies, few contributions to the appeal were forthcoming. 'Even though we went on to win the Cup, some damage had already been done by irresponsible journalism. This made me realize that if I was hanging around in England as a non-playing captain, waiting to overcome injury, and the team happened to be doing badly, my fundraising campaign could be hit,' wrote Imran in the *Daily Telegraph*. 'As long as cricket and the hospital project were complementing each other it made sense to play for Pakistan, but now that there was a conflict the only sensible thing to do was to opt out of the tour. My priority in life had shifted from cricket to the cancer hospital.' What further decided him was the shoulder injury he had incurred just before the World Cup. He would not be able to play on the tour of England until mid-June at the earliest.

The impetus gained from winning the World Cup was considerable. Imran regretted that he had become so carried away that he had given the building of the hospital the same national significance as Pakistan's victory, and had failed to mention the players; he was to apologize for doing so. Nonetheless, his speech was shown all around the world through satellite television. Never again would there be the opportunity for such publicity.

Imran felt that if Pakistan had not triumphed, the appeal would have collapsed. His embarrassment at returning home to face the people who had contributed, especially the poor, would have

115

been acute. They had known it to be an ambitious project but had believed Imran would bring it to fruition. What he termed his 'emotional, disjointed and egotistical-sounding speech' was the result of success taking the pressure off him. He knew now that the hospital would be built.

Chapter 9

Two cricketers, Imran and Javed Miandad, were at the epi-
centre of Pakistan's greatest, most tumultuous years in the
game for longer than either could have envisaged. As cricketers
they complemented each other; as individuals they epitomized
their starkly contrasting environments and backgrounds. To
attempt to understand Javed's lodestar it is necessary to delve
not into history but into the teeming back alleys of Karachi,
where the rules of street cricket are interpreted without a sense
of perspective. It is not the game that was learned at Broad
Halfpennydown. The consequence is that the West has a com-
prehension of Javed Miandad no more complete than its compre-
hension of Islam.

At best, Imran and Javed rubbed along, as sportsmen on the
same side have to do. They had too great a need of each other's
abilities on the cricket field not to do so. At worst, when Javed
lost the captaincy of Pakistan in 1993 shortly after Imran had
become the Board of Control's special adviser to the International Cricket Council, they were not on speaking terms. Javed
is credited for the considerable tactical knowledge brought to
Imran's captaincy over many seasons, even if Imran would pay
greater heed to the advice of Mudassar Nazar. Imran admired
Javed's talent as a batsman and knew that he could rely on him
to fight, as it were, like a cornered tiger, although he felt that
more of his half-centuries should have been turned into centuries. Away from cricket, they did not socialize. Imran, while
appreciating that Javed came from a very poor background, disliked his materialistic outlook. He has an appreciation, though,
of the compassionate and religious side to Javed's nature. 'Most
of the time we got on all right,' said Imran, 'although sometimes
when the press in Karachi campaigned for him to be captain he
would go along with them and egg them on.'

Given a preference, the players, with one or two exceptions who turned to print or who felt the cancer hospital appeal was benefiting ahead of their own pockets, would rather have had Imran captaining them. When Javed first led Pakistan, ten players were adamant that they did not want to carry on under him. When last he captained them, more than a decade later, he said he could not control the side he took to New Zealand and asked the Board for Imran to be sent out as manager. Communication was never his strength: in Australia on that same tour he hardly spoke to his vice-captain, Ramiz Raja. He wanted a guarantee to remain captain for two years, which was impractical. In between times, in the 1980s, the captaincy swung between him and Imran with extraordinary frequency and extraordinary results. It was most certainly not a sinecure for either of them. Sinecures are not an option for anyone involved with cricket in Pakistan.

That Javed came to captain Pakistan at the age of twenty-two was in part because they had just been heavily beaten – the introduction of youth is always thought to be the best remedy for defeat – and also because of the influence of two predecessors, Mushtaq Mohammad and Asif Iqbal, who pushed him forward for promotion on account of what they felt was his exceptional understanding of the game. Fast bowlers traditionally did not make good captains, which meant that Imran was initially overlooked by the Board and by Pakistan's selectors. In one respect Javed was unfortunate: he had less use of Imran's bowling than Imran had of his batting. It is a point cited by critics of Imran's leadership, who tend to be based in Javed's home city of Karachi.

Captains in Pakistan are afflicted more by public criticism than anything else. Having lost three consecutive one-day internationals to India, even the prospect of competing against them in the cauldron of Sharjah was too much for Javed. He reverted to playing under Imran, who was resolved to reshaping a side that he felt had lost all semblance of team spirit, in the stadium where he felt more pressurized than anywhere else.

One-day cricket played a more significant part in Imran's

career than he would have wished. Under him, Pakistan did beat India in Sharjah in November 1985, but lost yet another limited-overs series to a strong West Indies side 3–2. Imran, now batting at number five, was at the crease when Pakistan beat them at Lahore for the first time in this form of cricket. A capacity crowd of 25,000 saw them do so, which emphasized that overkill was not a description that could be applied to one-day cricket on the subcontinent.

The following February, in 1986, Imran led Pakistan on a three-Tests tour of Sri Lanka, having made it quite evident to the selectors that he would go as captain only if allowed to take the side of his choosing. They had attempted, he felt, to usurp his authority by not announcing the names of the captain and the players until four days before departure. The machinations of what Javed Burki called 'a nasty lot of political administrators' were such that shortly beforehand Imran told Sarfraz Nawaz, by now a member of Parliament, that he would not play for Pakistan any more. He could have signed a further lucrative contract with New South Wales and was, said Sarfraz, 'cheesed off with all this aggravation'. Sarfraz complained to high-ranking government officials and heard nothing further until told of Imran's appointment to lead Pakistan in Sri Lanka.

Imran's lack of side and his disdain for the politics of the game endeared him to his players, if not necessarily to Pakistan's administrators. He was able to transcend all petty jealousies, rivalries and intrigues, which in Pakistan was the most vital attribute a captain could have. 'Although Javed knows more about the game and followed a policy of greater containment as a captain, he would demand respect whereas Imran would command it,' said Arif Ali Abbasi, one of the Board's most prominent secretaries.

In spite of this, Imran had the greatest difficulty controlling Pakistani players who felt vehemently that the whole of Sri Lanka, let alone their umpires, were united against them in 1986. Pakistan's ambassador had told the Board that the country was not in a fit state to stage a tour. This was not because of any civil unrest but because of the disaffection Sri Lanka's players had felt towards their hosts on their visit to Pakistan. The three-match series in Sri Lanka ended 1–1 and was marred by numerous squabbles that were mostly to do with allegedly biased umpiring. In the first Test the umpires took the players off the field after Arjuna Ranatunga had been called a cheat by Pakistan fielders, and in the second Test, after Javed Miandad had had an altercation with a spectator who threw a stone at him, Imran and the manager, Salim Asghar Mian, drafted a statement to their Board to the effect that there was no point in continuing the tour. On one occasion, Salim brought a copy of *Wisden* on to the ground to show the umpires they were incorrect in their interpretation of the laws. The intervention of General Zia, Pakistan's president, was needed for the series to continue.

Although Imran had one of his most unproductive tours with the bat, making just 48 runs in three Tests, few fared any better. That he was completely recovered from his stress fracture was evidenced by his bowling more overs and taking more wickets, 15 at 18 runs apiece, than anyone else on either side. Pakistan then stayed on in Sri Lanka until April for a one-day tournament, the Asia Cup, that also involved Bangladesh and featured, for the first time in a country which was a full member of the International Cricket Conference, neutral umpires in all the matches. Dickie Bird and David Sheppard came from England and Mahboob Shah from Pakistan. Sri Lanka met and beat Pakistan in the final, as the organizers hoped they would, and, however imitative the competition was of other one-day events, a public holiday was declared to commemorate the result.

No cricketing issue has preoccupied Imran more than that of neutral umpires. He became obsessional about this, although he accepted decisions, whatever he thought of them, in a manner that would not upset the crowd, and complained in victory as much as in defeat, even if on occasion his views could have been interpreted as an excuse for being beaten. He had first lobbied for so-called neutral umpires in Test cricket in 1978, when it was far from a pressing topic. 'I believe that the home side is subconsciously favoured by the umpires. There will always be tight situations in Tests but in my experience the home side gets the benefit of the doubt on more occasions than not,' he wrote in 1983 in *Imran*. 'Neutral umpires, backed up by electronic aids, would help in that direction. It would be a move towards professionalism, and if gadgets could help make the umpires' job easier, why not try them?' Imran felt umpires should be able to take criticism in the same way that players had to, although he appreciated their task had become more difficult owing to the all-seeing eye of television.

Such a viewpoint, ardently yet eloquently expressed, was radical at the time. Patriot that he was, Imran disliked insinuations that Pakistani umpires who made poor decisions were cheats, whereas English officials simply made mistakes. He saw such opinion as widespread in England, be it expressed by Mike Gatting in his infamous row with Shakoor Rana, Tom Graveney ('they've been cheating us for thirty years') or even by his friend Jeffrey Archer, who put it to Imran 'as gently as possible' that Javed Miandad 'was never out lbw in Pakistan'. Imran felt in the early 1980s that umpiring standards in Pakistan were improving – even if there was no one to match Bird – and felt this was a view supported by the Australians and the Indians of 1982–3, despite both being beaten heavily.

'All Test captains have had to face biased or incompetent umpires. It does not mean we have turned around and condemned the whole nation for that,' said Imran, who felt Pakistanis were still being treated as natives out to cheat colonial masters. The untrustworthy native was 'the white man's burden', as Kipling put it, and had to be taught the higher British values. Imran felt the more sensational English newspapers still seemed to believe that the native was going to cheat whenever the Englishman was off his guard.

Imran invoked this argument whenever Pakistan were accused of ball tampering. If his feelings about international umpires were most strongly expressed in England in 1982 and 1987, they encompassed standards in every country. Once, in Australia, he was asked if he felt the umpiring in a series of one-day matches was inconsistent. 'Not inconsistent,' he replied. 'Just consistently poor.' In *The Times*, John Woodcock wrote that 'from someone whose views are widely respected, that is a crushing indictment, the more so as it was made after Pakistan had won'. New Zealand, Imran believed, had a fixation that Pakistan were trying to cheat them. In Imran's first series against them in 1976, he asked the Pakistani umpire in Urdu to stand back from the stumps. The non-striker immediately demanded that he should speak in English to the umpire. On an unofficial tour to Sri Lanka in 1988, the Pakistani ambassador suggested that it would be a good thing for relations between the two countries if the Pakistan side desisted from appealing altogether. 'Hardly an Indian–Pakistan series is completed without an accusation from one team that an umpire is biased,' said Imran. 'There are so many instances when an umpire may or may not give a batsman the benefit of the doubt, especially on slow, low pitches. In some countries he is under added pressure from fiercely partisan crowds. Despite the importance of the umpire, this aspect of the game is widely neglected.

'We have to realize that incompetent and, sadly, biased umpiring does exist. If discipline is to be imposed on the players then umpiring standards all over the world will also have to improve. Otherwise efforts to impose discipline by fining players will prove futile,' he declared.

Later in the decade, Imran's advocacy would be a factor in the International Cricket Council (as it became) embracing international umpires to the extent of wanting to use them in as many Test series as possible. When, after he retired, Imran became Pakistan's special delegate to the ICC, he was able to put his point even more forcefully. He was able to criticize the fledgling system of match referees who, he felt, were policing the players while protecting the umpires from criticism. And if that did not have effect, he always had the medium of the *Daily Telegraph* to expound his opinions. They gave him quite sufficient space to do so.

Not all the solutions were as straightforward as he imagined and hence he, as well as the game, profited from his decision to become a part-time administrator after he had retired. His strictures also did little for umpires' confidence. This came to a head during a tournament in Sharjah in 1990 when an Indian official, P. D. Reporter, threatened to walk off the field after a dispute with Imran. It arose over Reporter's interpretation of the regulations concerning wides and no-balls in one-day cricket. A remark by Imran led to Reporter setting off for the pavilion until Javed Miandad, of all players, managed to calm him down.

On several occasions in the 1980s Imran would pass judgement on the umpiring. If, at times, he might have had too much power for the good of Pakistan's cricket, making such unchallenged statements, saying that he would not play unless certain players were chosen and questioning whether Test matches and one-day internationals should be played in the heat of September and October, it was not least because he was constantly having to deal with administrators who were not intent on consulting him. On the field, his equilibrium was too important to Pakistan's side for him not ultimately to have his own way. Without him, they were a shambles.

By the mid-1980s, Zaheer having retired and Javed Miandad too contrary a character to lead Pakistan for long, the only cricketers who tried to overturn Imran's authority were disaffected ones. There was also continuing discontent in some of the press; rivalries between north and south in England had nothing on the antagonism between Karachi and Lahore. Imran's preference for Abdul Qadir, a Lahorite, over Iqbal Qasim, a left-arm spinner from Karachi, caused considerable anger in his city's press. In terms of figures and averages they were both successful, but Imran had an unassailable belief in Qadir's leg spin, primarily because it was so difficult to pick.

It was not the Pakistani press but an English tabloid newspaper that proved to be the conduit for the dissatisfaction of one player. Qasim Omar, a batsman who did not hit it off with Imran, gave an interview to the *People*, accusing him of being 'a negative, arrogant, spiteful leader who picked on players for no reason'.

No one stood up to Imran, not even Javed Miandad, he claimed, because everyone was scared of him. In a letter to the Pakistan Board, Omar claimed he had been forced to carry drugs for Imran in his batting gloves. Paid for the article, he was banned for seven years following an inquiry ordered by President Zia. Then, in the same newspaper, Younis Ahmed, who had been recalled to play for Pakistan at the age of thirty-nine, accused Imran (after subsequently being dropped) of openly smoking pot and taking girls back to his hotel room on tour. Neither played for Pakistan again. The allegations were denied by Imran and were unproven, the scandal dying away. Had they arisen after Imran had begun his campaign to raise funds for the hospital, the implications might have been more serious.

However autocratic Imran may have been in the dressing room, there was no denying he had presence. 'A lot of our players were useless but if the atmosphere was not right, we were not going to win,' said Javed Burki, who became chairman of selectors at the end of the 1980s. 'His contempt for the opposition gave the players complete confidence. Some of our captains had been rather dull, whereas Imran had presence and the highest IQ of anyone in the side, as well as being better educated than anyone else.' Imran has always maintained that he would choose players whom he did not personally like if they were good enough, although Qamar Ahmed, who reported on most of Pakistan's Test matches, felt he purposely excluded Asif Mujtaba. When Salim Malik was dropped in 1992, Imran was thought to be responsible. He denies having had any influence, distancing himself from team selection after he retired.

Throughout all the intrigue and counter-intrigue, Imran retained his enthusiasm through his great love for the game. Captaincy was not an intellectual challenge for him as it was to Mike Brearley; but it was a challenge nonetheless. Other captains, his cousin Majid included, would not have stood for any attempts at undermining their authority. Imran, though, was spurred on by wanting Pakistan to become the best side in the world – unlike some, he was happier playing West Indies than

Sri Lanka – and his own sense of pride meant he never became complacent. Imparting his ambition and aggression to players brought up without a positive outlook on dead, doctored pitches was in itself enough to occupy any captain.

Above all, Imran's ambition was to beat West Indies, who in this period were unquestionably the strongest side in the world. He stood a better chance of beating them at home than in the Caribbean, if only because one or two of their foremost players would choose not to tour Pakistan for reasons of health. In 1987 West Indies were to come to Pakistan at the start of an exhaustive year. That would be followed by Pakistan touring India, where they had never won a series, then going to England, and finishing with the World Cup on the subcontinent. Small wonder that Imran felt this would be his last year of international cricket and his reputation would stand or fall on the results. There would be little left for him to have a tilt at after that.

Although Imran felt the standard of umpiring in Pakistan had improved, he impressed upon the Board the desirability of inter-national umpires. He was intent not only on beating West Indies but on doing so in such a manner that there would be no scope for complaints or excuses. Indian officials were appointed for all three tests, resulting, according to *Wisden*, in 'a welcome absence of bickering over decisions'.

Pakistan were undoubtedly helped by Joel Garner and Michael Holding not touring, although Malcolm Marshall was then at his peak and Courtney Walsh, Patrick Patterson and Tony Gray made for formidable support. If Imran had by now lost a yard of pace, it was none too apparent from the boundary or, perhaps, to the opposition. He did not have such an array of fast bowlers under him, but in Wasim Akram he had a twenty-year-old whom he felt even then was going to become the best all-rounder in the world. 'I have never seen another cricketer with Wasim's ability,' Imran said at the time. 'It's a compliment that he has supposed to have modelled his game on mine but really it's a joke to compare us because he is way ahead of what I was at his age. And Botham come to that.' Imran is often credited with discovering and developing some of the young Pakistanis who came to prominence at the end of the 1980s, although in this instance, Wasim was first spotted by Javed Miandad. Imran's judgement of a young cricketer was exceptionally sound. His willingness to include anyone with an unusual talent at the first possible opportunity was indicative of what an attacking captain he was. 'Imran was very good with the young players,' said Wasim. 'He taught me to be positive, never to lose my head. I wanted to be as good a cricketer as him and to last as long and he helped me both on and off the field.' Wasim, like Waqar Younis in later years, became not so much a friend as a disciple and was introduced to several of Imran's friends. He was particularly drawn to Emma Gibbs before he had an arranged marriage. 'He became a very good friend,' said Susannah Constantine. 'He was so very humble and sweet and quite gauche – like Imran used to be.' On the field, however, they metamorphosed into pugilists.

Between them and Abdul Qadir, Pakistan won the first Test against West Indies at Faisalabad. It was a match in which courage played as big a part as skill, as was the case in all matches involving West Indies. On the first day, Pakistan having lost five wickets cheaply, Imran was struck on the shoulder by a rising ball from Marshall: he knew that if he went off for treatment, the remainder of the order would most probably collapse. He batted on to make 61 out of a total of 159. In the second innings he likewise persevered after having stitches in the index finger of his right hand, and Salim Malik, who broke an arm, batted with a cast on it. Such fortitude deserved reward, which duly came through the bowling of Wasim, who took six for 91, and Qadir, who bowled West Indies out in their second innings for 53, their lowest total in Test cricket. It was an extraordinary collapse for a side containing Greenidge, Haynes and Richards.

The remainder of the series was no less compelling. Imran was not a captain to ask for groundsmen to prepare pitches in a particular way – Board member Arif Ali Abbasi felt this to be a positive aspect of his nature – but he could have done now with

126

the pitch on his home ground at Lahore being less quick than it was. Normally lifeless through having a high water level, it was now ideally suited to West Indies fast bowlers. Imran took five for 59, Pakistan dismissing their opponents for 218, but their own batting was alarmingly suspect. They could muster only 131 and 77 and lost by an innings.

Runs were no more plentiful in the final Test at Karachi. Again Pakistan's batsmen let them down. They lacked a settled opening pair, which was too much of a handicap against such an attack. Half-centuries from Ramiz and Javed enabled them to make 239, a creditable performance in the circumstances, following which Imran's best spell of the series, five for 11 in 33 balls and six for 46 in all, left Pakistan needing 230 to win. They had collapsed to 125 for seven on the final day when, with nine overs remaining to be bowled in the last hour, the umpires (it was as well that they were neutral) decided the light was too bad to continue. Imran, who was undefeated on 15, was given the man of the match award on his thirty-fourth birthday.

As if he was not playing enough cricket, Imran went next to Perth for another one-day competition staged in conjunction with the America's Cup. It was while he was there that he learned that the side for India had been chosen without his consultation, which infuriated him. Even when Javed Burki, his first cousin, became chairman of selectors, Imran was not given total control in selection meetings. 'Imran would listen to the views of the players but he would be short with selectors who did not give proper arguments for taking a particular individual,' said Javed. 'Being an objective man, his selections were always fair, but we had to show him some of the young players. He would criticize the system of cricket in Pakistan irrationally without knowing the structure. Anglo-Saxon systems could not be duplicated.'

Imran had long been critical of Pakistan's domestic cricket, which, owing to a shortage of funds, was run under the aegis of commercial organizations. Imran felt this devalued first-class matches; that no one cared whether a bank beat a railway even if there were decent players involved. Pitches, he felt, were underprepared, groundsmen were not held accountable, and it was only through a natural abundance of gifted players, many of whom joined counties in England, that Test cricketers were developed. 'But every boy is a discovery to Imran because he has not seen them in domestic cricket in Pakistan,' said Qamar Ahmed. 'He says the best players are developing through going to England and playing under-19 representative cricket but the standard is good in Pakistan now.

'More money is coming into the game so new grounds could be built. Also, Imran is contradicting himself because he wrote in 1989 that "county cricket is so poor it cannot prepare a cricketer for Test manhood". There is no denying he has guided and recommended players to counties but he does not understand that the commercial organizations in Pakistan have provided jobs for players to fall back on if they lose their places,' said Qamar.

In addition to his trenchant opinions on the structure of the game in Pakistan, Imran took a dim view of the administrators who governed the Board of Control. Unlike most, if not all, of the other players, he was prepared to enunciate his feelings. His authority was challenged by administrators only when his own game was weakened through injury and hence he was not a requisite member of Pakistan's side. 'When he was at his peak, Imran was totally indispensable and no one would challenge his power,' said Qamar. Imran himself admits that he failed to understand the Board's oligarchy, and that they were accustomed to more pliant players. Success could not temper his frustration with incompetence in the game and corruption in the country, which spilled over to his friends. 'The only thing that is working in Pakistan is his hospital,' said Emily Todhunter.

In spite of not taking part in domestic cricket in Pakistan, Imran never seemed to be in any quandary about the make-up of his sides: he trusted his own judgement entirely. He paid due attention to the suggestions of Javed Miandad, whose idea it was that Younis Ahmed should join Pakistan's party in India in 1987. Such opinion he would respect, even though he himself championed youth ahead of this kind of experienced batsman who had

128

Ascot. Imran has long cherished the English summer (*PA*)

Susannah Constantine at the opening of Gianni Versace's shop in
Bond Street. She had a relationship with Imran after breaking up
with Viscount Linley (*Sunday Telegraph*)

Opposite: Emma Sergeant. The only girl Imran has ever truly loved (*The Times*)

At the Rainforest Ball with the Marchioness of Worcester in 1988.
They were patrons of the event, which highlighted the destruction of
the Amazon Forest in Brazil (*PA*)

Surrounded by Oriental furnishings at his flat in Draycott Avenue,
South Kensington (*Sunday Times*)

Congratulations from England captain Graham Gooch after winning the
World Cup in 1992. It was Gooch's third final – and third defeat (*AP*)

The Pakistani flag flies over the Melbourne Cricket Ground. The World
Cup is won and the future of Imran's hospital secure (*AP*)

A model of the hospital commemorating his mother (above) and (below) nearing completion

Shooting has long been a favourite pursuit. Even at the remote North-West Frontier, a crowd gathers to view Imran's expertise (*The Times*)

Phil Edmonds is one of the few cricketers with whom Imran has an affinity. They played for Paul Getty at his ground at Wormsley, Oxfordshire, in 1992 (*Sunday Telegraph*)

Imran gives a lecture to cricket followers at London's National Theatre, 1993 (*Daily Telegraph*)

Modelling could have been more time-consuming had there not been other commitments (*Sunday Telegraph*)

not played Test cricket for several years. The selection proved less inspired than others. Yet the Board at least was supportive of Imran. Although the Pakistanis were not so well received as they had been on their previous tour – there was tension on the border between the countries that on occasion was reflected in the behaviour of the crowds – they realized Imran's ambition of winning a series in India. Thunderous praise – and a stricture – was forthcoming from *Wisden*. 'Imran's sporting approach to the niggling problems which occur on a tour of India helped keep matters from getting out of proportion, including those instances when his own colleagues were guilty of over-dramatization on the field. Their orchestrated appealing and various other practices designed to put umpires under severe pressure, gave an unhappy aspect to their cricket.' Another reason for Imran's dissatisfaction with standards of umpiring was that he felt some officials, especially in England, could not always differentiate between a leg spinner's various deliveries. In addition, in countries such as India, umpires were under pressure from the communities within which they lived. Although Iqbal Qasim, the left-arm spinner, proved to be effective on the 1987 tour of India, and Tauseef Ahmed, the off-spinner, was more successful there than any other Pakistani, Abdul Qadir was Imran's key bowler for many years. Critics of over-zealous appealing were dismissed by Imran as having scant knowledge of the game in Pakistan, since (he maintained) joyous enthusiasm had not been stifled by too much cricket, as happened in England, where professionals were generally not only older but more world-weary. Imran knew that cultural differences were also a factor. Accordingly, he was not one to counsel moderation from his players or managers, as was noted by journalists such as Henry Blofeld and John Woodcock who were far from myopic observers of the game. 'Imran appears to allow young players on occasion to push laws to the limit and sometimes beyond,' wrote Blofeld. It was a point taken up by Richard Hadlee, who said that Imran 'didn't always exercise control over his players'.

In India, there were errors of judgement by the umpires which affected both sides. The International Cricket Council member countries had yet to react with any enthusiasm to Imran's calls – pleas – for neutral officials, and *Wisden*'s correspondent was surprised that, after winning the Test series 1–0 and the one-day internationals 5–1, Imran should pursue the matter, for 'Pakistan got away with a considerable amount'. If Imran's remarks resulted from any one match, it was the third Test at Jaipur, where after the rest day the pitch was sprinkled with sawdust. Indian officials said this had blown in from the outfield but the Pakistan side reckoned it had been used purposely to dry the surface. Imran threatened to refuse to bat, reasoning that in accordance with the laws the pitch had to be in the same condition as it had been left the previous day, whereupon the umpires abandoned play for the day.

Crowd trouble ensued in the fourth Test at Ahmedabad when Pakistan's deep fielders were pelted with stones. Having sought the consent of the umpires to take the players off, Imran was reluctant to continue. When play did resume after tea, six fielders came out in helmets, which was interpreted as a humorous gesture, but was in actuality a decree by the captain for their own protection, as Mark Shand, who was travelling with Imran, recognized. 'Imran had the ability to defuse possible tension between two passionate sides,' he said. 'What Imran says goes. I always thought he was a proper sort of captain, a bit aloof with very strict ideals. He was a jot higher than the others in the dressing room.'

The series was won by Pakistan, who beat India in the final Test at Bangalore after the previous four had finished in dull draws – for which, much to Imran's chagrin, India's captain blamed him. Kapil Dev went so far as to issue a statement criticizing Imran for what he regarded as Pakistan's negative cricket. He was, Imran felt, defending himself against the criticism he would inevitably face if India did not win the series.

The nature of the pitches was evident from Imran's return of just eight wickets in five Tests. That his batting was becoming as potent as his bowling was evident from his making 324 runs at 64.80, including an unbeaten 135 in the first Test at Madras. It was his third Test century, an innings best remembered for the manner in which he drove the spinners, Maninder Singh and Shastri, down the ground. His five sixes and 14 fours were recorded on television and highlighted on video, making for notably correct strokeplay.

The final Test at Bangalore was held during a Hindu festival, various players taking the field wearing coloured paint and dye. Imran now had his own chance for avengement over Kapil Dev's comments. Pathans do not miss such an opportunity. It took courage to leave out Qadir on a pitch that had clearly been prepared for the Indian spinners. It was a match in which there were likely to be all too few runs scored, hence the necessity, as Imran stressed, for every batsman not to give his wicket away. India gained a first innings lead of 29 and, as a result of some defiant batting – Ramiz 47, Imran 39, Salim Malik 33 – Pakistan made sufficient runs to leave India 221 to win.

The pitch was taking so much turn and bounce that Imran did not bowl a ball in the second innings. It was a dilemma for him whether or not to keep the spinners on during the last day. Tauseef Ahmed and Iqbal Qasim operated unchanged – and did so with great success. Sunil Gavaskar played the finest innings Imran had seen in international cricket, 96 made through a masterly exposition of technique. India lost by just 16 runs, Qasim taking nine wickets in the match. Qasim had joined the tour late, on standby as it were, which made his performance even more creditable. Yet he never played for Pakistan again under Imran's leadership, which only fuelled the belief that Imran stood for the interests of Lahore against those of Karachi. Javed Burki's impression that he liked only to field leg spinners was more plausible, not least because Qadir and, later, Mushtaq Ahmed, were hugely effective.

When the Pakistani party arrived back at Lahore, having not merely beaten India in India for the first time but having also gained what was only their third victory away from their own country, the crowd to greet them was estimated at 200,000. The chief minister, Nawaz Sharif, was among them. He was not only ignored but knocked around by the heaving throng interested only in chanting for Imran and obtaining a sight of the other players. The future prime minister was not amused. It was an occasion he was not to forget when re-routing Imran's return from Australia after the World Cup had been won five years later.

Chapter 10

I f any one issue other than short-pitched bowling bedevilled cricket in the 1980s and 1990s, it was ball tampering. In that this was both hard to prove and fraught with legal complications, it became one of the most complex issues for the International Cricket Council to try to resolve. The nine Test-playing nations realized they were in a dilemma and yet were undecided as to how to sort it out. If the issue afflicted every side, it was inextricably linked with Pakistan.

'There were periods in Pakistan, particularly during one tour by New Zealand, when the ball was being messed around with,' admitted Javed Burki. In Pakistan, where the ball becomes scuffed on the hard grounds and bare pitches within a few overs, and the umpires can be bought, the first-class game is being spoiled. Fielders are roughing up balls now that television cameras constantly zoom in on bowlers, highlighting the slightest picking of the seam.

There was the odd inference of ball tampering on Pakistan's tour of England in 1982, although not by the England captain, Bob Willis. Dark mutterings became outright allegations only when Imran, Wasim Akram and Waqar Younis perfected the art of reverse swing, whereby one half of the ball is allowed to roughen with use and the other is dampened and polished so that it swings towards that side. This started occurring in England after 1981, when the seam was altered. The following year, when Pakistan played at Lord's, the worn square meant Imran was able to reverse swing the ball while England's bowlers attempted in vain to move it in the conventional way. This was, Imran maintained, the only way to swing the ball in Pakistan, 'where we have been practising it for years'. He always maintained that it was ignorant of critics to say that reverse swing could only be obtained by ball tampering. While fast bowlers of

133

the calibre of Wasim and Waqar struggled to bowl properly with a new ball, even club cricketers knew how to achieve reverse swing on dry pitches and rough outfields.

Fair or foul, this was an innovation, the first in genuinely fast bowling, according to *Wisden*, since overarm was legalized in 1864. The allegations rumbled on in the 1980s, and Imran reacted angrily when England hinted that the Pakistanis were up to no good in a ten-day tournament in Sharjah in 1987. Some of the England players, he reckoned, had accused his side of gamesmanship, of putting the umpires under pressure through constantly asking for the ball to be changed. These English players were declaring that English umpires would not tolerate their behaviour. Such controversies continued throughout the 1987 series in England.

Imran's viewpoint, other than seeing attacks on his country in a racist, anti-Muslim light, was that ball tampering had gone on in one form or another since the game had begun. If Pakistanis were to gouge chunks out of the ball then that, he felt, was no worse than lifting the seam, which he had seen Dennis Lillee, John Snow 'and almost every seamer' do.

Seam lifting, Imran felt, had almost become an accepted practice. And he knew that it was hard for an umpire to spot methods of applying substances such as cream and hair oil, which might be intermingled with grease and sweat. This had gone on without anyone being called a cheat. Even if any bowler or fielder did gouge holes in the ball, it would be hard for the umpires to know if the scratches were made by the roughness of the pitch, the advertising boards or a player's nails.

Imran's belief that in one way or another every seam bowler doctors the ball and that this varies only by degree, poses the question: has he ever tampered through methods that have gone beyond picking at the seam? 'I believe scratching was no more a crime than lifting the seam and you can only scratch a ball when it is well marked,' he said. 'I have occasionally scratched the side and lifted the seam. Only once did I use an object. When Sussex were playing Hampshire in 1981, the ball was not deviating at all. I got the 12th man to bring on a bottle top and it started to move around a lot.' Adrian Jones, the 12th man that day, was in his first season with Sussex and was nonplussed. The batsmen, umpires and assembled journalists spotted nothing untoward, probably because they were expecting nothing untoward. Sussex won the match – comfortably – even if Imran's figures did not noticeably benefit.

As the innuendoes and mutterings against Pakistan's whole approach to the game – alleged ball tampering, vociferous appeals, supposedly biased umpiring, over-loquacious managers, little fraternity with the opposition even if this was because of language and cultural barriers – reached a clamour in the late 1980s with headlines such as 'Paki Cheats' and the row between Shakoor Rana and Mike Gatting, Imran began to perceive this as a slur on Islam. 'Pakistan cricketers are treated somewhat like Islam in the West. Most of the time, such images are depicted by terrorists, fanaticism, veiled women and so on. Similarly, our cricketers are looked upon as an indisciplined, unruly mob who pressurize umpires, cheat, doctor cricket balls, whinge about umpiring decisions and are generally unsporting. Consequently, English umpires make mistakes but Pakistani umpires cheat,' he said.

Although he never spurned an interview, such stereotyped thinking infuriated him, not least when he was depicted as believing in veils one side of the Indian Ocean and mini-skirts on the other. No matter that other Pakistan cricketers – Majid, Asif Iqbal, Intikhab Alam – had been just as popular cricketers in England, Imran was regarded as a product of English society, nurtured by Oxford and moulded by the English press. He would always have a platform. He was the one individual who could conceivably alter Western perceptions of fanatics and fundamentalists.

In England on the 1987 tour, he was almost the only Pakistani who was not regarded as a zealot. Haseeb Ahsan, who managed the touring party, was thoroughly voluble and provocative to the extent that there was a feeling that Imran was using him to his own ends, especially over negotiations with the Test and County Cricket Board. There were leaks and counter-leaks, statements and counter-statements. It had been a rag-bag arrival: Imran, Abdul Qadir and Javed Miandad, the three key players, for one reason or another all missed the start of the tour. The captain was exhausted after Pakistan's tour of India, having lost half a stone. Qadir, whom Imran had taken under his wing in England in 1982, did not appear because his wife was apparently possessed by demons (he had married her when he was fifteen and never introduced her to Imran since she rarely left home) and Javed was awaiting the birth of his child and doing battle with the customs over a car. Neither was it a propitious start to the tour in the middle, although that is customary for Pakistan. Imran recuperated in South Kensington and trained at Lord's as if he were a scarred picador, or perhaps merely John Woodcock's latter-day maharajah. He joined his side in time for their match against Essex, one which Pakistan won with ease. With his first ball of the tour Imran bowled Graham Gooch, who made a pair, a contributory factor in his not playing any Test cricket that summer. Imran then had to have seven stitches inserted into his face after edging a ball into his cheekbone.

The mistrust between Pakistan and the TCCB had much to do with the appointment to the umpires panel of David Constant, who had incurred Pakistan's wrath in 1982. Imran felt that the chief executive, Alan Smith – whom he had never liked – leaked details of Imran's lack of regard for Constant to the press, who predictably reacted with much ire. Haseeb (not Imran) was denounced by tabloid newspapers which had become less impartial since Pakistan's previous tour, and even Imran, loyal by nature, felt that at times Haseeb went too far; but the gulf had widened between the Pakistanis and the quorum of Smith, Micky Stewart, the team manager, and Mike Gatting, the captain. In terms of outlook and background they differed considerably from Imran, who felt that the game in England was becoming run and played by a type of 'uneducated individual' who did not have such authority when he had first toured England. He believed

Smith leaked the TCCB's decision not to accede to their request to remove Constant and Ken Palmer from the panel of Test umpires. Imran was aggrieved that the TCCB had complied with India's desire to have Constant replaced in 1982. Whether he was more circumspect than he had been five years earlier, or whether it was simply that he preferred to let his voluble manager do the talking, Imran was less overtly critical than he had been. This could have been taken as evidence that he had more to say about umpiring standards when his side had lost a series, but in fact he could be just as outspoken when they won.

In such cricket as the Pakistanis managed before the first Test – it was a markedly wet summer – Imran took five wickets against Sussex (this was not the ideal year for him to take his Benefit since that was his only appearance of the season at Hove) and presided over two defeats and a victory in the Texaco Trophy one-day matches. Javed, who had finally arrived, was in considerable form even if his team-mates had yet to reconcile themselves to the wet conditions. This was no more or less than England or the English press expected: having just regained the Ashes in Australia, England were more complacent about the series than they should have been. At Edgbaston, in the last of the three one-day matches, the cricket was marred by fights in the crowd provoked by racial pride and alcohol, all of which only heightened the tensions between the two countries that resulted in so much animosity later that year in Pakistan.

Half of the playing hours in the first Test at Manchester were lost to the weather, which worked to Pakistan's advantage since Imran had strained a stomach muscle two days beforehand and Abdul Qadir had still not arrived. This Test was indicative of what Mike Gatting had in mind when he made the (admittedly fatuous) remark that England won the series on points: in reply to their total of 447, Pakistan had mustered 140 for five when rain put paid to such play as remained. Tim Robinson, as was his wont, took a century off a weakened attack. Other than an innings of 75 by Mansoor Akhtar, without whom Pakistan would barely have reached double figures, there was little else that was memorable. Imran was fit to bowl in the second Test at Lord's just nine days later, and indeed to bowl 34 overs in the one innings possible without slipping on the wet run-ups. In that there were only seven hours of cricket, this hardly mattered. England compiled 368, Bill Athey making a century and successfully hitting Qadir off his length. It was testimony to Imran's belief in his leg spinner that he not only included him in his side but had him on in the 12th over of the innings. This contrasted oddly with the declamation by Mike Brearley that Imran did not know when to bring Qadir into Pakistan's attack. Of greater concern at this stage of the tour was that the attack could look distinctly ordinary; later it appeared to be of the highest class.

By the time of the third Test, played at Leeds at the start of July, Imran was fully fit and, given that the weather was dry and the pitch and the footholds firm, was able to bowl considerably more quickly than hitherto. The conditions at Headingley always seemed to assist swing bowling and the first morning, even though England won the toss in what seemed to be ideal batting conditions, effectively decided the series. After an hour England were 31 for five, Imran taking the wickets of Robinson, Athey and, crucially, David Gower, who played on trying to withdraw his bat from one that lifted and was leaving him. Imran's figures at this point were 7–1–16–3. Wasim Akram, whom he had very much taken under his wing, had gained the wickets of Chris Broad and Gatting, out without playing a stroke.

Here was endorsement, if it were needed, of Imran's belief that Wasim would become the best all-round cricketer in the world. He was to take 39 wickets on the tour, more than any other bowler, and even though he was coming in as low in the order as Imran had on his first tour of England, he made useful runs to boot. England had need of Ian Botham to bat in his most responsible manner, vigilance underpinning a sound technique. He batted for nearly two hours in spite of being hit on an instep by Mudassar Nazar, who eventually had him caught at the wicket through his gentle but under-rated medium-paced swing bowling. There were wickets, too, for Mohsin Kamal, three in nine balls. This was his finest moment: he did not play again for his country after the tour. These wickets included that of David Capel, who made his maiden Test half-century. This enabled England to muster a total of 136. It was of no consolation to them that Imran would also have batted had he won the toss.

Neither was England's fielding impressive. In the 27 overs Pakistan had to survive before the end of that first day, three catches were put down. The dropping of the nightwatchman, Salim Yousuf, proved particularly costly since he batted for all of the first session the next morning. He finished with 37, assisting Salim Malik in ensuring that England would have scant chance of drawing, let alone winning. Salim Malik was out one run short of a century after batting for five and a half hours. The flat-track bully, as Imran depicted him over his career with some disregard, had shown he could make good runs when the ball was darting around. A half-century by Ijaz Ahmed that included nine fours and 43 off 41 balls from Wasim enabled Pakistan to gain a first innings lead of 217 which, for Headingley, was highly significant. Imran varied his pace and swung the ball prodigiously, removing Broad in his first over and Robinson, also for single figures, shortly afterwards. It was now that he was criticized – if only in a muted way – for tolerating some extravagant appealing, especially from his wicketkeeper. Salim Yousuf looked to have caught Broad on the bounce and appealed later in the day when Botham was batting for a catch when he had clearly already dropped the ball in front of him. Imran, who wrote later that Salim was trying to even the score because he thought Athey claimed a catch off a bump ball, gave him what *Wisden* described as 'a dressing-down in no uncertain manner'. Neither were Botham nor umpire Ken Palmer impressed. To the press and xenophobic Englishmen everywhere here was evidence that Pakistanis did not play the game.

Botham made only 24. Other than Gower, who struck a half-century before he played on to Imran for the second time in the match, and Capel, who again batted for three hours, no one inconvenienced Imran for long. By the sixth over of the fourth day, victory had been achieved and he had taken seven wickets for 40, making the most of the uncertain bounce in the pitch. It was one of his best returns in Test cricket. When he had Jack Richards held at forward short-leg he took his 300th Test wicket, becoming only the eighth bowler so to do. Other than Lance Gibbs and Fred Trueman, the others to do so – Ian Botham, Richard Hadlee, Dennis Lillee, Bob Willis and Kapil Dev – were all from Imran's era, an era in which there was more Test cricket than ever before. Interestingly enough, only Trueman conceded fewer runs per wicket. No one else in Pakistan's history had taken as many as 200 Test wickets, which was a measure of Imran's achievement. Whether he was a better bowler for the greater craft he could substitute for the pace he had lost through his stress fracture was questionable; Trueman had probably been a more formidable opponent in his later years, but then Imran had had greater control than him in his youth – if his first tour of England could be discounted. At Headingley Imran's experience, accuracy and changes of pace were all crucial to his performance. The speed he possessed – and he could still be genuinely quick – he retained until into his thirty-sixth year. Trueman may have bowled with greater devastation on beer; Imran reckoned that, for him, milk was a better stimulant.

It was noticeable that Imran played in only as many matches on the tour as he needed to. He had paced himself carefully with Sussex over the previous few years and, although he admired the commitment to county cricket of the likes of Neil Foster, England's best bowler in this series, Imran reckoned that he would burn himself out (Foster had to retire at the age of thirty-one owing to a succession of injuries). In addition to conserving his energies for the most important matches, Imran was also fortunate in that, other than when he was out of the game through his stress fracture, he was rarely unable to bowl through the niggling kind of injury, a groin strain or hamstring, that is a fast bowler's lot. That or he simply put up with it. Had he chosen to play in every Test series until his final retirement, he would not only have beaten Hadlee's tally of 431 Test wickets but would in all probability have set an unassailable record.

He was required, or required of himself in the fourth Test at Edgbaston, to bowl 41 overs in England's first innings and to ensure that, by bowling unchanged with Wasim Akram in the final session, the match would be drawn. His batting, too, was more disciplined than that of any of his team-mates in ensuring that England were kept in the field until the start of the final hour. England should have won, in that 124 in 18 overs should have been far from beyond the capabilities of players with much experience of run chases in limited-overs cricket.

For the twenty-first time in Test cricket, Imran had taken five wickets or more in an innings, and this in an England total of 521. He gained more from the pitch than any bowler on either side had done hitherto. Even on this placid pitch he could hold the ball up, as he did when he bowled Athey, who was anticipating the in-dipper that remained Imran's most potent delivery. A century by Gatting gave England a first-innings lead, whereupon it seemed as if Pakistan would lose the match and their chance of winning a series in England for the first time through their reckless faults of old. Half the side went for 104 and they required all of Imran's watchfulness and defensive qualities to reach a total of 205. Imran made but 37, yet stayed at the crease for two hours in a manner that he would not have been able to do without losing patience before he became captain.

Imran and Wasim then bowled unchanged throughout England's attempt to score at nearly seven runs an over. They were able to do so, of course, without restrictions as to field placings or balls bowled wide of the wicket. Broad made 30 out of 37 in the first five overs but the inevitable reckless shots and run-outs (three) followed. Athey, though, managed just 14 off the last seven overs – it cost him his place in the final Test – and although England finished only 15 runs short of victory, they had just three wickets intact.

Imran took no active part on the second and third days of the one remaining county match before the fifth Test – other, that

141

was, than to berate Mark Nicholas, Hampshire's captain, for not batting for longer in their first innings and hence not giving Imran the chance to test an injured hip. Nicholas hoped that his side would be left a target on the last day through the kind of contrived finish that was anathema to Imran. Hampshire, Imran felt, were putting out the equivalent of a second eleven with Gordon Greenidge and Malcolm Marshall absent. This rather childish argument with Nicholas, whom he does not like, erupted in front of the pavilion at Southampton, to the astonishment of the members, and was not properly resolved. Thus Imran did not bowl at all between the fourth and the fifth Tests.

In spite of an entreaty by Javed Miandad – his obvious successor – who generously said that for the good of Pakistan's cricket Imran should not give up the game, he had no intention of changing his decision. Imran was insistent that he would retire after the forthcoming World Cup on the subcontinent. After such an intensive year, in which Pakistan had beaten India and England (if they were not to lose at the Oval) in their own countries for the first time, and in which they had provided the only credible opposition to West Indies' supremacy, he had run out of challenges. Building his proposed cancer hospital was now his pre-eminent ambition.

Imran would be retiring when still on top of his game, as he proved in this Test: it seemed a crying shame that he was to do so. For the first time since Old Trafford he won the toss and by the second day he had realized what he felt was his last remaining ambition in the game. Pakistan's first innings total of 708, compiled in almost 14 hours, was their highest in Test cricket, surpassing their 674 for six against India in Faisalabad in 1984–5. Imran made his first century against England, as did Javed Miandad, turning his into a double century. A measure of how well Imran played was that on this easy-paced pitch he went from 57 to 100 while Javed, who by then had tired, did not score a run. Imran batted in all for four and a quarter hours, hitting an elegant six off Emburey through moving down the pitch and lofting him over long-on. It was his characteristic way of attacking the spinner, as Ravi Shastri – for one – had discovered in the past. There were also 11 fours, including some fine pulls off Botham and Dilley.

This was a match that Pakistan really should have won. Qadir, whom Imran had insisted on selecting even though he had been so patently out of form, at last found a bouncy pitch which suited his art and bowled England out for 232. His figures of seven for 96 were his best in Test cricket. Imran removed Broad, as he did so often during the summer, with the ball that he angled across his body. England followed on 476 runs in arrears and lost their first four batsmen to Pakistan's spinners relatively cheaply; but with Wasim absent on the final day through having an appendix operation, and catches going down, the fifth wicket pair of Gatting and Botham survived to the close of play. There was one further dispute involving the umpiring of Constant, whom Pakistan felt should have given Botham out when he had made 20. At a press conference afterwards, Imran accused him of treating Mudassar as 'some kind of cheat'. Haseeb went further and called him 'a disgrace'. They felt Constant had been imposed on them since 1974. It summarized the distrust prevalent between the two countries that even the advent of international (or neutral as they were commonly if mistakenly known) umpires could not improve. Gatting, missed five times in the course of making an unbeaten 150, was named England's man of the series; Imran, for the second successive tour, gained the nomination for Pakistan.

For the remainder of the summer he had to attend to his Benefit, organized by his friends in his necessary absence. He was chosen, as a leading player, to take part in MCC's bicentenary match against a Rest of the World XI at Lord's. It was a memorable match in which he had a full part, if more through his batting than his bowling. He made a spirited 82 in partnership with Sunil Gavaskar, once striking Emburey high into the President's box above the Tavern. If this was to be his last match at Lord's, it was an enjoyable finale.

Winning the World Cup in 1987 would have made Imran's year – and his retirement – complete. It would have been almost too perfect a departure from a game he had adorned for nearly two decades. If he no longer had the same relish for its pleasures, then this was because the ceaseless politicking, the travelling and the sheer daily grind, not least of one-day matches, had exacted a heavy toll. Had he been married or played county cricket regularly during the 1980s, it is fair to suppose he would have long since turned to a different career. If Pakistan had won this fourth World Cup, which was becoming an increasingly prestigious competition, Imran would most likely never have been tempted back into the game. He could, in all probability, have had any job he chose. Limited-overs cricket did not hold the appeal for him that Test cricket did, but he was not aware, until Pakistan were eliminated, just how much it meant to the populace on the subcontinent.

Expectations were enhanced: Pakistan were favourites and the competition was to be staged in Pakistan and in India. Yet one-day cricket, as Imran knew only too well, did not always result in victory for the strongest side. That had been proven in the previous World Cup, in 1983, when India quite unexpectedly beat West Indies. Moreover, Pakistan were in the stronger of the two groups, theirs including West Indies and England, and only one weak side in Sri Lanka.

It transpired that the tournament was the finest yet in terms of competitiveness and colour. The organization, too, was markedly impressive even though as many as twenty-one venues were used, sides having to be shunted around the subcontinent, spending as much time in transit lounges as in the middle. Pakistan began by defeating Sri Lanka and England, albeit by narrow margins. Imran took part in the second of these matches in spite of suffering from food poisoning. He batted, making 22, but neither bowled nor fielded. At one stage this appeared crucial, for England, with six wickets in hand, required 34 from the final four overs. They made such a hash of this that they lost all six in 16 balls. Next, Pakistan beat West Indies at Lahore in a finish that was closer still: their last wicket pair, Qadir and Saleem Jaffer, needed 14 off the last over, bowled by Courtney Walsh, and astonishingly managed to make them. Off a West Indian fast bowler! Imran had contributed in no small way to this victory, his four wickets including that of Viv Richards, who was in domineering form.

When Pakistan beat England for a second time, Imran again taking four wickets, they were assured of a place in the semi-finals. This was a more conclusive victory. Imran was not required to bat owing to the dominance of a partnership between Ramiz Raja and Salim Malik, who put on 167. When, in their penultimate qualifying match, Pakistan overwhelmed Sri Lanka by 113 runs, few doubted their pre-eminence. The one concern came when Imran did not complete his eight overs, pulling up in his approach to the wicket and feeling an ankle; fortunately nothing more serious than bruising was diagnosed. This was five victories in succession, an achievement marred only by defeat in their final match, in which a century by Richie Richardson enabled West Indies to make a total of 258 for seven that was beyond Pakistan. Imran was dissatisfied with his side's performance and said as much in public. It seemed their victories, if anything, had come about too easily. Five years later Pakistan were to work up to a crescendo after a poor start to the fifth World Cup: now, the concern was that they might have peaked too soon.

The hope of the organizers, the sponsors and, of course, the entire subcontinent, was that India, who would play England in the semi-finals, and Pakistan, drawn against Australia, would compete in the final at Calcutta. Each had finished on top of their group, India by dint of superior run-rate over Australia. Pakistan were to play at Lahore, Imran's home ground. Their advantages were manifest, familiarity of conditions apart. They had numerous players in form, sufficient all-rounders of requisite standard for this level of one-day cricket, the backing of a vociferous and wildly partisan crowd. Australia, lacking an exceptional attack, relied to an inordinate extent on two or three gifted

145

batsmen. No one had held a candle to them at the outset of the competition.

Imran subsequently was to describe the match as 'a complete nightmare', in which everything that could conceivably go wrong indeed did. Mudassar was injured and badly missed; so, too, was Salim Yousuf, who actually played but was hit in the mouth and had to be replaced during Australia's innings by Javed Miandad. Imran bowled more economically and effectively than anyone, but his three wickets were all taken at the end of the innings, by which time Australia, as *Wisden* put it, 'came of age'. Saleem Jaffer, of whom Imran had once expected so much, conceded 57 in six overs and Wasim was not the performer he had been in earlier matches. A half-century by David Boon, who put on 73 with Geoff Marsh and 82 with Dean Jones, enabled Australia to score at more than five an over.

Even so, a total of 267 for eight from the statutory 50 overs should have been within Pakistan's compass. It could have been even after Mansoor Akhtar, Ramiz Raja and Salim Malik had been out relatively cheaply. Upon Javed and Imran, much, if not everything, depended, as it so often did. Australia's attack was far from experienced, let alone potent. Javed's great ability lay in milking such bowling and with his captain he added 112 in 26 overs, which meant that from the 15 which remained, 118 were needed. Yet Imran felt Javed was not batting at anything like his best and took it upon himself to increase the scoring rate. Having made 58 off 83 balls, the lure of Allan Border's left-arm spin proved too enticing. He did not surmount the challenge or a disputable decision by Dickie Bird. Javed went for 70, swinging at Bruce Reid, and the return of Craig McDermott meant too much was left for the tail. Australia won by 18 runs, went on to defeat England in the final, and Pakistan, losing semi-finalists in 1979 and 1983, melted away from the ground. For Imran, there was scant acclaim on the day of his retirement. 'I shall never forget the calm dignity and bemused sadness Imran showed at the prize-giving afterwards,' said Henry Blofeld. 'If Pakistan had won the semi-final and gone on to win the World

Cup, I wonder if he would have allowed himself to be persuaded to return.'

It was but one factor in his decision to return to Test cricket. While Pakistan were defeating England and Shakoor Rana and Mike Gatting were doing their worst to strip any remaining veneer of honour and decency from the game, Imran was indulging himself in his other great sporting passion: shooting. He accepted invitations from friends which he had had to put off for years. He was correct in his assumption that a series tagged on to the World Cup would be anticlimactic; he was not to guess, though, that it would be so thoroughly ill tempered.

There were three other particular reasons for Imran being lured out of retirement in 1988. The hospital appeal, if it was to take off, evidently needed him to remain in the public eye. He himself had to have a challenge. If that would provide a part of it, then so would the opposition, West Indies in West Indies, where Pakistan had not won a series. But the impetus for him to return was provided from the very apex of Pakistan's autocratic society. The state president himself.

Imran had long been coy about his friendship with the president of his country, General Zia. 'I would not call us friends, exactly,' he said at the time. 'But yes, we know each other and he is a great admirer of cricket.' There was no doubting the regard in which he was held by Zia, who would speak to him regularly on the telephone. Pakistan had been besmirched, at least in cricketing terms, during the series against England, and diplomacy, which would be a requisite in the Caribbean, was clearly not Javed Miandad's forte. Pre-empting any aggravation, Javed had told the selectors he did not wish to be considered for the captaincy again, preferring to concentrate on his batting. Zia, who was also patron of the Board of Control, could circumvent cricket officials who, Imran felt, 'were gunning for me'. Imran had made enemies within the Board through his intolerance of any administrator he considered to be self-seeking. That, and the desire to retire when still an outstanding player, had led to his intention to quit for good. 'Without doubt the hardest problem for a sportsman is knowing when to retire,' he said. 'Ideally, he would like to leave at the top, going out in a blaze of glory. But, sadly, very few achieve this ideal.'

It was at a dinner, hosted by the president, in honour of the side's successes in India and England that the president made his public appeal to Imran to make a return to the colours. After presenting the players with gold medals, he praised Imran's decision to retire while at his peak, but added: 'A sportsman is like a soldier who is always ready to help the country.' Imran was left with little choice but to respond: 'I am always ready to serve the nation and the game.'

As the news spread that Imran had agreed to come out of retirement, jubilant supporters danced in the streets. When the selectors, chaired by Haseeb Ahsan, had begun the search for a successor to Javed, Imran's supporters staged processions, threatened hunger strikes and held a vigil outside his home, begging him to play in one last series. Now the burden of expectation, enervating enough for Imran over the previous decade, could not have been greater.

Unlike Richard Hadlee, Imran was motivated not by personal targets but by the will to beat the very best – and West Indies were nothing less than that. The drawback to a return was more a lack of fitness than of form. Although shooting and trekking had kept him active, thirty-five was an advanced age for a fast bowler, especially on the bone-hard pitches of the Caribbean. And yet through a combination of suppleness, sheer will-power and match practice Imran was bowling as quickly as any bowler of comparable age and pace had ever done by the time the series started. It was hard to envisage anyone else managing to do so, if one accepts that Hadlee was a different type of bowler. Fred Trueman, the first man to take 300 Test wickets, had found it nigh-impossible to sustain a second burst at the same age and as a consequence his Test career had come to an end when he was thirty-four. By common consent, the age of thirty was a watershed for a truly fast bowler. Imran, more than anyone else – Hadlee was comparably quick only in his youth – defied nature.

The correlation with not smoking or drinking was still not fully appreciated.

At the start of the tour, though, Imran had wondered if he would ever again be able to bowl quickly. His leap at the crease, the fulcrum, was dependent on his body being in the right condition to cope with the jarring it would have to contend with on such surfaces. In the midst of the one-day series at the start of the tour, throughout which he had a back strain and in which his bowling was pummelled as much as his body, he thought he had lost his art for good. Such a concern affects all sportsmen from time to time, but especially those on the brink of retirement. Now Imran gained the impression that his team-mates were thinking along the same lines as he was. Pakistan were thrashed in the five one-day matches, which was bound to be of concern even to a side accustomed to erratic beginnings. The particular worry for Imran was that, after returning adequate figures in the first three of these matches, he was hit for 76 off his eight overs at Port of Spain and 59 off his next eight at Georgetown. Other sides might have taken to recuperation on the beach; Imran ordered reparation in the nets.

The upshot was that, in spite of preparation which amounted to one-sided one-day skirmishes and just two first-class matches, Pakistan surpassed themselves in the first Test at Georgetown. West Indies had not been beaten in any of their islands since Australia won in 1978, also at Georgetown. Neither Richards nor Marshall was fit and the four-man pace battery was not as formidable as it had been in the days of Roberts, Holding, Garner and Croft; yet few of Pakistan's victories the world over can have been as memorable.

The rumour that Imran was over the hill was widespread before the match, when in fact all that was questionable was his fitness: his latest ailment was an infected toe. He would have batted had he won the toss, not least to give the toe time to recover. Instead, in Richards's absence, Gordon Greenidge opted to bat on a newly laid pitch. Tentatively at first, before thrusting more weight on to his front leg, Imran bore much of

149

the responsibility himself. He immediately had Haynes caught at the wicket but by tea, when Richardson, Greenidge, Logie and Hooper had taken the score to 219 for four, the decision to bat seemed to be the correct one. Upon resumption, Qadir had Logie leg before for 80, and it was then that Imran produced one of his most telling spells in Test cricket. If a fast bowler is evaluated by how quickly he accounts for the tail, then Imran is rarely found wanting. He swiftly took the last five wickets, including a burst of four for nine in three overs. Two of these were bowled, two lbw, which tells of his accuracy. Bouncers, of which there were far too many during the series, were wasted on such tailenders. Imran finished with seven for 80, which proved to be his best return against West Indies. He gained more wickets against them than any country other than India, and at a more impressive strike rate. To take these wickets at only 21.19 apiece at a time when their batting was nothing less than formidable was a remarkable achievement. Where was the bowler who could match that?

Imran had been guilty of overdoing the bouncer on his last tour of the Caribbean. Now he knew what to expect. There were, on average, three or four bouncers an over from West Indies fast bowlers. Imran had known this would occur and consequently warned Pakistan's batsmen that anyone retreating to the square-leg umpire would be sent home. Drastic action maybe, but no idle threat – and it was heeded. The onus, insisted Imran, was on the umpires to ensure short-pitched bowling was not overdone, and indeed one West Indian, Winston Benjamin, was warned during this match; but the onus was by now too great for any umpire.

That Imran was able to recuperate was because Pakistan batted so impressively in response. One of Javed Miandad's finest centuries, and his first against West Indies, occupied six and three-quarter hours (no great length of time against four fast bowlers) and there were several useful supporting innings besides. Salim Yousuf made a dogged 62, Shoaib Mohammad took obduracy to new extremes in compiling 46, and Imran, whose batting throughout the series had to be relegated in his priorities, contributed 24. Aided by 71 extras, 38 of which were no-balls, Pakistan reached a total of 435. That and the rest day enabled Imran, pumped up on antibiotics, to recover, even though initially he could scarcely walk on his infected toe. A first innings lead of 143 gave Pakistan sufficient runs to play with, sufficient indeed to win them the match. After the rest day, Imran, who had bowled only two overs in the last session on the third day, took the vital wicket of Greenidge followed by that of Logie, with whom Greenidge had added 65. At the end of the innings he finished off the tail. He was greatly abetted by Qadir, whose three victims were all important ones: Simmons, Richardson and Hooper.

There was no question that Imran was man of the match and that Pakistan had won a victory which was all the more astonishing in light of their previous form. The drawback of such a tour – Imran complained about the itinerary afterwards – was that just as the one-day internationals were lumped together at its start, so were the Tests towards the end. There was just one further match before the second Test at Port of Spain. Imran was still only half fit from his toe infection when he strained a leg muscle during fielding practice two days prior to the start. Two specialists told him he should not play if he wanted to be fit for the third and final Test which would begin only three days after the second finished. He counselled Javed and Intikhab Alam, the team manager (this was not the last time they were to have similar deliberations over his fitness), and realized that he had to play for the sake of the morale of the side, who were not informed. On the first morning he gambled with his fitness, reckoning that he could contend with a certain level of pain. As unconcerned as ever about taking a risk, Imran put West Indies in upon winning the toss. Starting by bowling medium-pace inswingers and working his way up to something faster by his second spell, Imran had Greenidge out in his first over and took three other wickets besides. When he dismissed Walsh, he became the fourth highest wicket-taker in Tests.

Neither was Wasim fully fit and yet he bowled with sufficient

151

pace to make the important early breakthrough. Qadir took four more wickets, including that of Richards, who, in the kind of cameo that told of unimpaired ability but faltering concentration, had made 49 in 43 balls. West Indies were dismissed for 174: here, surely, was the opportunity for Pakistan to increase their lead.

Yet by the end of the first day, Pakistan were 55 for five. They recovered somewhat to reach 194, but the return of Marshall proved as timely, indeed as necessary, as that of Richards. He took four wickets. It was now that Imran was to rue his dependency on his own bowling, giving him scant time to practise his batting: although he was to prove that he had by no means lost the ability to make important runs at important times, his lack of first-class cricket over the previous months had affected his game in the same way that his cousin Majid had struggled when he took time off during the previous decade. Although Imran was to bat purposefully and defiantly in the third Test, he could muster only single-figure scores here, falling first to Marshall and in the second innings to Benjamin. A half-century by Salim Malik enabled Pakistan to scrape a first innings lead, but they were unable to enforce their superiority thereafter. Ijaz Faqih, the off-spinner, was not fit and Wasim was still afflicted by a thigh injury, which meant that Imran and Qadir had to bowl almost continuously.

On a pitch that was becoming progressively slower, Imran still managed to remove the first four batsmen – Greenidge, Haynes, Richardson and Logie – relatively cheaply. West Indies were 81 for four and then 175 for five; twice Imran reckoned he had Richards lbw, protesting to the umpire after one of these appeals led to Richards waving his bat in anger at Salim Yousuf. West Indies captain went on to make what was, at this stage of his career, a rare century. Ably assisted by Dujon, they finished with a total of 391 which left Pakistan 372 to win, much more than had seemed likely. It was not an impossible target, not, at any rate, while Javed was in. It was typical of him that, having made one century, he should swiftly follow it with another, batting for more than seven hours and eliminating any semblance of risk. His problem was that he did not receive sufficient support. Just before the start of the last 20 overs, 84 were needed with five wickets in hand, a feasible proposition even against four fast bowlers. But wickets fell: Javed was followed by the tail, ultimately leaving Qadir, Pakistan's last batsman, needing to play out the last five balls from Richards, who had taken two wickets as they had continued to attempt to reach their target. Somehow he did so. Imran could not bring himself to watch that final over. His side finished 31 runs short of a spectacular victory and an unassailable lead in the series, having fearlessly pursued their goal until the very end.

Thus to win the series, Pakistan had only to stave off defeat in the final Test at Bridgetown, where West Indies had not lost since 1935. Their first innings was akin to the curate's egg: good in parts. Ramiz and Shoaib made half-centuries and everybody other than their last batsman reached double figures. A total of 309 was not insignificant but it was not as commanding as it had promised to be. West Indies likewise seemed as if they would make a large score but finished, in the face of Imran and Wasim taking three wickets apiece, with a three-run deficit. This in spite of another exhilarating cameo from Richards, who struck 67 off 80 balls.

Again Shoaib compiled a gutsy half-century, but Pakistan, collapsing to 177 for six by the end of the third day, simply did not make enough. Imran and Yousuf, batting in spite of dizziness incurred through breaking his nose in the first innings, put on 52 for the eighth wicket, sufficient to give them a total of 262. Imran finished unbeaten with 43, his highest score of the series. Thus West Indies needed 266 to win. At 150 for four, Richardson contributing a half-century, they looked as if they would do so with relative ease. The constant menace of Qadir and an excellent spell by Wasim, who matured rapidly during the series, meant that nothing was determined until the final exertions. When West Indies eighth wicket fell, 59 were still required for victory. Amid great tension they achieved it, Dujon and Benjamin seeing them through. It was an unhappy finish for Pakistan also in that out-of-court damages had to be settled after Qadir, aggrieved at a poor umpiring decision, had struck a heckler on the boundary. Three Tests had not been enough to decide which of these sides was the strongest in the world, yet only when Imran first competed against West Indies, in 1976–7, were five scheduled. It had been an invigorating series, one of the best since the war. West Indies had suffered their first moral defeat for many years. He had no regrets about having come out of retirement: he was nominated the player of a stirring series. Imran could still muster sufficient fitness and expertise to take on the best. The question now, as it had been before, was how much longer he could retain his motivation.

Chapter 11

Misjudgements among first-class cricketers are common-place. Yet for Imran to return to a moderate county side at a time when his interest in cricket was waning was a strange error. It suited him, of course, to be at his flat in London during the English summer of 1988, and he could play – more or less – in matches of his own choosing, which would mainly be of the one-day variety. But the spark had gone and by midsummer, when there was nothing left for his side to play for, it was evident he would not still be with Sussex come the end of the season. The parting of the ways at the end of July was messy and even unpleasant. There was to be no fond farewell. The groundsman, fed up with fielding telephone calls from ardent admirers, was not the only individual relieved by Imran's departure.

His appearances for Sussex had not been anything other than sporadic during the 1980s. Since 1981, when they almost won the championship, Imran had missed one season through injury and the best part of two through playing for Pakistan, and in other seasons mostly appeared in the one-day game. And yet he had been nothing if not consistent: it was a surprise if he was not at the top, or very close to the top, of both the batting and bowling averages. This was the case in his last two proper seasons with Sussex, in 1985 and 1986, when he took two wickets and made an elegant unbeaten half-century to enable Sussex to beat Lancashire in the NatWest final; and in a championship match at Lord's returned his best figures in county cricket, eight for 34, a stirring reminder that a great fast bowler was still in his pomp.

That summer of 1986 though, he played in fewer champion-ship matches than any other capped player on the Sussex staff apart from the injured Barclay. A contract for 1988 which would bind him to one-day matches but only a handful of championship appearances of his own choosing was clearly ill-conceived and became, as *Wisden* put it with succinct understatement, 'something of an embarrassment to the club'. John Barclay had retired, Garth le Roux had left and a new generation of players was not notably accommodating or deferential. Imran had played in just four championship matches (he still headed the county's bowling averages) when, at the end of July, he incurred the annoyance of his colleagues by arriving too late to play in a Sunday League match at Eastbourne. Although he had allowed three hours for a journey of 120 miles and had been delayed by roadworks, punctuality never was his strong point. A number of players, led by Paul Parker, the captain, were upset that Imran's conduct had gone unpunished – whereas some of them had been fined and suspended for what they regarded as lesser misdemeanours. The day after Imran's apology had been accepted, it was announced he would play only in the final match of the season. Sussex were out of the running for any of the competitions and this was an agreement which satisfied all parties. Imran was to miss that match as well, this time through injury.

It was a sad end to an eleven-year association in which he had scored 7216 runs and taken 407 wickets in first-class cricket. As Barclay said, he had played on for one season too many, having long tired of the structural deficiencies which had led him to reduce his appearances. Just as he had foreseen the desirability of an international panel of umpires for Test matches, so he was ahead of his time in advocating a four-day county championship. In a wide-ranging analysis for *The Times* on the state of English cricket, Imran said that the objective of the three-day game, to produce Test cricketers, was not being achieved. 'I am so bored with this nonsensical contrived cricket where, with two teams level on the morning of the third day, you have to give the other side runs to set up a declaration, so you get these ridiculous hundreds being scored while the wicketkeeper is bowling. In one spell Sussex played 42 days out of 44. It's complete madness. They were worn out. One-day cricket has changed everything – travelling has increased, which is more tiring than people realize, and the extra pace of the one-day game adds to the physical demands. I just cannot see England producing pace bowlers with this amount of cricket.' The Sunday League, he added, 'was no use to anyone'.

Imran's experience with New South Wales in the Sheffield Shield had made him an enthusiastic advocate of the four-day game, believing it produced more competitive and enthusiastic matches. 'Four-day cricket is nearer to five-day Test cricket and is a better preparation for it. It obviously gives batsmen the chance to build longer innings. Because Sheffield Shield cricket is so competitive, it is fun to play. Dennis Lillee once told me he sometimes enjoyed it more than Test matches. I couldn't believe my ears because no English player would ever say that about county cricket – England players just go through the motions when they go back to their counties. Because Australians play fewer innings, each is a bigger occasion and teaches them to play under pressure.' The force of his argument was not appreciated until Australia beat England in three successive series between 1989 and 1993.

His concern for the well being of the game was not parochial, even if he held opinions which sometimes suggested otherwise. Much of his life was invariably taken up with trying to resolve Pakistan's problems, some of which seemed insurmountable. Returning home in September 1988, Imran decided to make his own stand against Australia's imminent visit. He felt they should have been prepared to come during their own season. He could have taken part and boosted his own averages as well as his captaincy record, but that, for him, would not have been any sort of challenge. So Javed Miandad again led Pakistan in his stead throughout another unpleasant series, Australia going so far as to accuse the umpires of cheating and the Board of Control of doctoring the pitch at Karachi.

Javed always courted controversy, whether it was through players ganging up and refusing to play under him or when, in 1987, Pakistan and England became embroiled in as unpleasant a series as there has been. Nevertheless, he was re-appointed captain for the short tour of New Zealand and, prior to that, a one-day tournament in Australia involving Pakistan, West Indies and Australia. Four days before departure, Javed decided to stand down in favour of Imran, whereupon Imran insisted that unless he was given his own way over team selection, he would resign the captaincy as well. As a bemused Allan Border once memorably said of the Pakistanis: 'You never know what's going on behind the scenes.'

Such a shemozzle was by now familiar to followers of the game everywhere. Why did Javed step down so frequently when, as he himself said, he 'looked after so many things' on the pitch, from field placings to being an intermediary between Imran and the bowler? 'I did so for the good of the side,' he said, 'and in retrospect I am glad that I did. There was nothing difficult between us.' Javed was aware that he and Imran needed each other. He had a regard for Imran's captaincy, although he did not rate him as highly as Mushtaq Mohammad, whom he felt was the best leader he had played under and who had pushed his own claims. Javed saw in Imran a gambler's instinct, and luck: 'It was easy for a captain if he had runs on the board', and that this was often the case owed much to Javed's own batting. Javed's point that for much of Imran's time as captain Pakistan had a decent bowling attack is also true: Sarfraz Nawaz, Abdul Qadir, Wasim Akram and, later, Waqar Younis and Mushtaq Ahmed, were all world-class bowlers. It does not take into account that Imran's greatest strength as a captain was his own batting and bowling.

In the estimation of Javed's immediate predecessor, Asif Iqbal, Javed has not had the recognition from the media that he deserves. Although his approach to captaincy contrasted sharply with Imran's, he was widely regarded as a better tactician. 'They were both positive captains,' said Wasim Akram, ultimately Javed's successor. 'Javed has one of the best cricket brains I know and Imran leaned on him for tactical advice, as captains always will. But the players were more relaxed with Imran.' There was no sense of envy – they both made the most of the gifts bestowed on them at birth – but their differing backgrounds and natures ensured they would never be close. The rules of street cricket in Karachi are not those of the Parks at Oxford.

Javed was aware that Imran was regarded as indispensable, not least by the state president – and nothing changed after General Zia's death. The fact that Imran had been lured back to the game by no less an eminence than Zia gave him a standing far surpassing that of any paltry administrator of the Board of Control. He could ride roughshod over them, and once did. This was to the benefit of Pakistan's cricket, even though it was not desirable that so much power should reside in the control of one cricketer. Imran could pick and choose his series and still continue to lead Pakistan, in the same way Greg Chappell had done when Kim Hughes was supposedly the captain of Australia. The common link was that neither Hughes nor Javed had the full support of the players – even if, in Javed's case, his ability as a cricketer was no less than that of Imran's.

Regardless of whether he was captain or not, Javed had one particular virtue: he never gave of less than his best. He was as competitive in a Benefit match as he was in a limited-overs competition in the desert or at Lord's in a Test match. In New Zealand, having relinquished the captaincy, he averaged 194 in the two Tests and 149 on tour. His bravery and performances against West Indies had been vital to Pakistan's success – although he had wanted the tour cancelled rather than lead it himself. He thought Pakistan would be annihilated. There is truth in Imran's criticism that in England Javed did not make the weight of runs he should have done – his first century was not scored until the final Test in 1987 and then, perhaps inevitably, it was a double one – and the suspicion lingered in Imran's mind that Javed was using the press in Karachi to his own ends. Yet none of this impaired their partnership at the crease or in the field.

As he demonstrated in New Zealand, Javed was at his peak in 1988–9. In the preceding Benson and Hedges one-day tournament in Australia, both he and Imran were their customary consistent selves, although this proved to be of little avail: Pakistan's preparation was inadequate and, in the case of Qadir, almost hilariously shambolic. Qadir arrived in Australia only three hours before the start of the opening match, in which Pakistan were thoroughly outplayed by West Indies. By the time they lost their second match to Australia, Imran admitted he had had no idea how lacking in practice they were. This was the drawback of picking and choosing his appearances on a point of principle. And for once, they could not be rejuvenated. Imran's unbeaten 67 from 46 balls enabled them to beat West Indies by 55 runs but still they finished bottom of the qualifying table by some distance.

Realizing that he had to re-exert his authority, Imran insisted that changes be made to the party originally selected for New Zealand in his absence. He had seen Aqib Javed, then a raw teenager, bowling in the nets and immediately recognized his potential. Imran was determined also to have Shoaib Mohammad, which was just as well since he made centuries in each of the two Tests, both of which were drawn. A third was abandoned.

It was an unsatisfactory tour in which there were yet more disputes over umpiring, drawing a rare stricture from *Wisden*. 'It seemed that the tourists, sensitive to the claims that umpiring in Pakistan was questionable, set out to show that New Zealand umpires also were incompetent. That was the word used by the captain, Imran Khan ... the Pakistan way of approaching the umpires almost en masse, and the filthy language that was used, caused great concern ... an exception should be made of Imran, who led a highly excitable team.' Every series in which Pakistan were involved seemed now to result in controversy over the umpiring, which only damaged the game, even if other countries complained about the umpiring in New Zealand. Still Imran pressed for international umpires, if, for the time being, with little effect.

There were two challenges for Imran: Pakistan had not won a series in New Zealand for ten years and Imran had not played against Richard Hadlee, fellow great all-rounder but hardly alter

160

ego, for the same length of time. Owing to an Achilles tendon injury to Hadlee, this confrontation turned out to be something of a damp squib, as indeed did the series. Imran was the man of the match in a dull draw at Wellington, taking six wickets and making 71 in Pakistan's sole innings. At Auckland, where only 18 wickets fell for 1118 runs, he became the third all-rounder after Botham and Kapil Dev to score 3000 runs and take 300 wickets in Test matches in the course of making an unbeaten 69. The one-day internationals were dominated, surprisingly, by New Zealand.

Thereafter, Imran was free of cricket during the English summer for the first time since 1971. After leaving Sussex there was conjecture that he might play for Yorkshire and he was officially approached by Middlesex, but he had never had a desire to play for seven days a week and even the lure of appearing in one-day matches at Lord's, close enough to his flat, was not sufficiently appealing. He was attracted to nothing more strenuous than country house cricket in 1989. In London there was socializing; in Scotland shooting; in the Himalayas trekking; in Bangladesh work for UNICEF. The upshot was that, come October, when he had his thirty-seventh birthday (*Wisden* erroneously states November) he was not fit enough to play international cricket, even of the instant variety in Sharjah. By now, however, Javed Burki was chairing Pakistan's selection panel and insisted that Imran journeyed there, whether fit or not.

It was while recovering from a virus caught in Bangladesh that Imran switched on the television in his hospital room and watched a remarkably supple teenager bowling with pace and rhythm in a fixture of little bearing in Pakistan. He had the same suppleness of wrist and body as Sarfraz Nawaz, Asif Masood and Imran himself. The story goes that Imran plucked Waqar Younis from nowhere, including him in the national side in a jiffy. This is apocryphal: Waqar was already practising within their training camp ('I was not sure I would get selected') but there is no doubt that Imran's encouragement greatly helped in his becoming an exceptional fast bowler in an extremely short time. The captain picked him for the Sharjah Cup straight away. 'Imran was my coach and my friend and my elder brother. I was bowling quickly but not very accurately at the time and I was not thinking in terms of playing for Pakistan so soon. But I really enjoyed his captaincy because he understood fast bowlers.'

In particular, Imran helped Waqar with his run up, with marking out his run and where his front foot would land. They would go out for meals together. On occasion, Waqar looked quicker than anyone in Sharjah. Later, when in London, Waqar would go round to Imran's flat for advice, especially if he was depressed. He worked for Imran's hospital appeal and was introduced to Mick Jagger, who had given around £15,000 to the fund. It was through Imran's solicitation in retirement that Waqar became vice-captain of Pakistan. In short, Imran took him under his wing.

Pakistan won both this competition in Sharjah and the subsequent Nehru Cup in India, enabling Imran to begin his campaign to raise funds for his proposed hospital on the ideal footing. What was more, he won the man of the match award in the final of the Nehru Cup in Calcutta – in front of 70,000 spectators – by making an unbeaten half-century and, saving his allotted overs until the very end of West Indies' innings, taking three important middle order wickets. In addition, he was made man of the series for his consistent, rather than exceptional, all-round performances, having been awarded four man of the match awards. In nineteen days Pakistan took part in eleven one-day internationals, encompassing two competitions, winning nine of them. The prize money for the Nehru Cup, another spurious competition held to celebrate the centenary of the birth of the first prime minister of India after Independence, was not exceptional (US $40,000) and for Pakistan it meant little more than staying on the treadmill. As for Imran, he at least remained in the public eye. The trustees of his hospital appeal were to insist that this should continue to be so.

Thus Imran opted to carry on leading Pakistan in a four-Test series at home against India in November and December of 1989.

162

Having already been victorious in India, he had no remaining personal ambitions for a series that meant more to his countrymen than any other, and yet, driven by his new project – the two sides played each other in a fundraising one-day match at the start of the tour – he felt he was batting better than ever before. His coordination of hand and eye had not been dulled by advancement towards middle age and his technique remained unimpaired. He gave the lie to the notion that a batsman reaches his peak on the subcontinent before the age of thirty. If his bowling had lost some of its former sting, this was of less consequence with the advent of Waqar and the increasing expertise of Wasim.

The four Tests were all drawn, although that fact alone does not tell of their competitive nature. A series involving Pakistan could never be anything else. The introduction of two international umpires, John Hampshire and John Holder, made for less friction and proved the worth of Imran's badgering of officials. Colin Cowdrey, when he began a second term as chairman of the International Cricket Council, was to discover just how persuasive Imran could be.

At Karachi, Imran made his fifth Test century, coming in at number six and batting for three and a half hours against an attack which had, in Kapil Dev and Prabhakar, penetrating new-ball bowlers throughout the series. This was necessarily urgent cricket, for Pakistan's innings had become self-engrossed on a sluggish pitch. Of the six centuries that Imran was to score in all in his Test career, three were against India, which would say something, perhaps, about how much it meant to his country to excel against them. The fact that Wasim and Waqar were now good enough, and quick enough, to share the new ball was a further factor in Imran being able to concentrate more on his batting. He could come on first change, as he did when Waqar was fit, and provide the ideal tutelage.

Wasim and Waqar did not quite manage to win this first Test for Pakistan – they took eight wickets between them in India's first innings – since Waqar had strained his back. He was to play in only one further match in the series. 'Imran probably had too much confidence in him and his muscles were still developing,' said Javed Burki. Imran opened the bowling in the second innings but could not prevent Sanjay Manjrekar making an unbeaten century and staving off defeat. This Test was also notable for Sachin Tendulkar making his debut for India at the age of sixteen and 205 days. He struck two half-centuries in the series, batting in the lower middle order, but did not initially impress Imran.

Manjrekar had much to do with Pakistan not winning the second Test at Faisalabad, making 76 and 83 in another high-scoring draw. On a fast pitch, Imran took four wickets in India's first innings, which subsided from 244 for four to 288 all out. A century by Aamer Malik was at the core of a Pakistan total that gave them a lead of 135, but it was compiled at a tardy rate. Another century by Mohammad Azharuddin, his first outside India, effectively saved the match. It was not often that Imran conceded 100 runs and was wicketless, but this was one such occasion.

At Lahore, neither side progressed beyond an innings apiece. 'A strip devoid of grass stood out in contrast to the lush outfield of the Gaddafi Stadium and caused the Pakistan captain no small amount of annoyance,' observed *Wisden*. There seemed to be scant possibility of a positive result, and so it proved. Again Imran took the brunt of the bowling upon himself, having 50 overs in India's innings, and he made 66 in Pakistan's reply, which amounted to little more than batting practice. Shoaib made a double century in response to one compiled by Manjrekar and, in his hundredth Test, Javed Miandad scored a century, as Colin Cowdrey had done.

There was more in the pitch at Sialkot for the quicker bowlers, but still not enough to bring about anything other than a draw. India had the better of the match, but time lost through rain and the pelting of missiles at fielders caused various delays. There was life in the match when Imran and Wasim reduced India to 38 for four on the fourth day, but it petered out into a draw.

Pakistan had to content themselves with winning the one-day internationals, in which Imran had a bit part.

So a disappointing series and, for that matter, an unnecessary one. Pakistan had had the option of extending their 1989–90 tour of Australia to five Tests rather than three. This would, effectively, have given them the chance to determine which of the two sides was the strongest in the world after West Indies, for although Pakistan had triumphed over the three Tests in 1988 that Imran had missed, they had never won a series in Australia.

So having opted to play India, three Tests it was to be. There was the customary chaotic arrival, or non-arrival in the case of two players. And Qadir, the great match winner of the 1980s, turned up on time but returned home before the first Test. Imran had been his staunchest supporter, having given an ultimatum more than once that if Qadir did not go on tour, he would not go either. Now, it appeared his faith in him was wavering. In the final Test against India, Qadir was given only two overs (both maidens) out of the 169 which his side bowled. At thirty-four he was fit and ambitious to overtake Lance Gibbs's 309 Test wickets, but, as John Woodcock wrote, 'even for a Pakistani he is highly temperamental'. Qadir felt he was bowling better than Imran did, although his figures – three wickets for 181 – were far from impressive. This was not the end of his Test career, but it was close to being so. Qadir had named his son, born in 1982, after Imran, and it looked for a while as if this might become an embarrassment to them both. In due course time healed their differences. Qadir, a devout Muslim, continued to pray for the man who until now had always stood by him. 'My loyalty was to players who were loyal to the side,' said Imran.

With Qadir in his most effective form, Australia might have been cauterized. Without him and, for that matter, Mushtaq Ahmed, Pakistan were always likely to struggle. They lost the first Test at Melbourne by 92 runs in spite of Wasim taking 11 wickets. Imran chose to open the bowling with him but was unable to correct, at the moment of delivery, a tendency to fall

165

away at the crease. This plagued him throughout the series and, having a combative nature, angered him. He found his rhythm, and thus his pace, increasingly elusive. He was a spearhead no more, which turned his thoughts once again towards retirement. He found solace in his batting in Pakistan's second innings, although they did not save the match. Numerous lbw appeals were upheld. Bowled out for 107 in their first innings, they at least made a better fist of the rest of their performance. Imran compiled 45 in support of Ijaz Ahmed, who in making a century batted as he can rarely have batted before.

That there were six lbw decisions in Pakistan's second innings, five of them given to Terry Alderman, only made Australia's victory contentious in the eyes of Imran, who for once said nothing about umpiring afterwards. It was not so much a matter of inconsistent umpiring (or consistently poor as he described it) which caused seething resentment among his side, as the feeling of persecution that so constantly troubled them. When Imran stood down from the captaincy for their match against Victoria, the Pakistanis refused to accept a ruling by the umpire that Mushtaq had transgressed the laws by running on to the pitch. Ramiz Raja, who was captaining them, took the players off the field, an action that was surprisingly supported by Intikhab Alam, the manager. As ever, this was not the sole problematical issue, merely the one which brought matters to a head.

There were less abominable moments on the tour. Quite the most memorable, especially so far as their captain was concerned, was Pakistan's recovery from what otherwise would have been a thrashing in the second Test at Adelaide. Having conceded a first innings lead of 84, Imran one of Carl Rackemann's victims in a mightily impressive spell, Pakistan collapsed to 22 for four. Imran had hardly had time to take off his bowling boots when he was required to go in, two places higher than normal, on account of injuries to Javed and Salim Malik. Had he been caught at short leg off Rackemann, it would have been 22 for five. Having survived that, and Pakistan collapsing further to 90 for five when Javed was out, Imran compiled the highest and, perhaps, most accomplished innings of his Test career. And to think that Susannah Constantine, who was travelling in Australia with him, became bored and returned to Melbourne. 'I got an earful later,' she admitted ruefully.

'As captains' innings go, it is hard to think of a better one,' wrote John Woodcock. Imran chivvied and nurtured Wasim, encouraging him to put bat to ball in a way that no one else had done in the match. The upshot was a riveting contrast in styles and a partnership of 191 that saved the match. Imran batted for 485 minutes, hitting ten fours in his 136, and Wasim for half that time in achieving his maiden Test century. Although for once Imran chose to wear a chest protector, nothing disconcerted him, especially not Merv Hughes's personality. Whether gliding him through the gully off the full face of the bat or pulling him through mid-wicket, Imran always seemed to know which ball to score from. His placing of his cover drives was another feature in what was his first century against Australia. He was even able to declare and give Pakistan a chance of victory, leaving Australia 304 to win in a minimum of 78 overs, a typically positive, challenging move. But for Dean Jones scoring his second century of the match, Australia would have been in considerable trouble. As it was they finished six wickets down, 71 runs short of their target.

Imran was lavished with praise. From the commentary box, Richie Benaud declared this to be one of the most exciting partnerships he had seen in Test cricket. Imran described it as one of the best innings he had ever played. 'Our team would have been destroyed had we lost. Because my bowling had fallen away, I could only justify my position as captain through my batting [he had never believed in a Mike Brearley-style leader who was not worth his place solely as a player]. In the context of the match and for my own self-respect it was an important innings. Our team would have been destroyed had we lost.' It was a performance which more than any other won him the cricketer of the year award; and a prize of a car, which he gave to the hospital appeal.

The third Test at Sydney was spoiled by rain, although there was still time for Pakistan to collapse again. On this occasion they were 51 for four when Imran came in. He was left undefeated on 82, made in four and three-quarter hours, by the time they were dismissed for 199. Australia had progressed to 176 for two in response, Mark Taylor achieving his second century of the series. A modicum of revenge for their defeat in the first Test was gained when Pakistan beat Australia in the final of the Austral-Asia Cup, a tournament contested by six nations in Sharjah two months later. In that this amounted to Pakistan playing four matches and gaining considerable pecuniary reward – US $30,000 – it was worth Imran's while; there was scant other reason why it would have been. His own performances were, for once, unimpressive.

Back home, Imran toyed again with the idea of retirement as he wrestled with the inexorable difficulties of fundraising. He took a stance against New Zealand's tour in September, objecting to a weakened side being sent. Amid allegations of ball tampering, New Zealand were annihilated by Waqar Younis, who took 29 wickets in the three Tests. Imran had appealed to Pakistan's Board to cancel the tour altogether, having declined their invitation to play in the series. By the time it was completed in November 1990, the only cricket he had undertaken since the start of May was indoor net practice at Lord's; and yet his presence remained almost imperative to Pakistan. Javed had spared the Board some embarrassment when he had voluntarily relinquished the captaincy for the tour of Australia, but he had been told when appointed against New Zealand that he would be captain 'for an indefinite period'. Now he announced he was resigning 'for the greater interest of the game and the country'. He added: 'I'm stepping down voluntarily and willingly and will extend support to Imran so that Pakistan can beat West Indies.' He had voiced his disquiet before the series against New Zealand at being considered no more than a stop gap, and had initially refused to take on the captaincy, but no doubt he was aware that Imran still had prior claims.

So Imran, knowing he needed to keep playing for the sake of his fledgling project, found himself back in charge only five hours after flying home from London. It was not so much cricket as musical chairs. He described Javed Miandad's decision as 'great' and declared that it was an honour for him to lead his country again. This was the third series between Pakistan and West Indies within three years, which amounted to ludicrous overkill. Each of these three encounters consisted of only a short series, which hardly helped determine which was the best side in the world.

This series, like the previous two, was drawn. Imran again compensated with his batting for what he was losing with his bowling – he gave himself only 19 overs in the three relatively low-scoring matches – averaging 50.33 over five innings. He also had the satisfaction of winning the limited-overs internationals, all three of them, for the first time against West Indies. His unbeaten innings of 53 and 46 played a considerable part in this. He had changed his guard from his customary leg stump to middle stump in Australia and found it easier to play the ball in front of his body, even if he was more vulnerable to lbw decisions. He carried his form into the first Test at Karachi, where he batted for five hours in making an unbeaten 73. Only two other batsmen reached double figures – but these were match-winning innings. A century by Salim Malik and an innings of 86 by Shoaib Mohammad that was in the vein of his father, Hanif, gave Pakistan an 84-run lead. Imran had not bowled in West Indies' first innings and did not take the field when they batted again, owing to having been struck on a leg while batting, but it scarcely mattered. Waqar took nine wickets in the match, Wasim six, and a West Indies side lacking Richards and its imperious strut of old could not cope with that. Desmond Haynes, deputizing as captain, made a century and 47, but his most damaging contribution was an allegation of ball tampering, which was, as ever, unproven.

What West Indies still possessed in abundance was fast bowlers, and even if Malcolm Marshall was not as formidable as he had once been, he had sufficient savvy to make the most of helpful conditions when he saw them. At Faisalabad, these were exactly that. Imran's decision to bat first did not come off in that only Salim Malik made a score of note. Javed was out of form and Imran, in this match, out of runs. Even so, West Indies exceeded a total of 170 by only 25. What decided the outcome was Marshall's bowling in the second innings. In 13 balls he took four wickets, including having Imran caught at the wicket without scoring. Salim struck 71 to add to 74 in the first innings, but a target of 130 proved comfortably within West Indies' compass.

The deciding match was to be at Lahore, where no one knew the conditions better than Imran. The pitch was supposed to be prepared for Pakistan's spinners – Qadir was recalled after being dropped for the second Test – but the groundsman succeeded only in producing something on which fast bowling was harder to play. The blame for this from the press was heaped not on him but on Imran, who was nonplussed, although he felt that 'the host country does have the right to produce, within reason, a wicket to suit its team and, ever since I can remember, teams have done so'. A century by Carl Hooper, one of the finest Imran had ever seen, enabled West Indies to reach 294 in their first innings, Wasim taking four wickets. Imran chose to bowl for the first time in this series, taking the new ball himself in light of Waqar's preference for coming on when it was worn. Whatever confidence Imran had lacked in his own abilities – and for that to be the case he really must have been bowling badly – he restored a measure of it by removing both Greenidge and Haynes in his first and only spell, having one leg before and the other taken by Pakistan's new wicketkeeper, Moin Khan.

In reply, Pakistan were hurried out for 122, Ambrose and Bishop taking five wickets apiece. Although West Indies in turn were dismissed for a lowly total, 173, Imran taking two further wickets and Wasim four in five balls, 346 was too tall an order on that pitch for a side whose batting was already vulnerable. Pakistan were 110 for four on the final morning when Imran joined the nightwatchman, Masood Anwar, and it was only through their cussedness that the match was saved. Anwar made

37 in over three hours and Imran's resolve was such that, in facing 196 balls, he hit just three fours. He was undefeated on 58 when stumps were drawn, having played one of his finest innings and ensured that under his captaincy Pakistan would not lose a series against the strongest side of the decade. On a pitch on which batting was as dangerous as it was arduous, Imran did not want for courage. It was ever thus.

Chapter 12

It was not a question of whether Pakistan would win the World Cup, but when. That, at any rate, was how Imran regarded the fifth staging of a tournament that was becoming increasingly prestigious. One-day cricket generally held no more importance for him now than it had at the start of his career and was, he knew, no substitute for Test matches. In terms of whether or not his hospital venture would succeed, the World Cup was the most vital event of his career. Pakistan had to win – he had to win – if the appeal was not to collapse. Imran's faith in his own ability, that he and his team were competent enough to triumph, was surpassed only by his faith in God, his belief that he would be willed to succeed. He urged his friends well before the onset of the competition to back his side, who were not even favourites to win. Imran told Jeffrey Archer three months beforehand that, because every time he batted or bowled the future of the hospital was at issue, he was more dangerous than anyone else on the field. Archer promptly placed £10 on Pakistan in addition to £20 on England.

Such cricket as Imran played in the run up to the World Cup he used to work out Pakistan's best side and the strengths and weaknesses of others. In October 1991, six months before the tournament started, Pakistan won their fifth competition in four seasons in Sharjah, the Wills Trophy, and US $30,000 besides. It was of no concern to Imran that the Indians left furious at what they perceived to be biased umpiring and organization: he was forming something of a settled side, although he was to be without Waqar Younis, who missed the entire World Cup through injury. Upon return to Pakistan, Imran even looked upon a three-Tests series against Sri Lanka as preparation for what was ahead, which showed, apart from his underlying motives, just how much the game had changed since he first played in a World Cup in 1975. Then, it was no more than a sideshow.

Imran did not realize it at the time, but this was to be his last Test series. His intention was to tour England the following year, partly because he would be in London anyway but also so that he could continue fundraising there. This was not the series he would have chosen for his swan song; indeed, in normal circumstances he probably would not have played. In the event, Pakistan only scraped one victory, which was sufficient to win the series. Still afflicted by falling away in his delivery stride, a fault he did not manage to correct until shortly before the World Cup began, Imran gave himself only nine overs in the three Tests, entrusting Waqar and Wasim with the task of bowling out Sri Lanka. His batting, though, remained pre-eminent.

Nothing emphasized more clearly Imran's concern for the greater good over and above his personal averages than when, in the first Test, he declared before he reached what would have been his seventh Test century. He had batted nearly four hours for 93 when he decided a lead of 153 was enough. Far from his batting having been affected by not playing as often as he once did, he seemed to benefit from less concentrated cricket. Five wickets for Waqar had accounted for Sri Lanka in their first innings: that they managed to draw this match had something to do with bad light and more to do with an unbeaten partnership of 79 for the sixth wicket between Jayasuriya and Tillekeratne.

The second Test at Gujranwala lasted for no more than two and a half hours, Pakistan reaching a total of 109 for two. Sri Lanka performed well enough in the third and final match at Faisalabad almost to achieve their first victory outside their own country. Only the bowling of Waqar, who took five wickets in an innings for the seventh time in only his 14th Test, brought about victory for Pakistan by a mere three wickets. It was a low-scoring match, as Imran's final Test innings of 22 and a duck might suggest.

The one-day internationals were a more straightforward

173

affair, Pakistan winning four of the five and discovering, in Inzamam-ul-Haq, a batsman from a remote area of the country who was truly a match winner. As before, Imran backed his initial judgement. In these first appearances alone, Inzamam made two centuries and two other scores of note. No longer could Javed Burki become cross with his cousin about Pakistan's record in international matches, as he had when he became chief selector.

Imran had succeeded in persuading Pakistan's Board that the party selected for the World Cup should go to Australia a month before the start, so as to acclimatize to the harder pitches. It was there that he experimented with resurrecting his old bowling action, which he had not deployed since the 1970s. Given that he would have to bowl in every match for Pakistan to maintain a balanced side, it was imperative that he found some rhythm beforehand – and he did. The confidence he possessed through his belief that his hospital campaign would prevail was heightened by satisfaction with his personal form. Even without the injured Waqar, Imran truly believed Pakistan would win. Nine countries were to participate in an event that was to become as colourful as the Olympic Games. South Africa and Zimbabwe were there, and so too were floodlights, a white ball and coloured clothing. Not that the paraphernalia impressed Imran at all: he was to tell the co-hosts, Australia and New Zealand, that their organization was the worst of the five World Cups staged. Since he was one of only two players to compete in all five – Javed Miandad being the other – the administrators had to take notice. These were five weeks, as the *Cricketer* put it, 'of contrivance, of excitement, of plausibility, of despair, of self-sacrifice, of the very good and the fourth-rate, of the accomplished and the crude'. For Pakistan, it was a case of a 'tide in the affairs of men' being taken at the flood.

Australia were not as good as they thought they were. India had the ability but not the cohesion. West Indies did not bring Vivian Richards, nor for that matter Gordon Greenidge and one or two others, and it showed. South Africa aroused interest and were prevented from a chance of reaching the final not through the abilities of their opponents but through a rule devised for interruption from rain that no one had properly thought through. New Zealand performed more creditably than expected, attracting numerous spectators in their own country as they did so. England progressed in the style of automatons and Pakistan in their own, wholly unpredictable vein. The old sweats were on course for a confrontation with joyous flair.

It was not always thus, in spite of the vision Imran had of himself holding the trophy aloft before the commencement of the competition. Two days before Pakistan's first match against West Indies, Imran damaged his right shoulder to the point that he realized he would be unable to play. His disappointment was no less acute than the pain, although he was aware seven more qualifying matches remained. Pakistan were beaten by nine wickets, which only increased his resolve to play in their next match four days later: if they lost this, they would almost certainly be out of the competition. Although they beat Zimbabwe comfortably, Imran neither batted nor bowled. He was in obvious discomfort in the field and strained his shoulder further when practising in the nets. He saw two specialists who told him that the more he played, the worse it was going to get. On one occasion he sat waiting for an hour and a half in Launceston for a report.

Hopelessness is judged as a sin in the Koran. So while Imran was given painkillers and massages, his trusty manager and first captain, Intikhab Alam, scoured the countryside for anything that would relieve a stress fracture. Ultimately he came up with an imported maiomatic machine which sent magnetic currents into his shoulder. 'I knew the pain and agony he was in but he never showed it,' said Intikhab. Between them they determined that he would have to bowl his allotted ten overs on the trot, for fear of seizing up. During matches he had to have two or three sessions of treatment, which no one else was informed about. 'If you are clean and work hard you will make your own luck and succeed,' said Intikhab. 'Imran would put across the message that things should be made to happen.'

175

For the time being, though, little was happening to Pakistan that was not deleterious. Imran left himself out of their match against England, who bowled them out for 74 and would assuredly have won had it not rained. This was Pakistan's lowest total in limited-overs internationals and the smallest by a Test nation in any of the World Cups. Under the complex rules which governed rain interruptions and showed up the artificiality of such cricket, there had not been sufficient play to be any result. The way Pakistan were performing, there was little purpose in Imran holding himself back any longer, pain or no pain. He included himself in their next match, against India, and conceded just 25 runs off eight overs, but this contest, too, was lost. His side were simply batting too indifferently. An unbeaten half-century by Sachin Tendulkar, who put on 60 in eight overs with Kapil Dev, was sufficient to give India victory without undue difficulty. There was no respite and no recovery. At Brisbane Imran opted to field first in view of an indifferent weather forecast and, although Pakistan restricted South Africa to 211 for seven from their 50 overs, without Javed Miandad and Ramiz Raja they slumped to another defeat. Inzamam made runs for the first time and Imran, going in at number four, struck 34 to add to his two wickets, but this was not enough. Pakistan lost by 20 runs and the mien of each player betrayed their feelings. They had lost all sense of belief in themselves.

One victory in five matches meant that everybody was writing them off, including the bookmakers and, it had to be said, themselves. Imran's sense of desperation was exacerbated by the knowledge that he, rather than his side, was the prime target for the press, who felt (he reckoned) that he was spending too much time on obtaining publicity for his hospital rather than concentrating on the cricket. He was all too aware just how his fundraising would be affected. It was now that he made the comment for which he was to be famed. He had taken to wearing a T-shirt with 'Tiger' – which had long been his favourite animal – emblazoned on it. In the dressing room he told his players that they had nowhere to turn and should fight with their backs to the wall like cornered tigers. He actually believed Pakistan could still win the World Cup and endeavoured to put this across to his players. His faith, both in his side and in his religion, had not wavered.

So in their day/night match against Australia (who were faring no better), Pakistan did indeed play as if they had nowhere to hide. Aamer Sohail, whom Imran initially had not wanted in the party, took his aggregate to 307 runs in six innings by making 76 in partnership with Ramiz and Javed. A total of 220 for nine would not have won many 50-overs matches, but in this one it did. Australia, lacking the belief in themselves that Imran had attempted to instil into his side, could muster no more than 172. Pleasingly for Imran, the wickets were shared, although Aqib Javed had a notably telling spell, removing Moody and Boon early in the innings.

Pakistan now had to beat Sri Lanka, who were already out of the competition after making a useful start. They restricted Sri Lanka to 212 for six and reached that total for the loss of six wickets, Javed and Salim Malik making half-centuries. Imran chose to go in at number three for the first time in the competition, having lost all confidence in Salim's ability against the new ball. He did not like his approach, either, although that did not affect his selection. Their differences came to a head over Salim's contention that he should have been appointed vice-captain, and over the problem of whether gifts lavishly bestowed by generous businessmen should go to Imran's hospital or to the players themselves – although Imran never had any intentions that anything should be misconstrued.

To have any prospect of reaching the semi-finals, Pakistan had to beat New Zealand in their final qualifying match. This necessitated a flight to Christchurch where their opponents, not least because they were on home territory, were thoroughly cock-a-hoop. They had yet to lose a match. Yet such over-confidence told against them in the same way it had against Pakistan when the last World Cup was nearing its climax. Imran opted to put them in, reckoning the bouncy pitch would suit his attack, and so it proved. Many, perhaps most, captains look to keep run-scoring in check when they are in the field, reasoning that a bowler who returns an analysis of 10–4–25–0 is of greater value to his side than one who might take four for 58. Imran took the contrary view, partly because he was temperamentally inclined to do so, but also because he believed that was the surest way of winning a limited-overs match. Thus he told Wasim to bowl flat out, disregarding any wides and no-balls he might concede, and used Mushtaq Ahmed, his talented leg spinner, as an attacking bowler when other countries would not have played him at all. Against New Zealand Mushtaq bowled with astonishing expertise, conceding only 18 runs and no boundaries and taking the wickets of Greatbatch and Harris to boot. A century by Ramiz brought about victory for Pakistan by seven wickets with more than five overs to spare. Still they did not know until Australia beat West Indies later that evening in a day/night match whether they would qualify. Pakistan were fortunate in that the weather had played a part in their progression, England having bowled them out for 74 and scarcely been able to reply, and yet it was evident that their form and, crucially for them, their mood, was in the ascendancy. The very fact that they had reached the semi-finals gave them great succour.

As the country with the worst record to qualify, Pakistan, with just four victories from their eight matches, were pitted against New Zealand, who had suffered just that one defeat. This match, too, was to be staged in New Zealand, whose side could hardly acquit themselves as poorly as they had before – and indeed they did not. Their total of 262 for seven was dominated by a disdainful innings of 91 from Martin Crowe. Imran's ploy of introducing Mushtaq into the attack at the first available opportunity was on this occasion only relatively successful; less so was his own bowling. By now painkillers were having little effect on his immune system, so much so that he could not raise a glass to have a drink without great pain. Rather than leave himself out, he merely doubled the dosage. The result was that, hampered by lack of practice, his bowling was ineffectual. Tidy though it had been in previous matches, he now conceded 59 runs off his ten overs, 14 coming off the last.

Lack of practice had also affected Imran's batting. Although capable of seeing off Morrison and Watson when he came to the wicket with Pakistan 30 for one, he found run making a different proposition altogether. When he was out for 44, his dismissal to be closely followed by that of Salim Malik, Pakistan required a further 123 from 15 overs. The crowd of 32,000 were so confident of victory that they began to chant as much when the next Pakistan batsman took guard. That Inzamam did not speak a word of English was, on this occasion, a boon. With no time to play himself in, he attacked the bowling instantaneously. Audacious shot followed audacious shot – and most of them went to the boundary. In partnership with Javed he struck 60 off 37 balls, enabling him to play the more supportive role that he now preferred. By the time Inzamam had been run out the target had come down to 36 from five overs. With the assistance of Javed, Moin Khan finished the match in style, driving Harris for six over long-off and then pulling him to the mid-wicket boundary to bring about victory. His colleagues spilled on to the field, engulfing the batsmen. Among them was a mightily relieved Imran, whose smile, as the *Cricketer* put it, was 'like a Cheshire cat rather than a Pathan tiger'. His side had won an astonishing victory against all reason and expectation. 'I knew that God was on our side,' said Imran.

In the final, Pakistan were to meet England, who qualified through the ill-conceived rain rule coming into farce, as it were. With South Africa requiring 22 runs from 13 balls, a heavy shower held up play for ten minutes. It would have been as good a finish as in the other semi-final. Instead, when play resumed the target was revised to 21 from one ball. Television schedules, it seemed, were the deciding factor. When asked what he thought of this, Imran replied, 'Rubbish.' He appealed for a final which would be played to a decisive finish, win or lose. He was, according to Ian Wooldridge in the *Daily Mail*, 'utterly unimpressed by the street-salesmen Rotarians who by their elevation to some

World Cup committee find themselves a big deal with their neighbours and defenceless when subjected to international scrutiny.' Television requirements, Imran said, should have no part in deciding a cricket competition which came round only every four years.

The final itself was fortunately free of interference from the elements. Still Imran was not fully fit and yet, upon winning the toss in front of 87,000 spectators at Melbourne and around a billion the world over on television, he determined to go in at number three again, feeling that his and Javed's experience would be all-important against the new ball and that the likes of Inzamam and Wasim could make the necessary quick runs. And so it proved. They were together within ten overs after Pringle had removed Sohail and Ramiz, taking their strategy to such lengths that at one stage they contributed just four runs from the bat in 60 balls. Imran simply eschewed any risk or quick single. After 34 overs Pakistan had reached 113 for two, but in the next 16 they gathered 136 runs.

If, on the day, Wasim Akram was the crucial difference between the two sides, so, too, did the approach of the captains play a significant part in the outcome. Graham Gooch opted, as was to be expected, for a solidly professional, containing game. Imran, as was never to be doubted, went for performers with flair. Thus England chose Richard Illingworth, who bowled a flat line on or outside leg stump, and Pakistan had Mushtaq Ahmed on early in the innings, attacking the batsman with guile. That, coupled with the know-how of Javed and Imran, won the day (or rather the night). Luck, or perhaps God, was with Pakistan: Imran had made just nine from 16 overs when Gooch spilled a difficult, running catch. When Imran and Javed were finally parted, they had accelerated sufficiently to add 139 in 31 overs, Imran finishing with 72 and his longstanding accomplice 58. In the last six overs the strokeplay of Inzamam and Wasim enabled Pakistan to add a further 52. Their total, 249 for six, was some 20 runs more than anticipated and, as it transpired, 22 runs beyond England.

It proved to be a final that Ian Botham, Imran's great competitor down the years, would have no wish to remember. Having conceded 42 runs off seven overs, he was immediately caught behind off Wasim without scoring. Stewart soon followed, Hick was wholly deceived by a googly from Mushtaq, and when Gooch was caught at fine leg, swinging at the same bowler, England found themselves with a task that was beyond them. Lamb and Fairbrother added 72 in 14 overs but Wasim returned to great effect. Fittingly, Imran took the last wicket, when he dismissed Illingworth in his seventh over. The margin of victory was in reality more than a mere 22 runs, as Gooch admitted when he said England were beaten 'fair and square'.

Imran declared it to be his finest hour, holding the Waterford crystal trophy after Sir Colin Cowdrey, ICC's chairman, who had also participated at the very start of his international career, had presented him with it, and dedicating the triumph – and the proceeds – to his hospital appeal. He forgot himself, speaking as if at a dinner party, and failing to mention the contributions of the players. 'I would just like to say I want to give my commiserations to the English team. But I want them to know that by winning this World Cup, personally it means that one of my greatest obsessions in life, which is to build a cancer hospital . . . I'm sure that this World Cup will go a long way towards completion of this obsession. I would also like to say that I feel very proud that at the twilight of my career finally I have managed to win the World Cup. Thank you.' The problem of money was to raise its ugly head soon afterwards. But for the moment, Imran had triumphed on several levels. His team selection, mostly done by himself, had been a triumph, as had his tactics. His standing as the most influential figure in Pakistani cricket since Kardar (now an ambassador) was also confirmed. And who would dare to reject his pleas for money for his hospital now?

The elation that Imran experienced at what he felt was the greatest moment of his 21-year career was soured by those players who thought they were not gaining their rightful recompense. Their feelings were heightened both by Imran's speech and by his occasionally explosive language on the field during the World Cup, which they felt was aimed at them. 'I have never directly sworn at any player,' he insisted.

Disliking Singapore and the prospect of the duty-free shopping spree that his side were planning on the way home (customs officers in Pakistan were expected to turn a blind eye to their purchases), he remained, for a while, in Australia. He was exhausted, and not only by cortisone injections and pain-killing tablets. His shoulder would evidently take a while to heal: if he was to continue playing, he might well need an operation. Ultimately he rejoined the party for the return flight and, it was envisaged, a triumphant home-coming at Lahore airport. He was, at this stage, blissfully unaware of the resentment felt by some of the players – but by no means all – over what was happening to the bounty that was always forthcoming to victorious Pakistani cricketers.

The prime minister, Nawaz Sharif, did not have the same affection for Imran as General Zia had had. He did not even care to bask in the reflected glory of such a victory in the way that many in his position would have done. Remembering what had occurred previously at the airport at Lahore, when he had been pushed around by crowds chanting for Imran after Pakistan had beaten India in 1987, he decided to order the delay of the players' flight by four hours until it was dark. No one informed the thousands who turned up at the airport, united in a way that the populace rarely is in Pakistan, and yet still the majority waited. Sharif had thought of coming on the aeroplane with the players, only to conclude, Pakistani journalists reckoned, that no one would have paid any attention to him. It was hard to imagine that a prime minister in the West would not have milked the adulation, even if this was understandably and rightly reserved for the sportsmen, and turned it to his own political advantage.

Such shenanigans only further exhausted Imran, who was reaching the point where he had simply had enough of internecine strife. He had given youth its chance whereas English officials had banged it into preordained shape. He had brought honour to a corrupt country, yet he was far more revered by the people than some of the senior players. Javed Miandad, whom he had embraced when the World Cup was won, had become a front for press attacks on him, complaining that the captain should be asking for money for the players instead of for the hospital. Javed had had too much savvy to clash head on with Imran in the past, but he was now telling journalists that the players were planning to tour the major cities so that an organized collection of gifts and prizes could be made from companies interested in rewarding them for winning the World Cup. 'He made it clear,' stated one report, 'that these shows have nothing to do with Imran's ambitions for a cancer hospital – they will be purely for the players.'

Disillusioned at what he saw as a deepening materialistic ethic in Pakistan, Imran retreated, as he always does when enervated, to his beloved mountains. In the tribal areas, now reached by the all-seeing medium of television, he was greeted by constant fusillades of gunfire and lavish hospitality. However poverty-stricken, the people of each village killed a goat or a lamb for Imran's shooting party and put out pink, yellow and orange milk sweets on small tables before a day-bed decked like a throne. In the words of Kate Muir, an English journalist who had to cover her head when she journeyed with him, Imran was received as if he was 'Gazza, the Beatles and President Kennedy rolled into one in a country famished for idols'. This helped allay his frustration that some press reports still implied that money intended for the hospital was going to line his own pocket. 'Normally, personal attacks don't bother me, but this is stupid because it has affected my campaign. If only they could look through this curtain of hatred, they would find they're actually doing themselves damage. Among the masses it doesn't matter but it has an effect on the people who give money,' he said.

Such disillusionment, coupled with his shoulder injury – in the weeks following the World Cup he still did not have freedom of movement and felt he had done some serious damage – meant that his desire to regain his fitness was not as great as it would normally have been. His thoughts were increasingly of dropping

183

out of Pakistan's tour of England, which was to begin in May 1992, and conceivably of retirement. If his fundraising was to go ahead as planned in England – the hospital was due to open the following year – it was imperative this should not be hampered by fighting over money. Pakistan Board officials and former colleagues such as Wasim Bari saw which way his mind was turning and tried to put his train of thought into reverse. Having initially declared his availability, Imran decided to pull out.

It would take him six months to be free of pain from his shoulder. Even so, he had been persuaded out of retirement at the eleventh hour before now and even when Javed, reinstated as captain, held a press conference at Lord's upon arrival in England, it was widely assumed that Imran would be appearing at some juncture before the Tests got underway. The Pakistani management was noncommittal, although they knew by then that he would be turning up only in the guise of a spectator and journalist. Finally Imran announced in the *Daily Telegraph*, who were paying him £1000 an article – now the main source of his income – that although he believed injuries could be willed to heal and that he could be fit by the middle of June, his campaign would be affected if the side did badly while he was hanging around as a non-playing captain. 'As long as cricket and the hospital project were complementing each other it made sense to play for Pakistan, but now that there was a conflict the only sensible thing to do was to opt out of the tour. My priority in life had shifted from cricket to the cancer hospital. In cricket I have no other ambitions left,' he wrote. He was referring to having to distance himself from 'a few senior players' who felt the players' fund should have benefited more than it had from the World Cup. Salim Malik had already said that 'with no superstars in the side, we are happier'. Imran, who watched the first of the one-day internationals of the summer from Paul Getty's box at Lord's, retorted: 'You don't come back from the low point we were at in the World Cup if you have an unhappy dressing room. It is just not possible to fight back from that situation. But if Salim takes it that way then that is up to him.

184

If he is happier without me then that must be good for Pakistan cricket.' In print, Imran was notably critical of Salim, whom he felt was unreliable and did not practise enough, opinions which the selectors took on board later when Salim was dropped from Pakistan's tour of West Indies. Imran had by then been appointed special adviser on International Cricket Council matters to the Board of Control, for which he was paid expenses only. 'I didn't want my hands tied,' he stressed. 'I deliberately wanted to keep away from the whole set up.'

That summer, while Pakistan under Javed were en route to winning an engrossing but at times unpleasant series, allegations of ball tampering constantly to the fore, Imran went on fundraising visits to Saudi Arabia, South Africa – a country he would not have involved himself with had apartheid not been dismantled – and the United States, where his sister Robina was working on his behalf. He saw enough of the Test series to write copious columns and to defend Pakistan from charges of doctoring the ball. He called again for independent umpires and complained bitterly of stereotyped Western images of Pakistan of 'fanaticism, veiled women and brutal dictators'. The Pakistanis missed his presence more than they did his ability, for Wasim and Waqar were too good and too quick for England's batsmen. Had the tour been a disaster for Pakistan in terms of results, Imran would doubtless have been pressurized to return. It seemed now that Javed's position was strengthened and that there would be no way back for Imran, yet later that year Javed was unable to control Pakistan's players to the extent that he asked for Imran to return, if only as manager. This Imran declined to do, partly because the hospital was his priority but also because he had no interest in that kind of role. When Javed was subsequently sacked from the captaincy, he blamed his longstanding team-mate – understandably, said Imran – although the reality was that Imran had more to do with the appointments of Wasim as captain and Waqar as vice-captain. For several months Javed would not speak to Imran. When he was left out of the tour of New Zealand in 1994, he accused Imran of influencing the selectors once more.

In September 1992, shortly before his fortieth birthday, Imran announced his retirement. He had not played any first-class cricket since the World Cup final, when he took the decision in principle. 'There was never really any question of me playing after the World Cup but I wanted to be doubly sure so that I did not have to face the embarrassment of a second comeback,' he opined. He wrote in the *Daily Telegraph*, which used a close-up colour picture of him over two-thirds of the front of their sports section, of Pakistan having rid themselves of their inferiority complex and the colonial hangover from the days when, he reckoned, the managers' ultimate goal was to be elected to MCC. 'As the colonial shackles were mentally broken, the racist element in the British media got progressively more intolerant and aggressive.' The most painful decision he ever took was to drop his cousin, Majid (although he never wrote as much, they were still not on speaking terms). The most satisfying moments were beating India in India, Pakistan's performances against West Indies in 1988 and winning the World Cup. The lowest point was when, after taking 87 wickets in 13 Tests, he developed his stress fracture.

He singled out Viv Richards and Sunil Gavaskar as the best batsmen of his time; Michael Holding as the fastest and most talented bowler; Dennis Lillee and Malcolm Marshall as more skilful, with great fighting qualities. Ian Chappell was the finest captain. Imran's criterion was value to the side in time of need rather than skill alone.

For all Imran's elation at winning the World Cup, he regretted that one-day cricket was eclipsing the five-day game: 'I foresee a drastic reduction in the amount of Test matches played in the future.' He focused on his faith. 'On three occasions rain was forecast during our last four World Cup matches. Had it rained once, we were out. Some call it luck, for me it is the will of God. I am fortunate that God has allowed me to leave cricket with so much dignity – a privilege He has denied much greater sportsmen. With the respect that He has given me in my country, I feel He has also put a responsibility on me to help the less privileged people. My greatest achievement will be when the cancer hospital is up and running.'

He had, as Christopher Martin-Jenkins put it, given 'his right shoulder time to heal and his emotions time to settle before deciding to retire on what is still a high note'. He was a man who was 'as pre-eminent in cricket in his own land as W. G. Grace in England or Sir Donald Bradman in Australia'. Six or seven times after retiring, Imran dreamed he was making another comeback, until one night he awoke in the realization that he would never play Test cricket again. The dream had turned into a nightmare: he would have hated to make another comeback. He has not had that dream since.

Indeed, he has hardly played any form of cricket since. He will appear, of course, in an exhibition that will benefit the hospital, such as matches between Pakistan and India at Crystal Palace in 1992 and 1993, but otherwise only for friends such as the Marquis and Marchioness of Worcester, who also named a horse after him.

After Imran had made it plain that he was finally retiring for good – Mushtaq Ahmed, for one, still nourished the hope in 1993 that Imran would play Test cricket again – he was inevitably in demand once more to enter politics. Ahmed Mobashir, one of his few close friends in Pakistan, urged him to do so. He was offered a post in an interim government following Nawaz Sharif's fall from power but settled instead on an unpaid position as ambassador for tourism, the appointment bestowed by the ministry. It was a new, loosely defined post that required someone as renowned as Imran to fill it, even if in the opinion of his friend Charles Glass it was 'several rungs beneath him'.

As a foreign correspondent, Glass knew more than most about such roles. And yet the post carried an intrinsic challenge for Imran, as all of his projects had to do. At the time of his appointment there was rioting in Pakistan, and the country was not, even in a good year, a tourist destination. Imran saw his task as ridding the country of its image in the West, which had everything to do with Botham's mother-in-law, fundamentalism and suppression, and not enough to do with the Himalayas and the Karakorams. It attracted trekkers, not sightseers. There would be easier posts, but by that very definition they would not have appealed to Imran. And by not taking a full-time position in any Pakistan government, he would still have time to undertake social work in education, the environment and health, as well as his writing and advisory work on International Cricket Council matters for the Board of Control.

As ambassador for tourism, he planned to attend functions, to write books or documentaries promoting Pakistan and to bring out influential visitors two or three times a year. For this, he was given the use of tourist facilities. He truly believed his country had considerable potential. 'I don't want to go to a place where there are a lot of people, such as the south of France, where everybody knows everybody else. Pakistan has bad publicity abroad because it is branded with Muslim fundamentalism and a military dictatorship that leads people to think of suppression. Yet it is not as if you are beaten with sticks if a woman does not have her legs covered. Pakistanis love tourists, yet ever since the Crusades there has been a fear of Islam. It is always portrayed as an evil religion. Saddam Hussein is taken as an example of a Muslim, but he is totally unrepresentative of Islam.'

Although, through his fame, the hospital was a tourist attraction in itself, Imran was aware that Pakistan would never attract mass tourism – just as he was adamant that he would not want it. Fish and chips would never be a feature of a holiday in the Karakorams. What he envisaged was the building of ten luxury lodges of indigenous mud and brick as staging posts for safaris by jeep. He and Mermagen discussed with the London travel firm Worldwide Journeys & Expeditions how this could be organized. 'A great deal of the country could be seen without too much trekking,' said Imran. 'The areas I have in mind are on the snow line, areas protected by the weather for eight or nine months of the year. There would be designated areas for camping, tents with portable showers such as used in Kenya, and good cooks. It would be possible to take only small groups with guards into the tribal areas, since tourism is not known there. The north would be the ultimate place because the mountains are so high that many valleys are cut off. The Deosai Plain is 14,000 feet high and from mid-September is covered with flowers. There are bears and snow leopards there and hardly anyone from Europe knows about it.' He felt that safaris could be organized to Cholistan Desert in southern Punjab, Thar Desert in Sindh and Sibi in Baluchistan, where one of the oldest camel fairs in Asia had been held for many years. People came from central Asia, Dubai and Afghanistan to buy and sell. A tent-pegging competition was undertaken by horsemen with spears, a tradition emanating from raids in the past when they would spear the tents of their foe. 'Mohenjodaro, the spring of civilization, where there are ruins of houses 4000 years old, is less sophisticated now than it was then. Not many know of the world's highest road, the 15,000-foot Khunjerab Pass at the Silk Route to China. Marco Polo sheep are almost extinct now, but they can still be seen there,' said Imran. 'All this has to be in collaboration with the government. I want to see historical sites, forts and tombs restored. There is very little money since sixty per cent of government expenditure goes on defence, but the project is viable.' Given his commitments to the hospital, however, it is questionable how much time he will have for such ventures.

There was a precedent for distinguished cricketers following such a path. Wes Hall, once a fearsome fast bowler, had turned senator and minister for tourism in Barbados. Even Sir Gary Sobers, whom Imran was saddened to see so motivated by money – though in fairness he had made precious little in his great career – was working for the Barbados Tourist Board. If anyone could draw tourists to Pakistan, it would be Imran. The benevolence he always felt towards his country and his people was heightened when he spent much of the free time he had in 1992 journeying through the tribal areas, the part of the North-West Frontier Province that he had not hitherto visited, at the behest of one of his many cousins, Sohail Khan. His interest was in the Pathans, his own tribe, who were continuing a way of life they had maintained for centuries. It was in part to have a greater understanding of his own character, how it would have been shaped by the ruggedness and hostility of the mountainous terrain. He had an affinity with their marksmanship, frugal lifestyle, even the high nose ridge of classical Greeks that was a trait of invading forebears. He saw in them the competitiveness he was born with and the determination not to show fear. They gave him cause to recall his father's words when, as a boy, Imran had asked him whether their family belonged to the middle or upper class. 'His reply was typically Pathan – that no one was above or below us, some were just more fortunate than others. It was only in the tribal areas that I saw what he had said being put into practice.'

To the outsider, the tribal areas had long been regarded as lawless lands inhabited by dangerous, barbaric people who lived by robbing and killing. Feuds are carried on for years, if not centuries, which means that any visitor has to travel with armed guards and permission from the Pakistan government. 'In fact, I found completely the opposite [to such a reputation]. I was impressed by the Pathans' hospitality and politeness – so unexpected in one of the world's greatest warrior races – and most of all by their value system. It is in many ways a far more civilized society than any I have seen,' he wrote. He even found that since the advent of television in the region in the early 1980s, many young people had taken to cricket with a zest that reminded him of his youth in Zaman Park. Imran vowed to establish a system of recognizing talent whereby a boy with ability could be brought to the attention of first-class clubs in Pakistan. He was so taken with tribes who lived by a system based on honour that he wrote a tribute to them, a glossy book called *Warrior Race* that was published in 1993. His previous book on his country, *Indus Journey*, had celebrated the tract of the famous river. *All Round View*, which led to Imran being cautioned by the Test and County Cricket Board for not obtaining clearance since he was then still contracted to Sussex, sold more than 20,000 copies in 1988 – he signed 150 in one two-hour session at Harrods – and he wrote an instructional book on cricket besides. 'He does not consider what he writes to be perfect prose,' said his agent, Abner Stein, 'but he wants it to be as good as it can possibly be and he always meets his deadlines. If he says he will do something, he does it. All his editors love him. He is motivated by challenge and curiosity but he knows where the money is. He turned down the original offer of an advance for *Warrior Race.*'

These books, which he wrote in long-hand with a biro, were now as important to his cash flow as his *Daily Telegraph* articles. Indeed, by 1993, when he gave £200,000 of his capital to the hospital appeal, he relied largely on writing for his income. Mermagen was becoming concerned he was not leaving enough for himself. 'Imran has never frittered money away and he does not need a lot of money to live in Pakistan, but there is a misconception that he is landed wealthy. His father was not money orientated. Now, he feels almost everything he earns should go to the hospital.' Imran, however, remained adamant that the hoarding of wealth is a sin in Islam. 'When you retain money you become a prisoner of your own greed.' His investment in a supermarket in Lahore was in the hope that it would develop into a chain – as well as on the understanding that a percentage of any annual profits would go to the hospital. He was invited to commentate for Sky television on Pakistan's visit to West Indies in April 1993 but disliked the experience. He had no wish to become involved again in cricket tours and had never had any interest in trips to the beach. He was, besides, far from a dispassionate commentator, just as his newspaper articles invariably were strongly partisan. His other work in that medium had not lasted for long. He undertook pilot interviews of Marie Helvin and Jeffrey Archer for satellite television but had greater difficulty with the lighting – he was soon gushing with sweat – than with asking the questions. Marie Helvin reciprocated by interviewing him for the fashion programme *Frocks on the Box*. 'People who had seen it would scream at him in the street that they would like to see him in such and such,' she said. 'Women like his vulnerability about fashion, that he doesn't know anything about it. And why should he? He has a good body so he looks nice in anything.'

Two cricket videos were brought out: one as part of the BBC's Legends series, which missed out important matches, notably those against West Indies, and *Leading from the Front*, which did not follow his career in a logical way. This did not unduly concern Imran: cricket for him was in the past and, like his father, he did not believe in looking back. Any role that he would now undertake within the game would be unpaid, so that he could free himself of it if necessary. In this capacity as adviser to Pakistan's Board, he attended, as their delegate, meetings of the International Cricket Council in 1993 – and soon wished he hadn't. He was intent on putting the case for the next World Cup to be staged on the Indian subcontinent and was appalled by what he (and others) saw as collusion among other delegates. If he had not already decided that the life of a cricket administrator was not for him, he certainly did now.

What, then, if he found for the first time in his life that he had not enough money to live on, given that much of his work was unpaid and that a considerable amount of his capital had been donated to the hospital? 'I'll be all right,' he insisted. 'I'm strong enough to work.'

Epilogue

The Koran, the sacred book of Muslims, confirms the significance of reaching the age of forty that Imran places upon it. It is the age of spirituality. Where once he was happiest partying in London, now he prefers his own company and a stimulating book amid the solitude of the Salt Range mountains. He would like to build a house on a mountainside overlooking a favourite valley, which would be blocked off so as to benefit the environment and animals. 'If you don't keep close to nature, you lose a sense of perspective,' he says. The man who was a byword for glamour and athletic prowess is feeling his way in spheres far removed from cricket and cricketers. Talking to him now, it is not always apparent that he was one of the finest performers in the history of the game. And that does not concern him.

'He rationalizes and reads and thinks,' says Jonathan Mermagen. 'But where will it all end?' Secrecy is not a word associated with Imran, but although everybody around the table becomes an intimate when he holds forth in London or Lahore (the gatherings he most enjoys are small dinner parties) he does not want anyone to think he is going into politics. He picks and chooses whom he mixes with in a way that he was not always able to do before he became established both as a socialite and a cricketer in 1982. He has no need to make a great effort at rapport and thus has become a little spoiled. He prefers to know his surroundings and to be among friends: surprising though it may seem for someone with his amorous reputation, he needs men around him as much, if not more, than he does women. His friends hope that one day he will marry, but they have their doubts. Abdul Qadir has had a mural made of his old captain in the Marriage Hall he owns in Lahore. It depicts a young Imran with thick, sensuous lips, becoming betrothed. 'He should get married as soon as quick,' said Qadir, 'otherwise there is a question mark.'

The span of his life may, as his friends fear, depend on whether he goes into politics. They might look upon the mystic he visits as an old man in a tree but they are aware, as Imran is, that assassination is an everyday hazard in Pakistan. Whatever the future holds for him, he will be a public figure until his life ends, not least because he says that he would die if he did not have a purpose. 'When God gives you success, He puts a responsibility on you to look after other people.' Imran is adamant that his religion has been a greater gift than his cricketing ability. He puts his successes down to his faith rather than his talent for cricket. 'My own inability to control my own future has made me realize there is another power,' he says.

Nothing that Imran ever does or becomes will obfuscate the vivid memories of him as a cricketer. The sinuous delivery stride and thrilling leap at the wicket. The elegance and haughtiness of his batting, the ball never speared or shovelled away. The aura of his persona, which meant that he was ideally suited to captaincy. It remains a peculiarity that, in a country which produces few gifted leaders, he should not be made captain until he was in his thirtieth year, even if it is true that fast bowlers rarely make natural captains. He can be a martinet when he chooses to be. Imran does not mean to behave as if he is above the common herd, but sometimes he cannot avoid giving that impression.

Statistics mean less to him than to others, but they are mightily impressive nonetheless. Only a very great bowler takes 362 wickets in 88 Tests. To average 37.69 with the bat in addition – and it would have been more without the responsibility of bowling – means that he truly deserves the citation of Geoffrey Boycott as 'one hell of a cricketer'. If, as Imran says, the only true test of a cricketer is how well he performs under pressure against the strongest opposition, then his performances as a bowler against West Indies bear out his greatness. Pakistan was the one country to give them a game during Imran's time. In 18 Tests he took

80 wickets at 21.18 apiece, a lower average than against any country other than Sri Lanka, who had only just been admitted to the comity of Test nations. In the 1980s there would have been easy pickings in his own country that would have boosted his bowling and batting averages, had he been inclined to take them. But he was motivated by taking on the best of sides, not the worst. Whatever the opposition, he never allowed any of his extracurricular activities to affect his own game.

Imran captained Pakistan 48 times, winning 14 Tests, losing eight and drawing 26. He had, of course, his own talents to draw upon, which others who led the team during his time mostly did not – and it is as an inspirational captain that he will always be remembered. He had confidence in his own judgement. The responsibility only served to enhance his game, and to a quite astonishing extent. In the 40 Tests he played when he did not lead Pakistan, he averaged 25.44 with the bat and took 175 wickets at 25.53 apiece. In his 48 matches as captain, he averaged 52.34 with the bat and gained 187 wickets at the considerably better strike rate of 20.26. Such performances helped achieve the desired effect of unifying a side which often seemed driven by fervour. No one else could do so. If, as John Woodcock said, a degree in insider dealing was required to comprehend Pakistan's cricketing politics, then Imran evidently possessed it.

Thoroughly fit and spurred on by pride, Imran returned his best performances between thirty and thirty-seven, when a sportsman, let alone a fast bowler, is supposed to be in decline. Sir Richard Hadlee was a wonderfully effective performer between those ages, yet only in his youth was he anything like as quick as Imran and thus was likely to have a longer cricketing span. Ian Botham, by contrast, was past his peak by 1983 – at least as a bowler. A back injury and disregard of his own fitness meant that, as an all-rounder, his best years were over before Imran's had begun.

Well after he had retired, *The Times* printed the following letter:

Howzat!

From Mrs Sian Dalrymple

Sir, Amongst his presents this Christmas, my father received a miniature cricket bat signed by Imran Khan. We were amused to see a tag attached saying, 'Imran Khan: Sussex and England.' If only . . . we might have beaten the Pakistanis then.

Yours faithfully,
SIAN DALRYMPLE,
12 Offerton Road, SW4.

This was a cricketer.

Imran Khan Test Match Record

Batting and Fielding

Season	Opponents	Venue	M	I	NO	Runs	HS	Av	100	50	Ct
1971	England	E	1	1	–	5	5	5.00	–	–	1
1974	England	E	3	6	1	92	31	18.40	–	–	2
1976–7	New Zealand	P	3	4	1	105	59	35.00	–	1	1
1976–7	Australia	A	3	5	–	86	48	17.20	–	–	2
1976–7	West Indies	WI	5	10	–	215	47	21.50	–	–	2
1978–9	India	P	3	4	2	104	32	52.00	–	–	–
1978–9	New Zealand	NZ	2	3	1	63	33	31.50	–	–	–
1978–9	Australia	A	2	4	–	90	33	22.50	–	–	1
1979–80	India	I	5	8	1	154	34	22.00	–	–	–
1979–80	Australia	P	2	2	–	65	56	32.50	–	1	–
1980–1	West Indies	P	4	7	–	204	123	29.14	1	–	–
1981–2	Australia	A	3	5	1	108	70*	27.00	–	1	1
1981–2	Sri Lanka	P	1	1	–	39	39	39.00	–	–	1
1982	England	E	3	5	1	212	67*	53.00	–	2	–
1982–3	Australia	P	3	3	2	64	39*	64.00	–	–	1
1982–3	India	P	6	5	1	247	117	61.75	1	–	4
1983–4	Australia	A	2	4	1	170	83	56.67	–	2	–
1985–6	Sri Lanka	P	3	2	–	69	63	34.50	–	1	–
1985–6	Sri Lanka	SL	3	4	–	48	33	12.00	–	–	4
1986–7	West Indies	P	3	6	2	115	61	28.75	–	1	1
1986–7	India	I	5	7	2	324	135*	64.80	1	2	–
1987	England	E	5	5	1	191	118	47.75	1	–	3
1988	West Indies	WI	3	5	1	90	43*	22.50	–	–	1
1988–9	New Zealand	NZ	2	2	1	140	71	140.00	–	2	–
1989–90	India	P	4	5	2	262	109*	87.33	1	1	3
1989–90	Australia	A	3	5	1	279	136	69.75	1	1	–
1990–1	West Indies	P	3	5	2	151	73*	50.33	–	2	–
1991–2	Sri Lanka	P	3	3	1	115	93*	57.50	–	1	–
Total			88	126	25	3807	136	37.69	6	18	28

* denotes 'not out'

Record against each country

Country	M	I	NO	Runs	HS	Av	100	50	Ct
England	12	17	3	500	118	35.71	1	2	6
Australia	18	28	5	862	136	37.47	1	5	5
West Indies	18	33	5	775	123	27.67	1	3	4
New Zealand	7	9	3	308	71	51.33	0	3	1
India	23	29	8	1091	135*	51.95	3	3	7
Sri Lanka	10	10	1	271	93*	30.11	–	2	5
Total	88	126	25	3807	136	37.69	6	18	28

Record on Pakistan grounds

Ground	M	I	NO	Runs	HS	Av	100	50	Ct
Iqbal Stadium, Faisalabad	9	12	1	345	117	31.36	1	1	1
Niaz Stadium, Hyderabad	2	1	–	13	13	13.00	–	–	4
National Stadium, Karachi	11	16	7	523	109*	58.11	1	3	3
Gaddafi Stadium, Lahore	11	14	4	525	123	52.50	1	3	1
Ibn-e-Qasim Bagh Stadium, Multan	1	1	–	10	10	10.00	–	–	–
Jinnah Park Stadium, Sialkot	3	3	1	124	93*	62.00	–	1	2
Municipal Stadium, Gujranwala	1			did	not	bat			–
Total	38	47	13	1540	123	45.29	3	8	11

Bowling

Season	Opponents	Venue	M	Balls	Runs	Wkts	Av	BB	5wI	10wM
1971	England	E	1	168	55	0	–	–	–	–
1974	England	E	3	672	258	5	51.60	2–48	–	–
1976–7	New Zealand	P	3	908	421	14	30.07	4–59	–	–
1976–7	Australia	A	3	964	519	18	28.83	6–63	3	1
1976–7	West Indies	WI	5	1417	790	25	31.60	6–90	1	–
1978–9	India	P	3	973	441	14	31.50	4–54	–	–
1978–9	New Zealand	NZ	2	663	255	10	25.50	5–106	1	–
1978–9	Australia	A	2	752	285	7	40.71	4–26	–	–
1979–80	India	I	5	914	365	19	19.21	5–63	2	–
1979–80	Australia	P	2	336	144	6	24.00	2–28	–	–
1980–1	West Indies	P	4	540	236	10	23.60	5–62	1	–
1981–2	Australia	A	3	902	312	16	19.50	4–66	–	–
1981–2	Sri Lanka	P	1	314	116	14	8.29	8–58	2	1
1982	England	E	3	1069	390	21	18.57	7–52	2	–
1982–3	Australia	P	3	620	171	13	13.15	4–35	–	–
1982–3	India	P	6	1339	558	40	13.95	8–60	4	2
1983–4	Australia	A	2	–	–	–	–	–	–	–
1985–6	Sri Lanka	P	3	724	271	17	15.94	5–40	1	–
1985–6	Sri Lanka	SL	3	696	270	15	18.00	4–69	–	–
1986–7	West Indies	P	3	638	199	18	11.06	6–46	2	–
1986–7	India	I	5	739	392	8	49.00	2–28	–	–
1987	England	E	5	1010	455	21	21.67	7–40	2	1
1988	West Indies	P	3	779	416	23	18.09	7–80	2	1
1988–9	New Zealand	NZ	2	620	198	7	28.28	3–34	–	–
1989–90	India	P	4	1113	504	13	38.76	4–45	–	–
1989–90	Australia	A	3	420	167	4	41.75	2–53	–	–
1990–1	West Indies	P	3	114	54	4	13.50	2–22	–	–
1991–2	Sri Lanka	P	3	54	16	0	–	–	–	–
Total			88	19458	8258	362	22.81	8–58	23	6

Captaincy

Season	Opponents	Venue	M	W	L	D	Toss won
1982	England	E	3	1	2	–	2
1982–3	Australia	P	3	3	–	–	2
1982–3	India	P	6	3	–	3	3
1983–4	Australia	A	2	–	1	1	1
1985–6	Sri Lanka	SL	3	1	1	1	–
1986–7	West Indies	P	3	1	1	1	2
1986–7	India	I	5	1	–	4	4
1987	England	E	5	1	–	4	2
1988	West Indies	WI	3	1	1	1	1
1988–9	New Zealand	NZ	2	–	–	2	2
1989–90	India	P	4	–	–	4	3
1989–90	Australia	A	3	–	1	2	2
1990–1	West Indies	P	3	1	1	1	1
1991–2	Sri Lanka	P	3	1	–	2	1
Total			48	14	8	26	26

Record against each country

Country	M	Balls	Runs	Wkts	Av	BB	5wI	10wM
England	12	2919	1158	47	24.64	7–40	4	1
Australia	18	3994	1598	64	24.96	6–63	3	1
West Indies	18	3488	1695	80	21.18	7–80	6	1
New Zealand	7	2191	874	31	28.19	5–106	1	–
India	23	5078	2260	94	24.04	8–60	6	2
Sri Lanka	10	1788	673	46	14.63	8–58	3	1
Total	88	19458	8258	362	22.81	8–58	23	6

Record on Pakistan grounds

Ground	M	Balls	Runs	Wkts	Av	BB	5wI	10wM
Iqbal Stadium, Faisalabad	9	1619	703	26	27.03	6–98	2	1
Niaz Stadium, Hyderabad	2	500	174	11	15.82	6–35	1	–
National Stadium, Karachi	11	2406	938	51	18.39	8–60	2	1
Gaddafi Stadium, Lahore	11	2443	987	56	17.62	8–58	3	1
Ibn-e-Qasim Bagh Stadium, Multan	1	192	89	5	17.80	5–62	1	–
Jinnah Park Stadium, Sialkot	3	513	240	14	17.14	5–40	1	-
Municipal Stadium, Gujranwala	1		did	not	bowl			
Total	38	7173	3131	163	19.20	8–58	10	3

Record in each country

Country	M	Balls	Runs	Wkts	Av	BB	5wI	10wM
Pakistan	38	7160	3131	163	19.20	8–58	10	3
England	12	2919	1158	47	24.64	7–40	4	1
Australia	13	3038	1283	45	28.51	6–63	3	1
West Indies	8	2196	1206	48	25.13	7–80	3	1
New Zealand	4	1283	453	17	26.64	5–106	1	–
India	10	1653	757	27	28.04	5–63	2	–
Sri Lanka	3	696	270	15	18.00	4–69	–	–
Total	88	19458	8258	362	22.81	8–58	23	6

Overall records

Country	M	Balls	Runs	Wkts	Av	BB	5wI	10wM
Record when not captain	40	10247	4468	175	25.53	8–58	11	2
Record when captain	48	9211	3790	187	20.26	8–60	12	4
Total	88	19458	8258	362	22.81	8–58	23	6

Ten wickets in a Test match

12–165 v Australia	Sydney	1976–7
14–116 v Sri Lanka	Lahore	1981–2
11–79 v India	Karachi	1982–3
11–180 v India	Faisalabad	1982–3
10–77 v England	Headingley	1987
11–121 v West Indies	Georgetown	1988

Index of Names